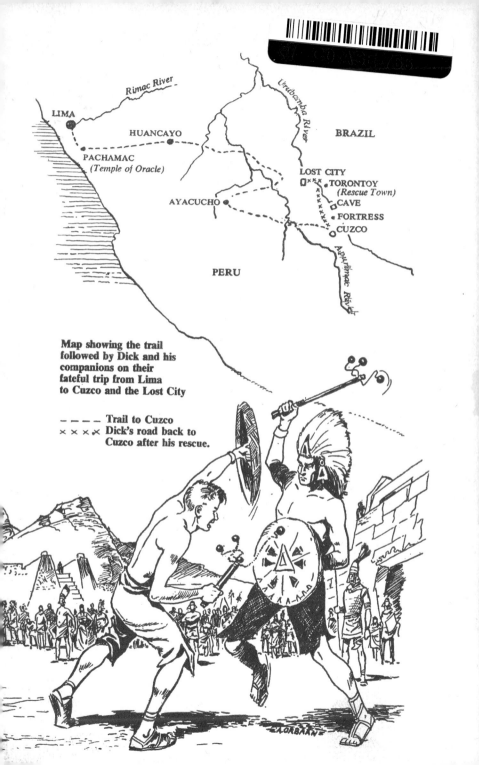

Map showing the trail
followed by Dick and his
companions on their
fateful trip from Lima
to Cuzco and the Lost City

– – – – Trail to Cuzco
× × × × Dick's road back to
Cuzco after his rescue.

On the Trail
of
Inca Gold

On the Trail of
INCA GOLD

by

Hector Lazo

A Lodestar Book

PRENTICE-HALL, INC.

Englewood Cliffs, N. J.

TO JIMMY

A UNITED STATES MARINE ON IWO JIMA

Table of Contents

On the Trail
of
Inca Gold

1

The Tombs of Pachacamac

"PROF! PROF! COME QUICK! MY PICK HAS SUNK INTO THE ground . . . I've found a deep hole!"

Dick was so excited he could hardly stand still. His voice rose to a shout, although Professor Bentley was only a few yards away, digging around the little pyramid.

Prof jumped to Dick's side and his own shouts brought Antonio and Pepe and Chico running. Pepe dropped his own small pick as he ran.

"What is it, Dick? What is it, Prof?" Pepe and Chico cried as they ran toward their companions. Only Antonio was quiet.

"Don't get excited! It may be nothing! Don't get excited!" But Prof's voice was also high and shaking, and if the boys had been listening, they would have caught the excitement in the teacher's voice. But they were all shouting—all except Antonio—and didn't notice. They crowded around Dick, whose little army surplus pick had indeed sunk right into the ground. The thin layer of hard-packed earth had cracked, and through the crack they could see what looked like a deep, dark hole. A curious smell, like the dank air from a cave, came up to them as they bent over.

"Is it the Tomb of the Incas, Prof? Is it?" Dick could hardly get the words out quickly enough. He was trembling all over from excitement. "Have we found it, Prof? Is this the Tomb?"

"Stand back, boys, this earth may give way at any minute!" Prof's voice was almost as excited as Dick's. "Stand back!"

An ominous cracking, snapping sound sent the boys scurrying backwards, bumping into each other as they pushed away from the spot. Pepe sat down hard but was up on his feet almost immediately, running even before he was quite up. It was only when the five explorers were a good ten yards away that Prof raised his hand.

"This is enough!" he panted, his breath coming short. "It won't reach this far out."

They stood there—the three boys from Lima, Dick's companions in the Instituto de Varones, the Boy's High School of the capital city of Peru; Dick, the blond son of the Ambassador of the United States and Don Horacio Bentley, their teacher, whom they all affectionately called 'Prof.' Sweat streamed down their faces under the hot sun, but they were shivering. The palms of their hands, in spite of the heat and exertion of the last few hours, were wet and clammy.

"We must stop now. Let's catch our breath. We'll eat our luncheon now and afterward we will see what we have found." Prof Bentley's face was very serious.

"Oh, *no!*" The cry of protest was unanimous.

"We can't stop now!" Dick's voice had never carried more indignation in his life. "This may be the secret tomb of a great Inca King! Prof, we can't stop now!"

Prof looked from one to the other of his young companions, and his eyes met the coal black eyes of Antonio, who stood very straight. He was pale despite his deep bronzed skin. Antonio returned the steady stare of the teacher. Between the two passed some unspoken message Dick could not understand, but it was as though they had spoken out loud. Prof turned to the other boys.

"All right, boys," he said, speaking very slowly. "We will divide ourselves into two teams and dig very, very carefully, and only where I tell you to. One team can rest while the other digs, and in that way we can make better progress." He stopped for a moment and looked down at his feet, thinking. Then he looked up again. Dick thought he would burst if Prof didn't give the word to start digging.

"Antonio knows more about digging than any of the rest of you, and he and I will start this," said Prof. Dick felt his heart sink. Words of protest jumped into his mouth. He had discovered this, and now he would not be allowed to dig! He looked quickly at Prof and caught the serious look in the teacher's eyes. Something in the look made Dick swallow hard, choking back the words he had intended to shout out. Antonio stepped to Dick's side and put his hand on Dick's shoulder.

"There will be enough digging for all of us, *mi amigo,*" he said softly, but there was no smile on his lips as he spoke. "And you can have the honor of going down the steps first when we open the mouth of the cave."

"Steps? How do you know it goes down?"

"If this is a burial cave, it will go down—deep down into the earth. The Tomb itself will be far down."

Dick felt a cold chill go over him. He was almost sorry when Antonio took his hand off his shoulder and without another word lifted his pick and started digging where Prof indicated.

Whoever invented that old crack about Latin Americans refusing to work with their hands was just crazy, Dick thought, as he watched Prof Bentley and Antonio working methodically, slowly, rhythmically. While the other three boys watched, Prof dug a circle about three feet wide around the spot where Dick's pick handle stuck up out of the ground.

"Get the crowbar, Dick," said Prof, without looking up. Dick rushed back to the truck where the tools were, and grunted as he lifted the heavy steel bar. Prof took it from his hands and handled it as though it weighed only an ounce or two, instead of the eighteen pounds of solid steel that, in the hot sun, seemed to Dick to weigh a ton. Prof lifted the bar high and let it slide straight through his uplifted hands. The bar sank a full two feet into the ground!

"Look out, Antonio!" cried Prof, waving his hand as though to wave Antonio and the other boys back. Carefully, he lifted the bar up again in both hands, and again let it slide down. This time the crowbar sank all the way, and as Prof tried to catch it, he almost fell forward on his face. The crowbar sank to Prof's wrists, and practically disappeared into the ground!

"A pit! A pit! We've found it, boys! Careful, now, careful!" Again Prof waved the boys back as they rushed forward, crowding around the spot where the crowbar had disappeared into the ground.

Prof knelt down and tapped the earth, as though he were tapping the lid of a drum. It sounded hollow underneath!

"We've found it! We've found it!" Everyone was shouting, in English and in Spanish, no one hearing anybody else.

And with the boys inching forward as close as they dared, peering down and holding their breaths, Prof tapped the ground with the knuckles of his right hand. About eighteen inches from where the crowbar had sunk into the ground, the hollow sound suddenly stopped. Prof tested the ground again, then narrowed the circle. There was that hollow thump again! Slowly, carefully, Prof narrowed the circle more and more, little by little working toward the sunken shaft of the crowbar.

"Get the large flat shovel from the truck, Dick," said Prof, stopping for a moment. His eyes, as he looked up into the faces of the boys, were dancing with excitement and anticipation. His face was flushed from stooping. "You can lift the earth off as Antonio and I dig, but you must be careful! Don't pound or hit the ground, just scrape it off!"

Dick was back in no time at all, his hands shaking so that the long handle of the shovel slipped through his fingers. He juggled it for a few seconds. Beads of sweat dropped from his forehead. He forgot all about the blisters he had raised earlier. He didn't even feel the hot burning of the sun.

For the next several minutes there was only the sound of the light tap-tap as Prof and Antonio broke the ground in a circle of about three feet in circumference, followed by the soft swoosh of Dick's shovel.

Suddenly the earth cracked with a sharp snap, and Prof fell into a hole up to his waist!

"Hold it, hold it!" Prof's voice sounded as though it, too, were cracking.

"Now with your hands! All of you!"

Dick dropped his shovel. Pepe and Chico pressed forward. Kneeling alongside Dick, close to where Prof was standing, the three boys lifted a thin layer of dry clay, barely the thickness of plywood, and widened the opening through which Prof had sunk. Only Antonio had withdrawn; now he stood, arms by his side, head high, his black piercing eyes watching intently while his companions widened the aperture. How could he tell his friends, especially this *norte-americano*, that as a small child in his native mountain village, he and the other boys had taken an oath never to betray to any foreigner the hiding place of Inca treasure? Suppose this were the tomb of an Inca, and the customary gold and precious stones were buried with the mummy? Would not this be a betrayal of his boyhood oath?

Antonio was brought back from his doubts by Prof's voice.

"I am standing on something that feels like a round stone, but the ground is solid all around," said Prof. He moved his foot cautiously from side to side, feeling his footing below. "Feels like a stone wall," he added.

The next half-hour—it seemed like ten ages to Dick—was spent clearing a round hole about two feet in diameter. As soon as he was sufficiently free, Prof worked with his hands from inside the small pit, and the boys worked from the top. Suddenly Prof gave a sharp cry.

"Wait a minute, boys . . . I think . . . I think . . . this round thing I am standing on . . . may be a skeleton!"

Dick gulped. His heart was pounding in his dry throat. All the boys stared at Prof, and for a long moment Prof stared back at them. Then he slowly reached down, keeping his eyes on the boys, and worked his hand back and forth in a slow digging motion. Sweat made little streams down his dark brown face. His hand worked something loose. Slowly he raised it. It was a skull, and the big eye cavities held large green stones!

"Hold this, Dick!" Prof lifted the yellow skull to the ground level. "There seems to be something else down here," he added, reaching down with his left arm.

Dick's stomach tightened into a hard knot. He felt the blood leave his face, and his arms felt so weak he thought he could not hold the gruesome head Prof had handed him.

"Look out, Dick!" cried Prof as he saw Dick sway.

"Oh, for heaven's sake! Here, let me hold it!" It was the quiet, pale-faced Chico. "I'll take it!" He snatched the skull from Dick's trembling hands.

Dick tried to smile, though he thought he was going to be sick to his stomach. A sudden hot shame rushed the blood back into his face. He fought back tears that threatened now to blind him. Then he felt Antonio's strong arm on his shoulders.

"I understand how you feel, Dick," said Antonio, almost whispering into his friend's ear. The pressure of his strong hand told Dick much more than his words. "I don't want to handle it either."

Then Prof straightened. In his left hand he held a dry and yellowed bone that looked like a forearm. And standing there in the hot Peruvian desert, looking down into the small pit in the hard ground, Dick stared down on a small pile of bones.

"This must have been the Guardian of the Tomb," said Prof, climbing out of his little pit. As he raised himself to his feet, his eyes met Dick's and he saw the faraway look that had suddenly come into Dick's eyes.

"What's the matter, Dick?" asked Prof.

"I suddenly thought of high school back in Indiana," answered Dick, slowly. In his mind he was seeing the wide limestone steps of Carter High, the kids streaming out, and he could almost hear the happy shouts as boys and girls tumbled out of the classrooms into the sunshine.

"Imagine, Prof," Dick said, "what the fellows back home would think if they saw me now. Imagine if this turned out to be a real Indian burial cave, and you and I and all of us here suddenly became famous! Wow!"

"Wow!" echoed Pepe, who had learned slang fast from his *norte-americano* friend.

They all laughed. That seemed to break the spell.

"And now," said Prof, "we will take that breathing spell you would not let me take earlier, Dick, and see what your mother packed in that luncheon basket!"

They turned eagerly and walked back to the truck. All but Antonio, who stood silently staring into the little pit. His lips were moving but they made no noise. He stood there perhaps a full minute, then turned and silently joined his companions.

After luncheon, with the hot sun pouring down heat that seemed almost as though the ancient Inca deity were angry at the intrusion, Dick lay back on the canvas sheet they had spread on the dry desert sand. He locked his hands behind his head and closed his eyes as the hot sunlight burned his eyeballs. But he was smiling.

"I was just thinking, Prof," he said, while his companions finished the delicious food Dick's mother had packed for them,, "I was just thinking what would have happened if Dad hadn't given his consent to my coming with you today. Think of the things I would have missed!"

"But you must not feel resentful toward your father, Dick," said Prof.

"Oh, I'm not! But I can't help remembering how close I came to missing this—all this! Wait till Dad hears about this tomb!"

"It is probably a tomb, Dick, but we cannot be sure yet," said

Prof soberly. "You must not get your hopes too high. We may be disappointed."

"But I was thinking of the other things too, Prof," said Dick, refusing to let his spirits be dampened. "Think of what we saw this morning—the actual remains of the Temple of Pachacamac, the Oracle Room, the view of the Pacific Ocean and that gigantic horseshoe it makes as the shore reaches out north and south from this hill!"

For a moment Dick and his companions relived that breathtaking sight as the early morning sun bathed the Pacific Ocean to the west of the hill. The high hill on which the once-famed Temple of the Oracle had stood rose right out of the desert. To the south, a silver-white river meandered through a valley of flowering trees. To the east and north stretched the brown, barren, dusty desert.

"It's like being in two different worlds, Prof!" Dick had exclaimed.

"They are two different worlds!" Prof's eyes had been serious, but his face wore the pleased smile of an older man who discovers a boy's interest. Dick's three companions from the Instituto de Varones of Lima had crowded around Prof atop the crumbled wall. Suddenly Prof had pointed down.

"See that big square rock down in this pit?" he asked. All the boys peered down intently, nodding. "That was the cornerstone of the Oracle Room. That is where the Priests came to consult the Voice of the Oracle. Sometimes even the Inca himself came up here to talk to the spirit of his departed ancestors."

"I bet not many boys from the United States have stood on the Oracle Stone!" Dick's voice was high with excitement.

"Not many of them know about it!" It was Antonio who had spoken, and his companions all turned to him. There was a strange ring in Antonio's voice.

"But they will after this!" Dick couldn't wait to get back and tell his father about it. Maybe the Ambassador would send a special dispatch to Washington! Or maybe the American Embassy in Peru would get out a special pamphlet that could be sent to the schools in the United States. It would interest a lot of boys and girls in the Land of the Incas. Then Dick's eyes suddenly clouded.

"I wish there were some book or some written record of those ceremonies, Prof," he said. "I'd like to read all about them, how they talked to the Oracle, what the Oracle said in turn . . ."

"But we do have books—some very good ones in English— and lots more in Spanish that I will lend you as soon as you know enough Spanish to read them."

"But I thought you said, Prof, that the Incas did not have a written language! I mean I wish there were some books written by the Incas themselves. Those books written after the Spanish Conquest—we don't even know if what they wrote was so . . ."

"Oh, I think we can believe them," answered Antonio gravely. "The Incas did not have a written language, but they did have specially trained historians whom they called *Quipu-camayocs*. They trained their minds from early childhood. They remembered everything. That's all they did—remember and recite the history of the Incas, and of the Priests, and of the generals."

"You mean they carried all that stuff in their heads?" Dick asked.

"No," answered Antonio, and again Dick saw that wonderful pride in his friend's eyes. "They carried it in their hearts. You see, our *Quechua* word for 'memorizing' is 'to carry in the heart.'"

"You use the same expression as Antonio's ancestors did, Dick," said Prof. Bentley. "You say in English, 'to learn by heart,' when you really mean to remember in the head."

"So we do, Prof!" Dick exclaimed. "I never thought of that. Do you suppose we got the expression from the Incas?"

"I rather doubt that," said Prof with a smile. "Your ancestors and Antonio's ancestors never knew each other. But it isn't really surprising—is it?—that all people should speak of the heart as the place where you remember anything you really want to remember?"

"But wouldn't it be awful if we didn't have books today, if we couldn't read or write?"

"There are many millions of people all over the world who can't read or write," said Prof.

Antonio had come close to Dick, and now put his arm around his North American friend. "And they are not necessarily less happy than we are, Dick," he said. "I don't think the Incas were unhappy. They just never knew such things existed!"

"I guess you are right, Antonio."

They were all silent for a few moments. Dick looked down into the broad valley at the foot of the hill, and the desert and hard-packed brown sand to the left of where they stood.

"Think what it must have been to be a High Priest up here on this hill, hundreds of feet above the river—able to see in all directions, see the sun rise, and the sun set, and the storms coming, and hear the voice of the God of Lightning, and the God of Thunder—and then see the skies fill with stars at night! No wonder they could talk to the Voices of their Ancestors!" Antonio's voice sounded far away. It was as though he was, himself, talking to some distant priest or relative, long since dead. He didn't seem to notice the others around him.

Dick turned to his tall Peruvian companion. Antonio had been very cordial when Dick had first entered the school. Classes had already begun, for the appointment of Dick's father as Ambassador to Peru had not been approved by the United States Senate until late in March, and it had been a full month before the family had been ready for the trip down to that exciting land on the west coast of South America about which they had read in their history books. The new school year in Lima had started in early April. And now here it was almost Christmas and very close to the summer vacation in this land below the equator. Between April and December, a fast friendship had grown up between Dick and Antonio, whose ancestors had once ruled the vast land that stretched more than two thousand miles along the whole west coast of the southern continent.

"You think maybe your great-great-great-grandfather stood up here once and listened to the Voice of the Oracle, Antonio?" Dick asked.

Antonio did not answer at once, but turned his head and stared at the vast Pacific Ocean to the west. Its deep blue waters shimmered in the early morning light.

"Perhaps," he said, not turning back to look at Dick. "One of my ancestors was a brother of the King, and was High Priest at the time of Pachacutec."

"I think we better start down if we are going to do any digging," said Prof. He had a way of bringing faraway thoughts right back to the present.

Climbing down from the high hill, one step at a time, single file, sometimes dropping as much as five or six feet down the face of the stone walls that once guarded the sacred temples, was a harder job than climbing up.

The muscles in Dick's legs hurt long before they reached the high dirt parapet. Once Pepe stumbled and slid on his pants. "Ay!" he cried, rubbing himself while the others laughed. For some reason, the tear in his pants worried him more than the bruise.

"That was a wow of a fall, Pepe," said Dick. They all joined in the laughter. Pepe grinned, half-embarrassed.

They reached again the vast plateau of Pachacamac. Under Prof's instructions, they had started to dig, Pepe, Chico and Antonio by the large protruding stone some fifty paces away, and Prof and Dick at the base of the little earth pyramid. They had each taken one of the small army surplus picks from the truck.

"The earth is caked awfully hard," said Dick, striking the ground with his pick and not making even a scratch on it. "And wow! Is this sun hot!"

"Only a sun like this could have dried out this plateau," said Prof, amused at Dick's discomfort. "Shining like this for hundreds of years it makes an ideal burial ground for mummies sent on their long voyages to their ancestors. This was the greatest of all pilgrimage meeting grounds, here at Pachacamac. That's why I have thought for a long time that this mound is some sort of sepulchre."

The reminder that they might be standing right over one of those enormous underground Inca tombs made Dick forget the heat of the sun and his aching muscles.

"Why don't we dig then, Prof?" Dick was all eagerness.

"Let's start. But don't try to loosen this hard earth with the mattock end, Dick. You'll never do it. Use the pick, the sharp pointed end."

Little by little the dry caked earth around the little pyramid began to crack. Prof's pick struck a hard *ping*.

"Is that a rock, Prof?" asked Dick.

"Perhaps," answered Prof, bending over to examine what looked like a hard, narrow strip about four feet long embedded in the hard earth. The edge was thin, not more than half an inch, and almost the same color as the brown desert. But it gave off a hard rasping sound as Prof rubbed it with the wide side of his pickax.

"It's hard to tell, Dick. The ground is so very dry and hard. But it could be a rock—a stoop of some kind. We'll step off three feet to the west, and start digging right here." He drew a line with the point of his pickax, bearing down hard, and found it almost impossible even to scratch the ground. But Dick didn't need any other boundary line. He was afraid Prof would notice how his hands were shaking. He took a firmer grip on his pick-handle.

"Here goes, Prof!" he cried. He struck the ground with all his might. A little dull *glump* was all he managed, and the pickax almost flew out of his hands. Prof didn't seem to notice. Dick saw Prof lift the heavy crowbar, and let the iron bar come down through his cupped hands. Its weight cracked the earth, making a little hole. Prof struck the same spot with his pick and made the hole larger.

"Try the crowbar, Dick," said Prof. "It works easier."

After that, the digging really started. Prof and Dick worked toward each other, widening the first thin crack into a little trench. Sweat ran down Dick's face, into his eyes, his mouth. It was discouragingly slow work.

Finally Dick stopped. "Whew, Prof! This is hard work!"

Prof went on methodically. "Want to quit?" he called out between grunts as he lifted the pick and with a regular swing struck the ground again.

"Quit?" Dick's neck was now very red, and very hot. "Oh, no . . . only it *is* hard work!"

Prof stopped and looked at his student. His eyes were smiling.

"Of course it is. Did you think the ground would crack open on command?"

Dick suddenly felt embarrassed. He glanced quickly at Prof, then at his three companions who were digging steadily thirty or forty yards away. On the very next blow Dick struck it happened. His pick stuck into the ground—he had struck a hole! They might be standing on the very edge of the tomb of the Incas!

2

The Cave of the Mummy

THAT FIRST OPENING, AS PROF HAD SUGGESTED, WAS ONLY the beginning. By the time the sun had crossed over to the western slopes of Pachacamac, the feverish thrill of the discovery had subsided. Dick and Antonio, then Prof and Pepe, took turns digging in the growing pit. Chico was given the job of shoveling the earth from the hole and spreading it over the surface outside the pit so that there would be no mound of dirt around the opening. Two feet farther down they came on a stone wall. Most of the stones were square and finely polished, fitting tightly one upon the other, but without mortar. In spite of having been years underground, the stones were reddish in color. They were about the size of large building blocks.

"I think this is the circular retaining wall, the vestibule to the tomb below," said Prof. "We'll dig around it and see."

It was slow, hot work. Here and there a small soft pocket of clay let the pick sink in, but mostly it was plain hard digging.

"Not much fun, is it?" said Dick, straightening up to get the kink out of his back.

"Did you expect this would be what you call fun?" Antonio's eyes were very serious. "The people who made these graves did not have much fun, either."

"I hadn't thought of that," confessed Dick, a little crestfallen. The boys turned to digging again.

"Time for relief!" Prof exclaimed half-an-hour later.

Dick looked up quickly. A large drop of sweat stung his eye and made him blink. But he was glad enough to stop digging and get out of the sun, even if it only meant sitting in the stifling car that had been in the hot sun all day. Dick sank into the back seat, put his head against the thin flannel blanket that protected the upholstery, and closed his eyes. He felt Antonio crawl in beside him, heard the deep sigh as Antonio also stretched his legs.

For a few moments the two boys sat in silence. Dick's muscles ached, he could hear his heart inside his breast.

"You know, Antonio," said Dick, without opening his eyes, "I feel tired out. I would just as soon stop now and come back tomorrow."

Antonio did not answer. After another long moment, Dick turned his head sideways and looked at his Peruvian friend. How brown Antonio's skin was! How yellow the deep furrows on his wrinkled forehead. But the tightly pressed lips barely changed color from the deep purple bronze of Antonio's cheeks.

"Aren't you tired, Antonio?" asked Dick finally.

Again a long moment passed. Slowly Antonio opened his eyes, turned his head and looked straight into Dick's eyes.

"I feel tired in my heart more than in my muscles, Dick," he said solemnly. The tone in his voice gave Dick a queer feeling of discomfort. "Somehow I do not feel we should be digging here at all."

Dick sat up straight and stared at Antonio.

"But wouldn't you like to become famous for discovering some important cave or something?" Dick was puzzled.

Antonio's big black eyes seemed even bigger and darker than before. The wrinkles on his forehead made deep grooves. His voice was very soft, but there was no smile on his lips as he answered Dick's question.

"The people of Peru need so many things—especially the young people, the poor, the Indians . . . I think I would rather be doing something to help them, instead of digging around in the past . . . You find it hard to understand that, Dick?" he asked, as Dick's face twisted in a puzzled frown.

"I'm trying to understand . . . and I think I do, a little . . . but you see, up north we sort of go for the great things your ancestors did—their history—their past is very interesting to us."

"Yes, their past, always their past! But we cannot live in the past any more, Dick!" Hearing the impatience in Antonio's voice, Dick looked away quickly, afraid Antonio would see his embarrassment.

"When I first came to the Boys' High School in Lima," Antonio said, "Prof told me that the people who live in the past cannot have much future. I have never forgotten that. I want the boys and girls of Peru to have much future, like they do in the United States, where all the boys and girls go to school!"

Dick's mind ran back quickly to earlier that morning when they had talked about books, and reading and writing. He remembered Antonio's wistful thought that the people of the Incas had not been unhappy although they could not read or write, because they had never known how.

"But today," Antonio went on, as though he read Dick's thoughts, "every boy and girl has to know how to read and write. It is because so many of them do not know that the people of Peru, and Bolivia, and the other South American countries are poor. And I want to help them."

Dick did not know what to say. A whole jumble of confused thoughts raced through his mind. Again he saw his friends back at Carter High in Indiana, boys and girls he had known since kindergarten, and it was hard for him to visualize boys and girls growing up without going to school. He closed his eyes and tried to picture what it would be like if he had never gone

to school. He couldn't do it. Suppose he couldn't even . . .
well, not even sign his name?

The quiet of his thoughts was interrupted suddenly by a
shout from Professor Bentley.

"Dick! Antonio! Come quick!"

Dick flung the rear car door open, stumbled as he jumped
out, and almost fell before he recovered his balance. Antonio
was already at his side, and the two ran to the edge of the pit.
Prof, Pepe and Chico were standing inside, only their shoulders
and head showing above the pit's edge. The circular stone wall
around which they had been digging now made almost a complete circle about five feet across.

"Look, boys, look!" Prof's voice was high with excitement.
"This *is* the vestibule and this is the wall around it! Here is the
round passage inside the wall, leading right down into the
ground. Pepe uncovered the first step. Down in there somewhere should be a great round chamber, and the mummy in its
burial clothes."

Both Dick and Antonio had jumped down beside the others,
and they all crowded around the round opening, that looked
like the neck of a giant bottle stuck in the ground, partially
filled with dry hard earth. At the top, coming in from the right
side, they could see a stone step marking the entrance. Dick
stooped down and felt of the step, then hit it with his pick. It
was solid granite.

"Let's open this up!" cried Dick, pushing to get into position
with his pick. Prof looked at his wrist watch.

"We'll come back tomorrow and finish this, boys," he said.
His eyes were filled with a new joy.

"Oh, gee, can't we at least open this entrance now?" Dick
wasn't at all tired; he had forgotten the sun, and the heat.

"Not today, Dick. We have to report this to the authorities.
It is getting late and we have to get back to Lima before they
close the offices. This is summer now, remember? And they close
the offices early."

Very reluctantly the boys picked up the tools, one by one,

and carried them back to the truck. Suddenly going back to Lima seemed like stopping a game at the end of the first inning.

"Shouldn't some of us stay here to . . . well, to sort of guard this tonight?" Dick was still not ready to go back to the city.

Prof's voice was full of laugher. "You think this tomb will run away tonight, Dick?"

All the boys laughed. Antonio climbed up into the cab of the truck, and the three boys piled into Prof's old Buick sedan.

"We will drive directly to the Ministry of Public Instruction, Antonio," said Prof, climbing behind the wheel of the sedan. He stepped on the self-starter and the old motor churned and roared into life. Behind them, Antonio's truck exploded into loud coughing, then settled down to the steady, explosive protests of old truck engines, echoing strangely loud from the stone ruins on the slopes of the mountain. The two motor vehicles rumbled slowly over the hard earth of the plateau, winding toward the road.

"Prof," said Pepe as they reached the paved highway, "my house is on the edge of the city as we go in. Can't you drop me off there?"

"Me, too," said Chico, "I live only a couple of blocks from Pepe."

"All right, boys, we'll drop you off, and Dick, Antonio and I will go to the Ministry and make our report. I'll let you know later what we do tomorrow. I only hope we get there before they close the office."

Nobody had much to say the balance of the trip back to Lima. Dick noticed many little things he had not seen on the way out that morning—the big white angel trumpet vines, for example, with their giant flowers and big leaves, that served as fences around the little enclosed yards of the native adobe huts. There was the occasional patch of irrigated land where some hardworking Indian grew a few vegetables, as well as the inevitable bony dog, and the equally inevitable runty pig, tied by one leg to a post stuck in the barren ground. Half-naked children played quietly by the side of the road with solemn, serious little faces that didn't know how to smile. Occasionally a dog ran out and barked indignantly at the turning tires, choking in the dust. Every so often Dick looked back at Antonio and the truck that followed, sometimes lost in the dust raised by Prof's car. But Antonio's motor growled steadily, rasping occasionally as Antonio shifted gears on specially rough spots or around sharp curves.

At last they reached the outskirts of Lima, the city that sprawled in the giant plain cradled in the foothills, and stretched, flat and sunbaked, as far as the Pacific Ocean eight miles away. A giant international plane circled once overhead and headed gracefully for the beautiful airport of Limatambo. Pepe and Chico leaped out of the car by the new housing development in the northern section, and ran, shouting, toward Pepe's house. Prof set the car in gear again, and drove on.

The streets of Lima were already crowded with going-home people, rushing to get out of the hot city. Fortunately, the Minister of Public Instruction was still in his office when Prof arrived. The news of the discovery brought other officials into the big conference room, and soon all time was forgotten as details of the discovery at Pachacamac were recited and repeated for others. Dr. Ortega, the Director of the National Museum, asked questions over and over again, excused himself, ran out to telephone, and returned, picking up the questions where he had left off. Although in four months Dick had made excellent progress and could speak Spanish quite well, he had difficulty following them now. Prof and Antonio did most of the talking, with Prof making rough drawings of the pit, the circular wall, the round opening that looked like a giant bottle neck top, the granite stone step half-hidden in the packed earth. At last the officials were satisfied. Another conference followed between the Minister, Dr. Ortega, and a thin-faced older man who turned out to be a well-known archaeologist whom Dr. Ortega had summoned by telephone from the University nearby. Now they all came forward and shook hands solemnly with Prof, with Antonio, and with Dick.

"These may be a great zing for Peru, Meester Dick," said the Minister, smiling broadly. "Your name will be very beeg!"

Outside the big white marble building, surrounded by flowering red and white hibiscus and carefully tended green lawns, Dick blinked as the last rays of the setting sun blinded him for a moment.

"Better take the truck back to the garage, Antonio," said Prof. "I'll drive Dick home and then go home myself. I am tired."

"Whew! So am I," said Dick.

They shook hands with Antonio. "I'll get in touch with you later about tomorrow, Antonio," said Prof, getting behind the wheel of the sedan. Antonio nodded. He smiled and waved his hand at Dick as he climbed back into the truck cab. It was an old American truck that had seen much heavy service, and it was very noisy.

A short hour later, Prof and Dick drove up the broad avenue of the beautiful suburb of Miraflores, where the Ambassador had rented a large establishment soon after their arrival in Peru. Dick was surprised to see people already gathering at a respectful distance from the big house, as people always do when a house suddenly jumps into news. Apparently, even in such a short time, the word had begun to get around.

"See how famous you are already, Dick?" said Prof, smiling.

Dick's shirt suddenly felt tight. He waved to Prof from the front door.

"See you soon, Prof!" he called. Boy, would a shower feel good!

He bounded up the stairs two at a time, tearing off his sweaty shirt as he ran. Raul, the pale-faced houseboy who had opened the door downstairs, followed Dick admiringly.

"I hear all about Pachacamac," he called as he ran up the stairs. Dick stopped short outside his bedroom door.

"You did? Already?"

"Oh, yes, we have the radios, here, too! And the newspaper men, they call up and ask much questions!"

"They did? What did you tell them?"

"Oh, not I!" Raul was alarmed at the question. "Your Mawther, she answer!"

"Aw, gee, and I wanted to tell her!" thought Dick as he pushed his bedroom door open and began undressing.

He came out of the shower room across the hall, wrapped in a big bath sheet his mother had bought him after they had seen them at the hotel in Lima. Dick drew up short.

"Gee, Mom, can't a fellow dress in private?" he asked, seeing his mother and his ten-year-old sister Dorothy seated on his bed.

"Your father has just phoned, Dick." His mother's face was more serious than usual. "He wants you to be sure not to talk to anybody about this—this cave you and Prof found. He says you are not to say anything to anybody, especially the newspaper reporters. And he says sister and I are to see to it that they don't take any pictures of you under any circumstances before he gets home."

"What's the matter with him, Mom? I haven't done anything disgraceful!"

"No, Dick, but you know what a stickler your father is about the feelings of the people down here. Anyway, he doesn't want you to talk to anybody before he gets home, and he said to tell you that those are orders."

"But good gosh, Mom . . ."

"Now, Dick, don't get all excited. You know your father is doing what he thinks is best. Anyway, he's coming home early and you can argue it out with him. I'm just telling you what he said to tell you. Dot and I are to see that no newspaper man gets to you before Dad gets home."

"Well, you can at least let a fellow dress in private, can't you?"

Mrs. Collins looked at Dick for a long moment in silence. Dick stared back. He wanted to say a lot of things, but after all, this was only Mom, and anyway, it wasn't her doing.

"Come, Sister," said Mrs. Collins, getting off the bed and taking Dorothy by the hand, "let's leave Big Brother alone to dress."

Dick glared at them as they went out the door. Swiftly he crossed the room and kicked the door shut with a loud bang. He dropped the big towel off his shoulders and stood naked, facing his bed. On his right was the study desk his father had bought him, and under it the round wicker hand-woven wastebasket. With his bare foot he kicked out at this basket. Crumpled papers from yesterday's homework piled out as the basket rolled crazily on one side across the room.

"What's the matter with everybody?" Dick said aloud.

He walked to the bed and picked up his socks, putting them on slowly, standing first on one foot, then on the other, as he always did. His mother had laid out clean underwear and a clean shirt for him. He knocked them off the bed with a swipe of his hand, let them lie on the floor where they fell. He walked over to his dresser, selected his own clothes, and deliberately chose a green sport shirt his father didn't like. To get his shoes, he had to pass the wastebasket again, and he kicked it viciously, sending the empty basket high in the air. As it fell, it knocked the reading lamp off his desk. He looked at the pieces, stepped over them, pushed his feet into his shoes and left the room, slamming the door behind him.

His mother was in the hall outside his room when he came out.

"What happened, Dick?" Her voice sounded anxious.

"Nothing."

"Something certainly broke, Dick, we heard it . . ."

"OK, Mom, so something broke. The lamp wasn't any good, anyway."

Mrs. Collins looked at Dick with reproving eyes.

"I'll have Victoria clean it up before your father gets home," she said. Dick didn't answer. He pushed past his mother, not looking up, and scuffed his feet as he reached the top of the long graceful marble stairway that led to the first floor.

"Where are you going, Dick?" asked his mother, catching up to him on the stairs.

"To find a place to hide . . . in the cellar, probably . . . so the big bad boys of the press can't find me!"

His mother made a gesture as though to put one hand on Dick's shoulder, but Dick dodged, took a long step at the bottom of the stairway, and made for the mahogany-paneled library to the right. He slammed the door shut.

Dick was just staring at the deep upholstered green chair in his father's library when he heard the commotion out front—cars arriving, several voices shouting. The Ambassador was polite but very firm to the newspaper reporters who had followed him out to the residence.

"Please, gentlemen, I beg of you. The Minister of Public Instruction will issue all the statements that will be made. My son . . . my son is tired, and he will have nothing to say tonight. Please!"

"What about you, Mr. Ambassador?" someone shouted.

"I repeat, I have nothing to say. Please excuse us, gentlemen."

Dick opened the thick library door a crack and peered out. He recognized the way his father was holding his head, which meant he was trying to hold his temper. Mrs. Collins walked quietly behind her husband as the houseboy closed the door on the disappointed reporters. She whispered something in her husband's ear. Mr. Collins nodded, and came toward the library. Dick could see how pale his father was.

"Your mother tells me you are upset, Dick?" said Mr. Collins, pushing the library door open.

"Ye gods, Dad, why all the orders? I haven't talked to anybody . . ."

"And I don't want you to talk to anybody. I don't want your picture in the papers. If I could, I would keep your name out of this entirely. I am sorry I let you go with Prof."

"What's so bad about finding an old cave full of old bones?" Dick was defiant.

"In the first place, *you* didn't find it. In the second place . . ."

"I didn't say I found it all alone, did I?"

Father and son stared at each other. Something inside told Dick this was not the time to argue further, but he was having a hard time keeping still.

A long moment went by. Then Mr. Collins sighed, shook his head.

"I have a hard time persuading you that we are only guests down here, Dick," he said finally. "You are the son of the Ambassador from the big United States of America. Everything you do reflects not only on you, but on me, on the United States, on all Americans. I'm sorry, Dick. I don't like it any more than you do, but that is one of the penalties of diplomatic life."

"Diplomatic life makes me sick!"

"Seems to me you are acting pretty childish about this, Dick!" The color had returned to Mr. Collins' face. "I had hoped you would understand. I don't want your pictures in the papers, and I don't want you giving out any interviews to the press. Is that clear?"

Again Dick stared at his father, noticing the tall massive head of gray hair that always needed combing, the sharp gray eyes that returned his own stare.

"Back home in Indiana if I had found a cave full of old bones, my name and picture would have been plastered all over the front pages. Aunt Martha would have put the picture in the store window. The kids at school . . ."

"For the last time, we're not back home in Indiana, Dick, and there will be no pictures of Richard Collins in the papers!" Dick knew what his father's tightly pressed lips meant.

"OK, Dad," he said finally, "if that's the way you want it."

"That's the way I want it!" Mr. Collins walked slowly toward Dick. There was a sudden softness in his voice that went right to Dick's heart when his father spoke again.

"Prof and Antonio are coming to dinner in a little while. I thought it would be nice if we were all together when the official announcement is made by the government after Dr. Ortega returns from Pachacamac."

"Have they gone out there?" There was alarm in Dick's voice.

"Yes, the government has taken official charge," said his father slowly. "I'm afraid you and the others won't be going back there tomorrow . . . or any other day. An official from the Ministry of Foreign Relations phoned my office to say that Prof's report seemed to indicate an important discovery. If it is what they think it is—and we ought to know pretty soon now —it may uncover the tombs of Inca noblemen, perhaps even the Inca himself. The government has already closed all the approaches to Pachacamac. Do you see now why I want to keep you out of this as much as possible?"

"But, Dad, we didn't do anything wrong . . ."

"On the contrary, Dick. But the Spanish invaders plundered these graves once, and took a lot of gold out of the country. Ever since their independence, Peruvians have been very touchy about anybody from a foreign country finding Inca treasures. Let Prof get the credit for finding it, let the Museum people give out all the publicity they want to. But don't you see how any one of the opposition newspapers could embarrass the government by saying that the son of the Ambassador from the Colossus of the North had got something out of an Inca grave, even if you hadn't at all?"

Dick felt the hot flush crawling up his neck. He swallowed hard. For a moment he stared at the floor. He was trying hard to smile when he finally looked up at his father.

"I'm sorry, Dad," he said. "I guess I was just thinking how the kids at Carter High would envy me when they heard the news . . . I didn't think of this other . . ."

"No, of course you didn't," said his father placing a warm

hand on his shoulder. "Let's forget about it and get ready for dinner. Prof and Antonio should be here soon."

Dick walked up the stairs with his father. He didn't notice that his mother and sister were peering at them from behind the big door of the family living room. They walked down the upstairs corridor together, and as he passed his own door, Dick gave his father a quick pat on the back and stepped into his bedroom, closing the door softly behind him. The maid had cleaned away the broken lamp pieces and picked up the clothes strewn on the floor. Dick went directly to his bureau and took out a white shirt. He threw the green shirt into the closet, and hoped his father hadn't noticed it on him. He selected the new gray tie his father had given him for his birthday, and tied an ascot knot. He looked at himself in the mirror over his bureau, and noticed his hair needed combing. The white comb had just been washed.

"Mom, again," he said, half-aloud, smiling.

He left the bedroom door open as he walked down the hall and down the wide stairs. Maybe Prof would bring some more news from downtown. They had lots to talk over.

3

The Secrets of the Mountains

DINNER WAS ALMOST OVER BEFORE THE TELEPHONE RANG. It was Anderson, from the Embassy staff. His voice was excited.

"Mr. Ambassador, Dr. Ortega has just returned. He has told the newspapers that this may be the most important single find in the past 25 years . . . those are definitely burial caves of ancient Inca nobility."

"Did the newspaper people call you up again, Anderson?" Mr. Collins could not hide the excitement in his voice.

"Yes, sir, but they understand there will be no statement from here."

"Good. If you hear anything further tonight let me know. Otherwise, I'll see you at the office tomorrow morning."

"Good night, sir."

"Good night, Anderson; and thank you for calling."

Eager faces awaited Mr. Collins' return. Dick thought he could not wait until his father spoke. His last mouthful stuck right in his throat.

"Professor," said Mr. Collins, smiling broadly, "I guess you did it all right. Dr. Ortega has just announced that those are genuine Inca burial caves. Digging starts tomorrow morning at daybreak."

"But we won't be there." Dick sounded as though he were feeling very sorry for himself.

"No, you won't. But I imagine we will hear a lot about it in the next few weeks."

Dick was not satisfied. But he knew he could not argue. He looked up quickly and caught Prof looking at him across the table with an amused but intense look.

"Dick, you look as though it was the end of the world!" Prof's eyes were smiling.

"Well, it is . . . almost. Gee whiz, we just barely got started and now it's all over."

"Oh, but it isn't! Antonio and I were talking over a possible trip as we drove out here tonight, and if your parents will permit it, we can plan to start very soon. Summer vacation will start, you know, in another two weeks."

"Summer vacation?" Dorothy's shrill voice sounded incredulous.

"Why, yes—you are living below the Equator now, and summer starts December 22 down here!" There was almost pride in Prof's voice as he answered. Dorothy's eyes were big.

"You mean just a line across the middle of the earth changes summer to winter and winter to summer?" she demanded.

"Well, it's not as simple as that, but that is the general idea. You see . . ."

"Gosh, Sis, you had all that in school," interrupted Dick, impatiently. "How about letting Prof tell us about our trip?"

"Hey, not so fast, young fellow!" Mr. Collins' voice was not angry, but it sounded judicial, as though he were reserving judgment. Dick's spirits fell again, especially when his father added: "We haven't heard what this is all about, yet."

"Well, sir," said Prof avoiding Mrs. Collins' eyes, having seen them fill with anxiety at the first mention of the proposed trip, "one of the things we have been looking for, for many years, is the remains of the Inca highway that stretched from Cuzco at the center, northward all the way up to Quito in Ecuador and the high Andes beyond, and southward into the farthest point of Chile almost to the Antarctic regions. Somewhere in the mountains east and south of us here lies the secret of that magnificent highway. We thought . . . that is, if you and Mrs. Collins would permit it . . . the five of us who have formed an unofficial explorers club could take a trip about one hundred miles inland during this summer vacation and see if we could find a part of that road."

"Any caves to dig up there?" Mrs. Collins apparently had an aversion to caves.

"No, not especially. The road, as far as we can determine, cut across the barren hillsides between here and Cuzco, crossed the deep canyons of the rivers that flow both ways, to the Pacific and to the Atlantic oceans, and connected the vast empire. Parts of the road, especially near and around Cuzco, are of course still in daily use. Other parts of it form the foundation for the Pan-American Highway. Some sections have been lost. We thought we might go out and look for at least one of these sections, up by the town of Huancayo."

"Is that the town way up on the mountains, fourteen or fifteen thousand feet high?" Dick's voice was all interest again.

"That's right. It was also where the Incas filled the river bed with rich soil and grew potatoes at 13,000 feet altitude."

"Potatoes, at 13,000 feet?" Even the Ambassador found it hard to believe that, thinking of the 'timber line' back in the States, usually far below any such height.

"Yes, they grew potatoes. You would have a hard time identifying these little half-frozen marbles grown up there as the ancestors of your magnificent Idaho baking potatoes, Mr. Collins, but they are. The potato came from Peru, and was taken from here to . . . well, to Ireland, and the United States, and the rest of the world."

"Incredible!" Dick's mother was now interested, too.

"How long would you be gone, Prof?" asked Mr. Collins.

Dick's heart leaped at the sound of his father's voice. He knew that sound. His Dad was sure one fine pal! Dick almost held his breath until Prof answered.

"Oh, perhaps a week, maybe ten days . . . we can drive up to Huancayo, and make that our headquarters. We would explore on foot."

"The same five of you—you, and Antonio, and Pepe and Chico, and Dick?"

"Yes, that is the plan," Prof answered. Then his mother spoke.

"Isn't that awfully dangerous in those high mountains?" she asked.

"No—not with ordinary care. I am sure the boys would all be careful. I should not want to take them on a dangerous mission, Mrs. Collins."

"Of course not!" Mr. Collins sounded reassuring. Again Dick's heart jumped. He knew his Dad would say yes, even though they might have to spend a little time convincing his Mom.

"Dick's mother and I would like to talk it over, Prof," said Mr. Collins after a pause. "Suppose you three conspirators make tentative plans while Mother and I go upstairs for a while. I'll join you in the library later."

"Can I stay here with Dick, Mom?" Dorothy was full of excitement. Dick glanced quickly at his mother, his eyes full of silent appeal. He was relieved to see that Mom understood, for she said:

"You come along with me, Sister . . . let the men hatch their schemes. I have something planned for you, too."

Mrs. Collins got up from the table and everybody else also stood up, while she walked gracefully to the door. Dick felt a warm glow of pride looking at his mother. How young she looks; and smart, too, he thought. At that moment he was very proud of his Mom. Mr. Collins waved a hand from the doorway. "I'll join you in a half-hour or so," he promised.

"Prof," said Dick as soon as they were gone, "do you think we can find that lost road?"

"We can try, Dick," said Prof, walking toward the hallway that led to the library at the foot of the stairs. Dick and Antonio, locking arms in silent pledge, followed.

Prof would not let the boys stray far from the task at hand, which was the planning of what might be needed for such an expedition.

"We'll take my car, of course," he said, as soon as they were all seated on the big leather couch in Mr. Collins' library. "But for this trip I think it might be better if we borrowed or rented a Jeep for Antonio to drive. They are better mountain-climbers."

"I want to go in the Jeep with Antonio, Prof," said Dick, seeing in his imagination the stub-nosed olive-drab Jeep churning all four wheels up the steep mountain side, himself on the front seat alongside of Antonio, the canvas top down, the sturdy little vehicle eating up the miles, not afraid of stones, or desert, or high mountains.

"You're not planning to drive it, are you, Dick?" Prof teased.

"I could! I drove a Jeep back home in Indiana."

"Well, we'll see about that when the time comes. We have a lot of planning to do so we can tell Mr. Collins when he comes back."

Forgotten were the mummy caves at Pachacamac; forgotten the excitement, the disappointment, the frustration of the last few hours; a whole new world of excitement and exploration opened before them as they discussed sleeping bags, extra blankets, hob-nailed boots, heavy woolen socks, picks, shovels, canes, axes, ponchos, hunting knives, first-aid kits.

"One thing none of us must forget is a good flashlight, with new batteries, and perhaps a couple of spare batteries just in case," said Prof.

"No electric lights up there, eh, Prof?" Dick was trying to figure out what the natives did for light in the mountains.

"No electricity," answered Prof, smiling. "You would probably scare the natives half to death if you ever turned on an electric light in their town. Most of them have never seen a flashlight, either; at least they have never held one in their hands. It's part of the new magic of our world."

Antonio had said little, but he had been making notes and lists of all the things they had been discussing, putting down alongside his idea of what the total cost might be.

"So far," he said, seriously, looking a little discouraged, "a rough estimate already runs up over three hundred dollars!"

"Three hundred dollars!" Prof and Dick echoed the words together.

"And that's without rental of the Jeep, nor any allowance for gas and oil," added Antonio, as though he were passing a sentence.

There was a deep silence that lasted several long seconds. Dick scarcely dared to look at Prof, but when he did, he was surprised to see Prof smiling.

"I have a special 'travel fund' I have been saving for a long, long time," said Prof at last, "and I can't imagine any better way of spending it than this way."

"I'm sure that Dad will let me pay part of it," said Dick, brightening, wondering just how much his father would consider a fair share.

"I cannot contribute much money," said Antonio, a little sadly.

"You don't need to, Antonio," Prof assured him. "We will get the money. But let's go over the list of things again . . . your father will be back any minute, Dick, and we must be ready."

They checked the items over, one by one.

"Oh, I almost forgot!" Prof exclaimed. "We must carry a supply of the new medicines and drugs. We can put them in Dick's first-aid kit. Against mountain sickness and stomach upset, terramycethin; penicillin; and that sulpha powder for cuts and possible snake-bites."

"Snake-bites?" Dick's alarmed question was out before he realized it.

"Just as a precaution, Dick," said Prof quickly. "You don't even have to say anything about it."

"Don't worry, I won't! If Mom ever heard about that, that would be the end of the trip, right then and there!" Dick was glad his Dad wasn't in the room either.

"And of course aspirin, and bandages, and a small bottle of merthiolate," Prof went on, listing the things on the fingers of his left hand. Antonio was putting them all down.

"Quite a drugstore!" said Dick, when Prof stopped a moment to think.

"Don't forget, in the mountain villages there are no drugstores," said Prof seriously. "We have to be prepared. What is it you say? 'Better be safe than sorry'? We want to be very happy on this trip, Dick."

"You bet we do, Prof. We'll have a wonderful time!"

The door opened and Mr. Collins strode in with that confident sure step Dick knew so well.

"Well, Mother is satisfied that you will be in safe hands with Prof," he said, smiling, addressing Dick but really looking at Prof. "Have you three figured out what you will need?"

"We figured it would cost more than three hundred dollars!" Dick exploded before the others had a chance to say anything. Prof opened his mouth to speak, but Mr. Collins spoke first.

"That's not such an insurmountable obstacle, Dick," he said.

"Oh, but I have a small fund for this sort of thing, Mr. Collins," Prof said, while Antonio watched the Ambassador's face. "I will be glad to . . ."

"You and I can straighten that out between us later, I am sure, Prof," answered Mr. Collins. "I am anxious to see how you three have planned for the trip. I only wish I could go with you!"

They crowded around the Ambassador's big desk as Dick's father, pencil in hand, checked off the list of things, noting the precise little numbers Antonio had written beside each item. One caught his eye especially.

"Five dollars for flashlight batteries?" he asked, half laughing.

"Fresh batteries cost fifty cents a piece. They are imported." It was as though Antonio were making an accurate inventory report in a business office.

"Oh, of course! I forgot."

"Aren't you conspirators ever going to bed?" said Mrs. Collins from the doorway. The door had been left open. How long had she been there, Dick wondered . . . and had she heard when his father read off 'penicillin, sulpha'? They looked up quickly and noted the clock over the mantel said almost midnight!

"Forgive us, Mrs. Collins," said Prof, as usual the first on his feet when Mrs. Collins entered the room. "We just forgot the time . . ."

"And everything else, almost," added Mr. Collins. "Let's all go to bed, tomorrow is another day." Then, on a sudden impulse, he added, "Would you and Antonio like to stay here tonight, Prof? You have no Mrs. Bentley to worry about your whereabouts," he said, smiling at Mrs. Collins, "and I am sure you would be comfortable in the guest rooms, you and Antonio."

"Yes, Prof, how about it?" asked Dick, taking hold of Prof's arm.

"You are very kind," said Prof, blushing a little in a way Dick had never seen him blush before, "but I think Antonio and I better get back to our Pension."

"But you will come tomorrow night for dinner again?" It was Mrs. Collins inviting them this time.

"Thank you, we will. There is still much to plan," Prof answered.

"Thanks, Mom—and Dad—for letting me go," said Dick when the door closed behind Prof and Antonio. Mrs. Collins put an arm over Dick's shoulder and gave it a little squeeze with her warm hand. Mr. Collins stood looking at Dick, a faraway look in his eye. Finally he said:

"You're a lucky fellow, Dick . . . I wish I could go with you!"

"You men are all the same . . . just big boys all your lives!"

said Mrs. Collins as they put out the lights in the hallway and started up the marble stairway.

Dick looked at his father. Suddenly the thought flashed through his mind that only a few hours before they had stared at each other like this, almost in the same spot. Things were different now.

"Thanks, Dad, for . . . everything," he said. Mr. Collins waved a hand at him, and nodded.

The next two weeks were the longest Dick had ever lived through. Final examinations, school closing, summer vacations, the nearness of Christmas—everything faded into the background in the preparations for the trip into the mountains above Huancayo. For a few days the newspapers were filled with details of the growing discoveries at Pachacamac, but other than discussing it very briefly one evening after dinner (by this time Prof and Antonio, and generally Pepe and Chico also, were almost nightly visitors at the big Collins residence in Miraflores) all thoughts and plans were on the trip to find the lost Inca highway.

At last the great day came. Dick was up long before daybreak. Prof and Antonio had slept in the guest rooms Mrs. Collins had prepared for them, and Chico and Pepe were to be picked up in front of Pepe's house on the way out of town. The road was the same that had taken them to Pachacamac; it passed that once-great Temple City, and wound up into the hills, climbing steadily after it left the plains around Pachacamac.

By noon the green valley was far behind, and they were up in the barren hills, nothing but desert sands all around them. After a long, hot dusty afternoon they arrived just at sunset on the outskirts of the mountain town of Huancayo.

"Look at that sunset!" said Dick, pointing, as Antonio pulled the hand-brake on the Jeep and stopped right in back of Prof's old Buick. The sky had suddenly turned crimson; then a jet black strip, like a black ribbon, crossed the entire sky, spread out, and swallowed up the crimson color. Suddenly, even before the boys had got out of the car, the sky had turned deep gray and it was night.

"Wow! That was quick!" said Dick, stretching his legs to free the cramped muscles.

"That's only a sample of what you will see up here in the mountains," Prof assured him, as Dick came alongside the big black sedan.

"By the way, Prof," said Dick, "I never knew a Buick that could climb like that old jalopy of yours." His voice was full of honest admiration.

"I should have told you before, Dick . . . my old Buick has a special transmission, and four-wheel drive. Otherwise I would never have kept up with you and Antonio in that Jeep."

They were in front of a pink-and-white stucco building. Its low second story and red tile roof set it apart from the thatch-roofed huts all about. The weathered wooden sign over the doorway read *Hospedaje*.

"Here's where we get our rooms for tonight, boys," said Prof, grabbing his canvas suitcase. "Might as well take everything out of the cars and up to our rooms now. Then we will be settled."

"Everything?" said Dick, his hand on the handle of his leather bag.

"See that mountain up ahead, the top just showing in the last sunlight? That's where we are going, but we are going on foot. You've had your last ride for a week!" Prof was already at the door of the little inn.

The rooms were small, but comfortable and clean. The cold night air from the mountains blew the little red and green muslin curtains at the window. Dick shivered. Antonio, who was to share the room with him, crossed over and closed the window.

"It gets very cold at night up here in the mountains," he said. "You will need the two blankets on your bed."

"I thought this was the beginning of summer!" Dick laughed.

"We are more than 12,000 feet high," Antonio answered. "In the mountains it is always cool . . . especially at night. The sun will be warm tomorrow, though; it always is." There was a special ring to Antonio's voice as he said "the sun."

"When do we start tomorrow, Prof?" asked Dick as the five gathered in the little dining room downstairs. A friendly little fire was burning in the fireplace, and Dick was surprised to feel how welcome the heat was. He stood with his back to the fire, facing the others nearby. A native houseboy, with white cotton shirt and cotton pants that once had also been white, announced that "the dinner is ready."

"If we are all feeling all right," said Prof, and Dick saw him exchange a glance with Antonio, "we will start as soon as it is daylight. The maestro here promises us breakfast before sunrise. Eggs, coffee, potatoes broiled in bacon grease, and homemade bread."

For the first time in more than two weeks Dick felt he could really sleep. He didn't notice that the little narrow bed was hard, its lumpy mattress barely wide enough to hold him. He was asleep almost before he had time to answer Antonio's "good-night." It was Antonio who blew out the candle. The mountain air smelled sweet and pure . . . and cold. Dick knew nothing until he felt a hand shaking him.

It was Antonio, and he was already dressed. And in the sky Dick could just see a faint gray light.

4

Lost Cities and Hanging Bridges

Several times that morning they had to stop to let one or the other of the party catch his breath. Dick was having difficulty breathing, and welcomed these stops. The air seemed to get thinner and thinner, his breath got shorter, and he wondered how the others, especially Prof and Antonio, could maintain their steady pace.

"It's mostly in your breathing," Prof told him after another short stop. Dick was leaning heavily on his mountain stick, panting, mouth open. "Pace your breathing with your walking," Prof went on. "You have to get more oxygen into your lungs, and the higher we go, the less oxygen there is, so you have to breathe faster. Breathe in every two steps, out every two steps. Keep it up steadily and you'll see how much less tired you get."

It helped, but Dick found it hard to keep up the regular breathing. There was no protest from him when Prof called a halt for luncheon.

They camped high above the town of Huancayo. They could

barely see the village, which from up here looked like a tiny toy town clinging to the slope of a toy hill far below. Before them lay the roaring canyons of the tributaries of the mighty Apurimac River; somewhere to their left, hidden by giant forests and buried under centuries of fierce, wild vegetation, the ancient north-south Inca highway stretched hundreds of miles in both directions. To their right, enormous mountains showed snow-fields, and sleet-gray precipices that rose thousands of feet into a wind-tossed ocean of clouds hiding the eternally frozen mountain tops.

Slinging their packs off their backs was about the most welcome thing they had done all morning, Dick thought. He unhooked his canteen, hunting knife, and small ax from his belt. He opened his shirt and dropped on the ground, panting.

"Be careful, boys," said Prof as Pepe and Chico followed suit. "The wind up here is very chilly and you are sweaty."

Dick shivered. It was cold! He looked at Prof, who didn't say anything, and then noticed Antonio busy making a small fire behind some stones he had gathered. Dick got up to help. Never had the smell of wood fire been so full of welcome fragrance. Never had broiling bacon sizzled and smelled so deliciously. Even the tough unleavened bread, which Dick had found so tasteless before, tasted suddenly good.

"Guess I was just hungry!" he said as they squatted around the fire. In spite of the sun overhead, the warmth from the crude little fireplace felt good.

"Put your sweaters on, boys," said Prof, joining them. "We will sit here for a while. I have something to discuss with you."

The boys slipped their sweaters on and looked expectantly at Prof.

"Somewhere in these hills, boys, may lie the real secret of the Incas' greatness. From these hills they carried water down into the valleys, and even to some of the cities, in marvellously constructed aqueducts. Through these aqueducts, which sometimes were underground, they brought mountain streams down to irrigate the fields. The water flowed from one slope to the next and finally reached the terraced gardens on the slopes of these mountains."

"That must have been some job to build those aqueducts!" Dick was genuinely impressed.

"The Incas had excellent engineers and architects," said Prof. "You will see in Cuzco and on the outskirts of their ancient Sacred City many buildings which they built centuries ago and which are still standing, exactly as they built them."

"What about the doors and windows and roofs?" asked Dick, who had seen pictures of roofless houses with silent stone walls looking sad and wretched and abandoned.

"Well, the doors are gone, if they did have doors. Many think they had heavy rugs and skins over the doorways, but they must have had some heavy wooden doors too because there are indications in some of the ruins in Pissac and Ollaytantambo that polished stone clubs held the massive doors in place, like stone locks. But as for windows, if you are thinking of glass, of course there were none. There was nothing in the windows except the opening."

"What about when it rained? Or up here, when it snowed?"

"Then it rained or snowed!" Prof's voice sounded a bit amused, but there was a ring of pride in it, too. "You must remember that the walls were sometimes several feet thick, always one and a half to two feet, and this naturally helped to keep rain out. But of course it did not keep the cold out. That's why many of the walls were solid, and windows were few and small. Even today, you will notice that most native huts are made without windows."

"Weren't the houses awfully dark inside?" asked Dick, trying to picture his father's house without windows.

"Probably. But you must remember that houses in the days of the Incas were only shelters for the workers and their families. They worked from sun-up to sun-down, and since there was nothing to do in the evening after sun-down, they mostly slept. And of course, they were ready for sleep: there were no 40-hour weeks in those days! It was work, work, work—every day and all day. Every man had his job given to him, and he was told what to do and where to do it. Some, like the guardians of the Inca's highways, passed their profession on proudly to their sons; also the gold and silver smiths. But mostly they worked in the fields, working everlastingly to grow crops to feed the subjects of the Inca.

"One-third of all crops belonged to the Inca, one-third to the Sun, one-third to the people. The Inca's share was used in his many palaces. All nobles and of course all members of the royal family were fed from the Inca's share. Out of this also came the share that was in the storehouses so that at all times there would be supplies for the Inca's armies in all places where they might be needed, and for travelers. Of course, only the nobles and the military traveled, and occasionally some merchant; the other people stayed home, very close to home, and only went to their place of work and back again. Never to another town or province, unless sent there as *mitimae*—workers sent by the Inca from one section of the country to another."

"Seems as though the Inca boss just about ruled everything in the lives of his people then," said Dick.

"You are exactly right, that is just what did happen," answered Prof, exchanging a smile with Antonio. "Everything about the people's lives was decided for them by the Inca or his representative: what clothes they wore, what food they ate, where they lived, what work they did, what holidays they could celebrate. Yes, Dick, believe it or not, the Inca even ruled how the people should cut their hair!"

"Imagine anybody trying that today!"

"No, it is hard for us who believe in personal liberty to imagine that today," said Prof.

Antonio, who had been listening attentively, as he always did when Prof or someone else spoke of the ancient Inca days, turned now to his *norte-americano* friend. His eyes were very serious, and there was no smile on his lips.

"But you must not think that people were abused, Dick," he

said in his crisp and very correct English. "Remember that because of the system, there was no poverty, there was no hunger, there was no unemployment. The sick and the old were cared for by the State, and every man received food and clothing in proportion to his needs. The father with ten children got ten times more than the man with none, or only one child. And if there was a crop failure, the people were fed from the great storehouses filled with food by the farsightedness of the Inca rulers."

"Antonio is right," Prof said, quickly, before Dick could offer any argument that might cause feeling between the boys. "The rulers ruled completely and governed sternly, but they were just and compassionate with their people. And everybody worked, except the very young and the old. Idleness was one of the three crimes punishable by death, that's how much the Incas valued work."

"What were the other two major crimes, Prof?"

"Stealing and killing. But, you see, there really was no need to steal. The people were provided with everything they needed, and there was no such thing as private property. So, nothing to steal."

The boys were silent, thinking that one over. Then Prof's voice came to them again.

"But that isn't really what I started to talk about," he said. "Look down over these mountains and see how the vegetation comes up sometimes to the very top of the mountain. Hidden somewhere in these deep jungle forests there are perhaps as many as one hundred lost cities, in their day complete with aqueducts, baths for the nobles, terraced gardens, sumptuous homes, and hundreds, perhaps even thousands of small one-room houses for the workers. The tradition persists that there were many such cities, and they have been lost. Maybe one of you boys will find them some day. That would be a real contribution to the archaeological history of Peru!"

"How did the people get to these cities, Prof?" Dick was puzzled.

"Possibly over the very Inca highway we are supposed to be looking for, Dick. They must have been accessible from the highways—the four main highways built by the Incas going north, south, east and west out of Cuzco, radiating like four spokes in a giant wheel. But though the tradition of the cities persists, their actual location has been lost for over four hundred years."

"Do you suppose some of those tombs in the desert might be near those lost cities, Prof?"

"Possibly, but I doubt it. You see, each city has its own cemetery, where the nobles were buried. In fact, one of the proud governmental posts in the ancient Inca cities was that of Aya Camayoc—the Guardian of the Dead. He had a large house at the edge of the cemetery, and no one could enter the cemetery without his permission. Not even the Priests! Later on this high post declined in importance, and finally the Aya-Camayoc was little better than gatekeeper. But I imagine that in the days of these lost cities the Guardian of the Dead was an important official in the town."

"Before we left Lima," said Dick, suddenly feeling a little homesick, although he didn't know why, "Dad said they had found some jars and earthen dishes in that tomb at Pachacamac, and he said you could still see the color on the dishes."

"I am not surprised at that," answered Prof. "The art of ceramics was very far advanced in the Inca days. Of course, the dishes placed in the tombs of the nobles were the best made, for they contained food supposed to last the departed spirit on his long journey to his ancestors. And sometimes, when they buried some of his servants or some of his chosen women in the tomb with him, the supplies had to be much greater."

"You mean they killed the nobleman's servants or his chosen women when he died?" Dick's voice betrayed his startled surprise.

"Not necessarily . . . some of them chose to walk into the tomb and be sealed in with the body of their departed master."

"Ugh!" Dick exclaimed. "Not for me!"

"No, not nowadays for anybody, Dick. But you must remember that it was a long-standing custom, freely accepted, and that since all the people believed in immortality, it was simply going to another and probably happier world."

"And what if they didn't want to die?"

"Well, sometimes they were put into the tomb just the same. At least some archaeologists think so, because we have found mummies, especially of women, whose bodies were tied up in the traditional manner with their knees under their chins, and their arms and legs tightly bound. The expression on their faces indicates that some died screaming and their features were frozen in terror or pain."

"Ugh goes for me, too," chimed in Chico, who up to this time had said nothing at all. "I am glad I live in the Twentieth Century!"

"Many things have happened in this century that reflect no credit on man or his so-called civilization." Antonio's voice was very quiet, but steady. His eyes were narrowed to mere slits, and his lips were tightly drawn.

"Let's talk of happier things, boys," said Prof, rising quickly to his feet. "Meantime we better get moving if we expect to reach Ayacucho down in the valley before dark."

Everyone seemed to welcome the end of the discussion that had ended in such gruesome conversation. But Dick made a mental note to ask Prof some more about these servants and chosen women who were buried, sometimes alive, with their noble masters. Perhaps in Cuzco they might even be able to see some of these mummies in the museum. Prof had said the museum in Cuzco was one of the finest of its kind in the world.

The going down, on the other side of the mountain, was almost more strenuous than the climb up had been that morning. There was very little talk. Every so often they stopped, and all of them took deep breaths. Once or twice Dick was annoyed, and a little ashamed, that he felt dizzy and light-headed. But he said nothing. They walked on and on. The sun had already left the deep valley, and the night coldness was beginning to chill them when they finally reached the little village of Ayacucho. Prof spoke quickly, in Quechua, to a dark-skinned, big-chested native who had greeted them impassively. The native bowed, and called something into the interior of the hut in front of which they stood. There was some commotion inside. A few minutes later the native bowed again and said something Dick did not understand.

"This is our home for the night," said Prof. "Supper is ready, according to Pahuac here. Let's turn in early. I imagine we are all ready for a good night's sleep."

Dick's cries aroused the others early the next morning. The whole sky was aflame! Deep reds, purples, brilliant coral were splashed above them and clouds chased each other with the speed of wind; the whole sky was a streaked mass of blood-red flames!

"Look! Look! The sky is on fire!" Dick cried, pointing.

The boys tumbled out in the cold half-light of dawn. Gold rimmed the jagged mountain tops to the east, ran along the scraggly edges. Excited natives ran out of thatched-roofed huts, shouting, pointing.

"Ccaya manchachicusc! Tatai hanacpacha! Manchachicusc!" they cried, running around, pointing, calling in at darkened doorways.

Men, women and children, some of the smaller ones almost naked, all of them barefooted, despite the cold, ran into the street, pointing to the sky, crying, shouting.

Prof, hastily pulling on his sweater, joined Dick and the other boys who had stopped in front of the hut in which they had spent the night. The narrow dirt street that formed the little village was now full of excited natives, dark-skinned and black-haired, shouting in Quechua things Dick could not understand. But from the tone in their voices, and the fear which was evident in all their faces, no one had to translate. Everyone was frightened.

"This is a terrible omen," said Prof, and in spite of himself, he, too, was shouting. "This is a Battle in the Skies. The Sun

God is fighting with Supay, the Devil-enemy. If Supay wins, he will push the Sun God back behind those mountains. Dreadful things can happen then. Earthquakes, avalanches, whole months of rain to ruin the crops. You see how the Sun God is running along the top edges of the mountains? The people believe that is his army fighting a running fight. Those red and purple clouds are blood, blood of the soldiers, thousands of them."

"*Tatai! Tatai!* Our Father! Our Father!" shouted the natives.

Women and children huddled in little groups. Some cried, some whimpered. Here and there one of them would scream. Men ran back and forth in the narrow street, pointing, throwing up their arms, yelling, throwing kisses with both hands at the mountain where the sun was having such a hard time to show its light. Dick ran back into the hut, and came out with his camera.

But he had no sooner reached the street than an angry, shouting group of men surrounded him.

"*Supay! Supay!* The enemy!" they cried, pointing at Dick.

"No, no!" shouted Dick. "I am a friend! Prof! Antonio! Help!"

Antonio jumped, pushed, clawed his way to his friend's side.

"*Sullca pana!*" he shouted, trying to protect Dick. "He is my younger brother! Do not hurt him!" He held up his right hand high over his head. The startled natives, surprised at the voice in their own tongue, stopped short. But a sudden growl from one of the older men roused them and again the shouting started. "*Supay! Supay!*" and they pointed to Dick's camera.

"*Jucha! Jucha!* He is to blame!"

They pushed closer, and one man tried to snatch Dick's camera from him. Dick looked wildly about, saw that Prof, Pepe and Chico had also been surrounded and were talking earnestly with an older man who kept looking over at Dick from time to time as Prof spoke earnestly. The older man pointed to the sky, then to Dick, and back to the sky.

Suddenly the red clouds broke. A flash of brilliant sunshine pierced the entire horizon. Like defeated armies in full rout, the red clouds scampered across the sky, and disappeared, as though they had dissolved away up above the mountains. The sun majestically climbed over the snow-covered mountain.

A great shout went up from the entire village. Dick was astounded to hear his own voice, shouting and mingling with that of the natives around him. Then suddenly, as one man, the men fell to their knees, heads bowed, deep silence taking over where only a few seconds before shouts had filled the air. Women and children stopped their whimpering and they, too, fell on their knees. All heads were bowed, and from the old man who had been talking to Prof came a long, low moan. Slowly he raised his head, then lifted his arms as he bent backward on his knees almost to a sitting position and raised his eyes to the Sun God. He groaned and mumbled, then very slowly brought his arms down, his hands to his mouth, and with great reverence threw three kisses to the sky. That was the signal. Now all the men were throwing kisses, rocking backward and forward, mumbling, moaning, deep guttural noises deep down in their throats. They kept their eyes down, not daring to look up at their Sun God.

Antonio had moved swiftly over to Dick, who was still very pale from his experience.

"Whew, Antonio," he whispered, "that was a close one. I feel like kneeling down myself and giving thanks."

"Don't do that! Come quick with me!" and Antonio seized Dick's arm, pulling Dick back into the hut. Prof, Pepe and Chico soon joined them. Once inside, Antonio let go Dick's arm. Dick felt his knees trembling, the cold sweat on his forehead. His throat suddenly was very dry.

"Gosh, Prof," he managed, after swallowing hard several times, "if Antonio hadn't reached me when he did, I'd have been a dead duck!"

"It is well the Sun won the Battle in the Skies," said Antonio in a low, even voice. Dick turned quickly and looked at his Peruvian friend. Antonio was staring straight out of the doorway, up at the sky, now brilliant gold. Then suddenly Antonio dropped to his knees, crossed his arms over his chest, bowed his head. He stayed that way for a long, silent minute. His lips moved, but no sound came from them. Then he, too, kissed both hands and smacked his lips as he threw three kisses to the winds.

Dick had the queer sensation of having stepped back into the pages of history. He felt like an intruder. When the natives had fallen on their knees in prayer of thanksgiving, the ceremony, for all his recent fright, had seemed almost quaint; but seeing Antonio do it made it seem almost sacred.

"Come, boys, let's get breakfast and be gone. We have a long way to go." Prof's voice sounded reverent, too. Breakfast was eaten in silence.

Two hours later Dick found out what Prof had meant when he said that the Incas had been fearless engineers and builders. The high stone platform on which they stood seemed to have been hacked right out of the mountain as though with a giant knife which had cut down, and then at right angles, making a wide, flat L-cut in the rock itself. The floor on which they stood reached the steep walls of the rocky mountain, and plunged steeply into the valley below. Clinging to the mountainside at what seemed impossible angles, carefully terraced gardens showed the tiny yellow sprouts of newly-planted corn!

"These are some of the famous terraced gardens of the Incas," said Prof, noting Dick's astonishment. "All the earth behind those retaining walls, and the stones of those walls themselves, were brought up here in baskets on the backs of domesticated llamas, and of course of men and women. Thousands of them!"

"But how did they get up here?" Dick couldn't get over his surprise.

"Over that Inca road I was telling you about," said Prof. "That's what we came out to find, remember?"

Dick looked back at the narrow mountain path over which they had come to the high platform. The path seemed lost at the edge of the precipice. And yet, on the other side of the deep gorge before them, through which they could hear the roaring of the river, they could see on the other side a cut as clearly as though it had been a giant scar on the face of the mountain. It seemed impossible that anything less than a gigantic upheaval could have lifted these rugged mountains right out of the earth's surface, with fierce and angry streams of rushing water cutting deep precipices on the face of the rocky mountains, refusing to be denied passage on their relentless way to the sea. At this particular point the precipice dropped hundreds of feet into the roaring canyon of the Urubamba River.

"I guess this is as far as we go," said Dick, standing on the platform, looking down into the deep gorge.

Professor Bentley joined Dick and stood silently by his side for a few seconds. When Dick did not speak, Prof said: "I guess you haven't become an expert mountain guide yet, Dick."

Dick turned. Prof was smiling.

"See how this path goes down here, clinging closely to the mountainside? It goes clear down to the water's edge, and goes up the other side."

"How come I didn't see it before, Prof?"

"It isn't traveled very often. And what you do see from here isn't part of the old Inca highway."

"How did they get across, then?"

"On suspension bridges," said Prof, looking now across the chasm of the river canyon.

"You mean bridges hanging from this platform where we are standing, and winging clear over to the other side?" Dick's voice showed how hard it was for him to believe a bridge could span three hundred feet or more of empty space over a frightening chasm.

"Yes, from right here. See those big boulders? They were the bridge anchors. The hole in the center was for the thick cable, made of tough fibers. Look at the size of the hole in the buttress: bigger than a man's body! That's how thick those cables were, woven by hand out of strand after strand of fibres from these forests."

"But how did they get across to the other side with these cables?"

"Specially selected men carried one end down into the ravine, across the river, and up the other side again. It was hard work."

"I can believe that! That cable must have weighed a ton!"

"It did, indeed. And that was not all. They stretched several of these cables across, sometimes five or six of them, put them through the buttresses on the other side, and locked them in place with heavy timbers. Then they lashed the cables together, and covered them with planks. Only a thin rope railing protected the traveler. The bridge swung from side to side over the river."

"But Prof, that's almost three hundred feet across here!" Dick still found it hard to believe these marvels.

"That's right."

"But didn't the whole thing sag?"

"Yes, it did. And you can imagine it must have been a frightening experience to cross over on such a bridge, dipping down almost to the water, swinging from side to side—and that river roaring underneath."

"I don't think I would like that a-tall!" said Dick.

"If you had been a soldier in the Inca's army you would not have been asked if you liked it or not." Antonio's face was impassive as he spoke from close beside Dick. His sharp black eyes were filled with a strange light.

"You think you could run across on a suspension bridge from here to the other side?" asked Dick.

"Run?" asked Antonio, still looking across the chasm. "No, not run, but I would march or walk across it."

Suddenly it seemed to Dick that he could see Antonio, stoically erect, marching across the bridge, swinging with the rhythm of the suspended cables—tramp, tramp, tramping in unison with thousands of other Antonios. Again he had that queer feeling of being in another age, hundreds of years ago. Antonio did not even notice Dick's stare.

"And then," Prof was saying, bringing Dick back, "these bridges were rebuilt every year. The Incas took no chances with having one of them collapse with several hundred fighting men on them."

"Every year, Prof?"

"Yes, once a year. Men were especially selected and trained for that one job. They were bridge builders, and nothing else."

Dick looked down into the deep ravine. The water foamed and tumbled over giant boulders that lay, like wounded soldiers, on their side in midstream. The fierce river seemed to be trying to push the mountains out of the way as it rushed on and on, day after day, ceaselessly fighting. Again Prof seemed to read Dick's mind.

"Every day those waters carry a little bit of Peru, maybe a little bit of Inca gold, to the Amazon, and so on to the Atlantic Ocean."

"The Atlantic Ocean? But that's thousands of miles away!"

"That's right, Dick, about four thousand miles. You see, this is almost the Continental Divide. The rivers in back of us, behind the mountain we just climbed, run west to the Pacific, little more than a hundred miles away in some places. But these others, these big ones like the Urubamba, they leave the mountains and go through the deepest jungles in the world, joining the Amazon where the jungle is so thick that very few white men have ever seen it. Eventually these cold waters are all turned into the warm muddy waters of the Amazon that sprawls through northern Brazil and eventually flows into the Atlantic Ocean."

"I'd like to follow the river some day and go down the length of it, Prof," Dick said after some moments of silence.

"Would you, Dick? That's a long, long journey."

"Dad told me about some of those tribes there in the upper Amazon," said Dick, "whole tribes that live in great big huts and have never seen a white man, and go around blowing darts from bamboo tubes, killing wild animals and their enemies with poison darts."

"If they have never seen a white man, how does a white man

know what they do?" Pepe was puzzled as he joined the conversation.

"Oh, I guess 'never' is not quite right. The Museum of Natural History sent an expedition down there and took some pictures of the natives."

"Wonder if the natives there were frightened by the cameras?" asked Dick.

Everybody laughed.

"That camera of yours will get you in trouble yet," said Pepe.

"Let's not start that again," warned Prof. "Anyway, we better cook a little lunch here and start back. We have a lot of travel ahead of us tomorrow."

"Where are we going tomorrow, Prof?"

"Tomorrow we go to Cuzco," said Prof, and the word 'Cuzco' sounded as though he said it reverently. "Cuzco was the Sacred City of the Incas. Now it is only a big town, but at one time there were as many as two hundred thousand inhabitants there. They were the chosen ones. Cuzco was the heart of the great Inca Empire."

"We walk there tomorrow?" asked Dick, beginning to wonder whether his feet would hold out.

"No," said Prof, "we double back out of the mountains here and drive from Ayacucho. Our cars have been driven there for us. It isn't as far as you think, but it looks impossible. It isn't. There is a very good stretch of the old road, used almost every day. But we'll come back and look for the lost road again."

"We are going to Ayacucho tonight?" asked Dick, remembering the two days they had been climbing around.

"Oh, yes, that town is just over this high hump in front of us," answered Prof. "We could have come directly over it the first day, but we went around through the river canyons."

"I am glad we did, Prof," said Dick seriously, as his companions watched. "That was some experience!"

5

Stairway to the Sky

AWAKENING THE NEXT MORNING IN THE LITTLE INN AT Huancayo, Dick knew he would not drive to Cuzco—or anywhere else—that day. Never in his life had he been so cold! Never had his head ached so that 'splitting' was the only word he could think of for it.

"Prof!" he groaned, "I feel awful! My head! And my stomach! It must have been that dinner last night . . . I'm poisoned . . . Oh, my head!"

"No, Dick," said Prof comfortingly, "you are just having an attack of *soroche,* what you call 'mountain sickness.' I am surprised you didn't have it before. Many people get it the first time they climb into high altitudes. The air is very thin, you know."

"Oh, my head! My stomach! Will I have this all the time we are here?" There was genuine despair in Dick's voice.

"Oh, no. It will pass. A day, half a day . . . you'll be all right in no time. I'll bring you some hot tea . . ."

"Ugh! Nothing to eat . . . I can't hold it down . . ."

"Prof," cried Pepe from the doorway, "something's happened to Chico! He's sick at his stomach, and says his head aches . . ."

"He, too?" Prof was more amused than alarmed. "Tell him to lie down and cover him up with all the blankets you can find. It will pass. But I guess this means we simply stay here today and forget about Cuzco until tomorrow."

Knowing that he was not alone helped Dick somewhat, but not much. In another half-hour he was shivering so that nothing seemed to be able to warm him, not even when Antonio piled his own blankets on top of Dick. His head ached almost beyond endurance. His stomach turned over and over as if it were trying to tear his insides out.

"Give in to it, Dick, relax. You'll feel better tomorrow," said Prof, as he hurried out to look at his other patient.

Dick wasn't sure there would be a tomorrow.

But he must have slept, for he awakened with a start. The gold of the early morning sun had rimmed the jagged mountain tops to the east, outlining them with a fine, brilliant line of light. Antonio was asleep in his own bed. The cool morning air smelled of mountain dew. From somewhere came the fragrance of hot coffee and frying bacon.

"Gee! I must have slept all day and all night, too!" Dick could not believe it.

Antonio stirred.

"You awake, Antonio?" asked Dick, sitting up in bed.

"The dead comes back to life," laughed Antonio, also sitting up. His tousled hair looked very black in the gray half-light of the room. His skin was deep bronze, almost purple.

"Have I been asleep all this time?" asked Dick, incredulously.

"You sure have," answered Antonio. "And you missed something yesterday. Prof and I went up the mountain in the afternoon and came face to face with one of those little bears they call 'spectacled bears' because they have large brown rings around their eyes, like spectacles. I don't know which of us was more startled, but we retreated very fast when we saw the mother bear coming out of the woods."

"Gee! I wish you had caught him and brought him in."

"Nothing to stop you from going up there and capturing him yourself, if you feel like wrestling with the mama bear."

"Was she very big?" asked Dick.

"Big enough! I don't want her. Beside her you would look like a guinea-pig!"

"Speaking of guinea-pigs, didn't you tell me that the people in these mountains ate guinea-pig for meat?"

"*Cucuy?*" laughed Antonio, "yes, they eat *cucuy*. You'll get to try it soon. You'll like it."

"The way I feel now, I could eat anything!" Dick suddenly realized he hadn't eaten for almost twenty-four hours!

They had breakfast in the little terrace outside the inn, overlooking the wild mountains all around. Far down in the canyon to the south the river sounded like muffled drums, pounding its way to the sea. Deep shadows clung stubbornly to the slopes of the hills immediately before them, yielding reluctantly to the climbing light of morning. This morning there was no Battle of the Skies. The lantern of the morning star—the lovely Shaska of Inca tradition—had lighted the path for the sun. It now climbed over the top of the big mountain to the east, flooding the valley with warmth and light. Suddenly it was day.

"We've lost a whole day," said Prof. "I think we should get started as soon as possible."

"Gee, I'm sorry, Prof," said Dick.

"You couldn't help it; neither could Chico. It might have been I, or Pepe, or even Antonio. It doesn't matter, I'm only glad you both feel well again. What do you say we get started?"

"*Adelante!*" cried Dick, pleased and proud of his growing Spanish vocabulary.

This time, Pepe was to ride with Antonio in the Jeep, and follow Prof; Dick and Chico would go in the closed sedan.

"You'll still be a little shaky from yesterday, you two," said Prof. "But you'll be fine by nightfall."

"We'll be in Cuzco then!" asked Dick.

"I certainly hope so!"

Two hours later they reached the banks of a wide river. The rough, narrow road wound in a general southwesterly direction to the right. But straight ahead, across on the other side of the river, which here flowed rather slowly in comparison to the turbulent rushing farther up the valley, the mountain rose steeply several thousand feet. Sheer gray rock blocked all passage, like a giant wall erected by a giant hand. "Thus far and no farther!" it seemed to say. Snow and white clouds hid the top of the mountain.

They had stopped the cars and now Dick and the other boys were looking across, where Prof had pointed.

Carved into the live rock, in regular, rhythmic intervals, a stone stairway reached upward and lost itself in the clouds.

"Wow! Look at that! A Stairway to the Skies!" cried Dick.

The boys stood in silent admiration. Carefully carved steps, one after the other, about one foot apart, showed polished faces some two feet wide, climbing up, up, steadily up, straight up the face of the mountain. A straight ladder hundreds of feet high, man-made, hewn right out of the rock! Thousands of hands had fashioned them, thousands upon thousands of hours had been consumed, cutting, carving, polishing!

"That was the Inca passageway to the north," said Prof after a long silence. "The mountain was there, so they went over the mountain."

"Soldiers and all?" asked Dick.

"Especially soldiers. Most of the Inca roads were military roads. Few people traveled for pleasure, or for commerce. These were utilitarian roads, for conquest and defense."

"But Prof, there must be three thousand steps up that mountain!"

"Maybe. Maybe more. And they had selected men who did nothing but keep those steps clean at all times, including when it snowed. It was a profession passed on from father to son."

"What a way of earning a living!" Dick was thinking how lonely such a job must be, and how monotonous.

"They were proud to serve their Inca, just like everyone else was," said Antonio.

Dick looked quickly at his friend. "How much would a man earn for doing that?"

"You mean in money?"

"Sure, in money."

"Nothing."

"Nothing? What do you mean nothing?" Dick's voice was full of disbelief.

"The people in the time of the Incas had no money, and no need for money. As you remember, Prof told us that each family head and each worker received food, clothing, shelter, according to the number of people he was responsible for. He did whatever work was assigned to him. There was no need to buy anything, so he had no need for money." Prof had been listening as his two young charges discussed the matter, and now nodded as Antonio finished his discourse on money.

"The people got their compensation in other ways besides money," he said. "One of the greatest was pride in their work."

Dick was still thinking that one over when Prof called: "Time to get going, boys." They got in the cars again, and soon the sputtering and coughing of the motors shot back at them from the granite cliffs on the other side of the river. The road left the river bank and started climbing, zig-zagging over barren, rocky slopes. One sharp turn followed another as they climbed higher and higher. Both Buick and Jeep were now in low gear, grinding up the mountain side. The river looked like a thin ribbon of silver far below. And still they climbed.

As they neared the top, the wind increased, chill, full of the frozen breath of the high snow fields on the giant mountain tops.

"Better close that window, Dick, until we start down into the Valley of Cuzco," Prof said. "It'll be pretty cold up here as we cross the mountain pass."

Dick felt dizzy as he looked down and back over the road on

which they had come. He could see ten or more hair-pin turns, each sharper than the previous one, like layers sliced into the mountain side. His heart skipped a beat or two when he suddenly noticed there were no guards of any kind on the side of the narrow road. The canyon looked like a bottomless pit, thousands of feet of sheer drop.

"What happens if you ever meet another car coming the other way?" he asked finally.

"You don't," said Prof after what seemed to Dick like a long wait. "You see that widening half-way down that looks like a small quarry? That's carved out of the mountain so cars coming down can wait if any vehicle is coming up. Traffic is light here as you can see. If a car were going down, then it would just wait for the car coming up to pass."

"What if it had already started down beyond that half-way station and another car started up?"

"It wouldn't. You first make sure nothing is coming down before you start up. You can see almost the entire way up from down below. You can also see all the way down looking down."

"No, thank you!" said Dick.

The wind was blowing almost with gale force when they reached the top of the pass. The mountains on either side rose almost straight up on either side, but ahead, bathed in sunshine and full of green vegetation, lay a wide valley.

"Oh, look!" cried Dick, not believing his eyes. They had been riding through barren, sandy and rocky terrain for more than six hours. Now suddenly the land was green, trees were either in full bloom or full of fruit, reaching almost to the very top of the pass where they were starting down.

"The sacred Valley of the Watanay," Prof said. "That very high mountain up ahead is Salcantay to the west; on the other side, Ausangati. Those two were high enough to guard the valley and the City of Cuzco; there is only one way in, and this is it."

Dick hadn't realized how hard the wind had been blowing until they started down the slope into the valley of Watanay.

Suddenly the whizzing and whining of the constant wind stopped, and in the silence that followed he could hear their own and the Jeep's motor in its steady pounding as it carried them closer and closer to the once-sacred city of Cuzco. But the distances were deceiving. They kept going and going, but they didn't seem to be making much headway.

"Oh, we have thirty or forty miles yet," said Prof when Dick mentioned it. "But we'll be there long before sunset."

"Will it be as cold down there as up here, Prof?" Dick gave another shiver.

"No, that is, not in the day time. But at night it gets cold, in spite of the summer weather. Don't forget, Cuzco is 12,000 feet high!"

Finally they reached a high mound that opened up into a flat plateau, as big as three or four football fields side by side. And just beyond, and below, they could see the red tile roofs and square one-storied buildings of the Capitol of the Inca Empire. Church towers rose high above all the other buildings on all sides of the city. The largest and most massive one soared right up in the center of Cuzco, majestic, gleaming white in the late afternoon sun.

"That's the Cathedral," said Prof. "It stands on the very site of the great Palace of Inca Rocca Yupanqui, mightiest of the Incas. Many of the stones in that high belfry were once part of the palace walls."

But it was a long half-hour before they reached the Cuzco Inn in the center of the city. Dick's legs were stiff; his muscles felt as though they had been tied up. He was thankful for the brown-faced lad in the green woolen uniform who ran out to get their bags.

"You came just at the right time," said the big smiling man behind the desk. He spoke English with a decided European accent, and Dick, who had learned to listen for the Latin R's and double S's, was surprised at the soft guttural R's of the desk clerk.

"Why is that?" asked Prof.

"Because they are starting tonight the revival of the great Inca theatre production, all in Quechua. They have been rehearsing for five years!"

"Five *years?*" Dick thought he had heard wrong.

"Yess! They had to teach the young men and women not only the play itself, but the language of the Incas. It hass changed much since those days."

"I'm afraid we are not much in the mood for theatre-going tonight," said Prof, looking at the way Pepe and Chico had slumped into the leather armchairs in the lobby. Dick was leaning heavily on the registration counter. Only Antonio was standing upright, talking to the young elevator operator in quiet tones.

"Do you know the Quechua language?" Dick asked the big heavy-set man at the desk.

"A liddle," he said, smiling. Then, as if he guessed Dick's unspoken question, he added: "I am Swiss. We are the best hotel-keepers, you know!" He said it with such pride that no one could possibly disagree with him.

"I speaking the English very good," boasted the little Indian boy as they started up in the miniature elevator. His green woolen uniform was stained from many years of service. The tiny elevator suddenly seemed very stuffy. Dick's nostrils quivered.

"Do you suppose he ever bathes?" Dick asked.

Prof looked quickly at Antonio, then at Dick.

"Probably not," he said. "At least not often. Bathing among the Indians was a sort of religious ceremony, limited mostly to the nobility. As a matter of fact, the Quechua language doesn't have a word for 'bathing.' They have words for 'washing the face,' 'washing the feet,' and even 'swimming,' but not for bathing."

"What do you know!"

"But all school children are required to bathe in school now, regularly," said Antonio, with pride in his voice. "The public schools in Peru are very good and getting better."

They reached their floor before Dick could think of anything to say, and in the excitement of finding their rooms and trying out the beds, which they found surprisingly soft, the little elevator boy and his odoriferous uniform were forgotten.

There was a bright fire burning in the enormous fireplace in the hotel lobby when they came down to dinner. Big slabs of cypress and eucalyptus wood sent fragrant puffs of smoke up the vast chimney. Night had fallen, swiftly and completely, and the warmth from the fireplace was a welcome one. The dining room seemed cold after that, but the food was tasty and, as usual, there was much too much of it for Dick.

"I can't eat all this, Prof," he said, patting his stomach. "I'm full."

"But we're not even half through yet," Antonio laughed. "I have ordered a special dish for you, Dick, and you must try it." Dick could not quite get used to the way Antonio pronounced his name. It sounded like 'Deek.'

"Special dish for me? On top of all this?"

"Oh, yes; they have prepared for you a special order of *cucuy!*" Antonio pronounced it coo-coo-eee. And suddenly Dick remembered.

"What! Guinea-pig—for me—now?"

"*Cucuy*—broiled in herbs and spices from the mountains," answered Antonio proudly. "You will like it!"

Dick had never been so stuffed in all his life. To his own astonishment, and the amusement of his companions, he finished every last bit of the tasty dish the waiter brought him. Everybody watched Dick.

"Now you are a true Peruvian!" said Antonio proudly, when Dick had finished.

"I feel like a real pig!"

The next morning Dick was awakened before dawn by a tremendous clanging and discordant pealing of hundreds of bells. There were deep bass bells in the high Cathedral tower; there were high-pitched metallic clangings from the church across the street; bells that rang as though in a tremendous hurry to get their shrill call into the morning air before their bigger brothers got all the customers; there were thin, reedy little bells that seemed to come from across town, from the direction in which they had come last night; and there was the steady clang-clang-clang from The Church of the Triumph, which had been badly damaged in the earthquake a few years before and was proudly proclaiming its reconstruction. Bells, bells, bells. Dick had never heard so many bells.

"What's happened? What's the trouble?" he cried, jumping out of bed and rushing to the little window.

Antonio laughed. "Trouble? No trouble. Those are the bells calling the faithful worshipers to church, reminding all the people that this is Sunday."

"Sunday! We've been gone almost a week!" Dick suddenly realized that he hadn't missed his family at all, had scarcely thought of Dad and Mom and his sister Dorothy all the time they had been gone!

"All that noise," said Antonio, sitting up in bed, "is because there are so many churches here. Cuzco is supposed to have more churches than any other city of its size in the world. You see, it was the sacred city of the Incas, and the Spanish built a Christian church over every one of the Inca temples. They had many temples; so we now have many churches."

"I believe that!" said Dick, looking out of the window again, trying to locate the different sounds. "Listen to that! Deep ones, high ones, shrill ones, soft ones. Listen to that!" he repeated.

"There are five churches around the main square alone," said Antonio, joining his North American friend at the window.

"Sounds like fifty!" Dick was still astonished.

"Do you go to the Catholic Church, Dick?" asked Antonio.

Dick turned quickly and looked at Antonio. He hadn't thought of it at all. But of course these were all Catholic churches. For a moment his mind raced back to Indiana, and the white steeple of the church where he had been baptized, where he had gone to Sunday school, where the minister had bidden them farewell as they had left that last Sunday to come to Peru.

"No, Antonio," he said finally, in a soft voice, realizing his friend was very serious, "I go to the Protestant Church."

"Perhaps you will join me in the Cathedral mass this morning?"

For a swift moment Dick thought of Mom, of Aunt Martha, of the minister back home. What would they say? But suddenly he felt a sort of joy and freedom he had never felt before.

"Of course I will!" he said, meeting Antonio's black eyes steadily, "I will be happy to, Antonio."

The big church was already crowded when they arrived. There were only a very few pews, away up front, and they were mostly occupied by women in black dresses, black shawls over their heads, most of them kneeling, heads bowed in prayer. But in the back of the church, where Dick, Antonio, Prof and Pepe were standing—Chico had chosen to go to the Church of San Augustin, his patron Saint—there were mostly men and children, all standing, holding their assorted hats in their hands, some of them praying silently, others just standing quietly in their places. Those around them turned and stared as Dick and his companions pushed a little farther toward the front, and one little fellow, his round, brown face smudged with crusted dirt, smiled a warm friendly smile at the *norte-americano*. Impulsively Dick reached into his pocket and gave the youngster a small coin. The lad's father, standing nearby, looked at Dick impassively, whispered something in dialect Dick did not understand. Immediately the little fellow's smile disappeared. He shook his head and returned the coin to Dick. The father's face had not changed expression.

"Better take it back, Dick," whispered Prof softly. "These are very proud people."

Dick felt a little ashamed, felt the red flush climb up his neck. He looked away. Up front by the altar the priest, in white cassock and a beautifully embroidered stole with gold threads over his shoulders, was now chanting in a sing-song voice. Dick was surprised to realize that the priest was chanting, not Latin or Spanish, but Quechua! Then the chant ended, and another priest, opening a big book, read quickly in Spanish a message concerning Peter, and how Christ had called to Peter to found a Temple; and then, more slowly, the same message was repeated in Quechua. Dick caught the name "Pedro" from time to time.

Now that was over, and from the side of the altar came a chorus of children's voices which answered a chanted word from the priest. Again the priest chanted, again the choir answered, untrained, sweet childish voices, and they were chanting Latin!

And while two men, dressed in black 'Western' suits, went through the crowd with little baskets collecting the small copper coins and offerings, the priest turned to the altar and swung his big incense urn, chanting and praying. Dick dropped an American dollar in the basket. The man stopped suddenly and looked at Dick. Most of the other coins were very small, some of them very dirty.

Dick noticed the sincerity and humility on the faces of the men and women around him. Most of them were very poor, dressed in Indian costume, red and blue woolens, with yellow and green in their blouses or rough one-piece shirts. Many wore the typical mountain hats worn by the women, others wore or carried the white straw hats denoting them as 'cholos.' A 'cholo,' Prof had told Dick, was a person of mixed Indian and Spanish blood.

"Is that supposed to set them apart?" Dick had asked.

"Some white people have tried to tell them that it makes them one rung higher than pure Indian," Prof had answered. And Antonio, who had been standing nearby, added: "But all full-blooded Indians do not believe that it makes the cholos any better."

Dick had wanted to answer, "Of course it doesn't," but he caught Prof's eye and thought he noticed an unspoken message, a little warning. And now, standing very close to many of them in the crowded church, he couldn't notice much difference in color of skin, or even in the features, between the cholos and the full Indians. Perhaps, he thought, the cholos tend to have rounder faces; their noses are not quite so aquiline, their cheek-bones perhaps not quite as high. But you would really have to look for differences.

The priest's voice rose high and clear. The choir answered and joined in a short litany. Little brown faces, serious and intent, little white gowns covering assorted clothes newly-washed for the occasion, thin childish voices joining in prayer and supplication. The priest swung the incense urn and prayed. People knelt down, the men mostly on one knee, and the women bowed, blessing themselves. Dick knelt down on one knee as Prof was doing. He bowed his head. "Just like we do in our church at home," he thought, feeling very quiet and at peace inside.

Dick was among the first to come out when the service was over. The people streamed out of the church, and as Dick waited at the top of the wide steps for Prof and the others, he got another chance to notice the multi-colored clothing of the Indians as they hastily descended the steps leading to the giant square in front of the Cathedral.

"This Cathedral," said Prof, joining Dick at the side of the huge carved door with giant nail heads in orderly pattern in the form of a cross, "is built on the ruins of the greatest Inca palace. From these steps the Inca Emperor called upon the Sun God to bless his people. From these same steps the Spanish Conquerors ordered the last Inca noblemen burned and beheaded. And a few years later, and from these same steps, they ordered the hanging and beheading of each other in the bloody struggle for power and for gold."

They walked down the long flight of steps together in silence. Dick was thinking of the hundreds of years of history, of sacred services, of bloody desecration that covered those very steps. At the foot of the long flight he stopped.

"Didn't you say that that road to the right leads to the fortress of Sacsahuaman, Prof?" Dick asked, pointing to the little street that seemed to lose itself underneath the wide stone archway at the far end of the square.

"That's right," answered Prof.

"Isn't that where we are going this afternoon?"

Prof didn't answer immediately. He was unusually thoughtful, Dick thought. Finally Prof said: "I—I have a queer feeling about that fortress, boys, something strange that came over me when we were in church."

"Queer feeling?" asked Dick, looking at Prof, trying to figure it out.

"I can't describe it," said Prof slowly, "it was—well, almost as though it was a warning of some kind . . ."

"You sure you're not coming down with *soroche,* too, Prof?"

Prof didn't seem to want to answer. Instead, he turned and started walking across the vast square. Although buildings had been built on all four sides, some right next to the Cathedral itself, there was an air of majesty and vastness to the giant Plaza. Four other churches besides the Cathedral flanked it to the east and south. Arcades, in the Moorish-Spanish style so characteristic of Spanish colonial architecture, completed the fourth boundary opposite the Cathedral. Set in among carefully arranged winding cement walks, giant trees and flowering shrubs, gave the immense Plaza shade, and an air of great expanse.

"This was the famous Huacay-Pata, the ceremonial square, largest by far of all the squares in the kingdom," said Prof, almost as though he were talking to himself. "In Inca days it was almost twice as big as it is now."

"Twice as big!" Dick glanced quickly around and realized that even today, the square occupied a good two city blocks! He tried hard to imagine what it must have been when those Spanish buildings were not there, and when a hundred thousand of the Inca's subjects stood in awed silence as their Inca spoke to them from the wide steps down which they had just come.

They crossed over to the arcade, and Dick was surprised to find most of the little shops open, many vendors hawking their wares, herbs, medicines, spices, books and newspapers, even microscopic 'ice cream cones' that sold for a fraction of a penny, and looked like frozen water with a little pink coloring.

"On Sunday?"

Prof smiled for the first time since church services. "Many of these people come to town only once a week, on Sunday. Often it is the biggest market day of the week. In fact, the Sunday market is an institution in many villages. We'll go to one in Pissac. Maybe we can ride up there this afternoon."

"But what about Sachsahuaman?"

Prof became serious again. He looked at Dick for a long moment. The boys had stopped in front of a little bookstore, where a wide assortment of paper covered books and pamphlets filled the little window completely. A copy of the Spanish edition of the *Reader's Digest* was suspended from the ceiling on a thin string.

"I don't know, Dick," Prof answered, and his face showed pain, doubt. "I can't tell you why, but I get that queer feeling every time I think of Sachsahuaman. It's probably nothing . . . but. . . ."

"Oh Prof, I want to see that great big fortification! I want to see those stone blocks that weigh eighteen tons you told us about. I want to see the water tower, and the drill-field, and the stone barracks."

"Yes, Dick, I know, I promised to take you there this afternoon. Just the same, I wish I hadn't. . . ."

They all walked on in silence, crossed the wide street, and walking on the flat cobble stones of the street itself as everyone else was doing, they turned toward the little hotel.

Dick couldn't make out why Prof was so thoughtful and quiet. Antonio walked up beside Dick and passed his arm through Dick's. Dick crooked his arm, holding Antonio's close. Antonio smiled but said nothing. The two boys followed Prof and Pepe into the hotel.

6

Captured!

"All right, dick," said prof, with just a trace of impatience in his voice. "I did promise, and we might as well go to the fortress."

They were seated on the wide oak benches in the sun-bathed patio of the Inn, under flowering shrubs that filled the air with strange and exotic fragrance, like cinnamon and honey.

"On one condition, though, boys," Prof added quickly, as Dick, Pepe and Chico jumped up and started for the door to the hotel lobby leading to the street. "That is, that we all stick together at all times. No separating into two's and three's. All of us, together!" he repeated, frowning.

"OK, Prof, together," said Dick. "Come on, Antonio, let's get our kits and flashlights!"

The narrow street at the north end of the great square before the Cathedral led past rows of low pink-and-green stucco houses, from whose occasional open doorways came the smells of food cooking in the flower-filled patios. A small herd of llamas came suddenly into view around a corner; their sandalled shepherd followed quickly, waving a thin switch and talking to his herd in soft, guttural, clucking noises. Then the houses suddenly ended and the dusty narrow road started climbing among cypress and eucalyptus trees that stretched long, thin trunks into the air, reaching for the sun. The road made a sharp turn, and seemed to be carved out of the side of the steep mountain that blocked the sun to the east, giving the narrow little gulch through which they climbed a feeling of dark unreality. The road narrowed, and rolling stones underfoot made the walking more difficult.

"How long is this road, anyway, Prof?" Dick asked, panting.

"Not tired already! We'll have almost two miles of this. After all, this was the fortress that protected the city in the old days. The hard going was part of the protection."

They were sweating when they finally came out on the edge of the plateau around which ran the high, irregular stone wall that guarded all passage to the north, east and west. Only the southern side was open, the side from which they had come, and here the natural contours of the two mountains which stood like sentinels toward the wide-stretching valley beyond, were molded as though in some prehistoric time a giant hand had crushed the two mountains together and kneaded and pleated them to form a narrow, steep passage that could easily be defended by a handful of armed men. The wide flat area that spread out before them was a giant field, totally enclosed by the walls of the fortress. Huge boulders, some twenty feet high, formed a series of three parallel walls with jutting bulwarks. On the summit of the hill to the right, Dick saw the foundations of what looked like giant towers. The walls were badly crumbled, but still showed solid stone foundations. On the hill to the left and carved into the sheer stone, was what looked like a giant throne, wide steps carved into the mountainside leading to it from both sides.

"Gosh, look at that!" Dick exclaimed.

"That was the Inca Throne," said Prof, "from which he and his generals could watch the drilling of his troops. This was the drill field . . . and they say that as many as ten thousand men could maneuver here at one time.

"See those narrow entrances in the center? They were made narrow so they could be defended and held against enemies; they are connected on the second terrace over those parapets; and they all lead to the top of the hill, to those towers up there."

"Were those the look-out towers, Prof?"

"One of them may have been. More likely, at least one of them was the great water tower. This was a self-sustaining fortress city, and water was the most important commodity. As many as four thousand soldiers were quartered here at one time, and fresh water was brought from those mountains, twenty and thirty miles away."

Dick and Antonio had reached the great Ttio Punchu, the large Sand Entrance, so-called because vast quantities of sand had been brought up to serve as beds for the giant boulders which, with the solid stone lintel on top, formed the gate to the south of the main entrance, fifty yards away.

"Better wait for Prof and the others," said Antonio, as Dick was starting up the narrow, steep pathway. "You remember our promise."

Dick stopped short and looked back impatiently to where Prof, Pepe and Chico were apparently engrossed in some detail of the mountain opposite. He reached down and pulled up a wild flower growing along the path, but quickly dropped it.

"Ouch!" he cried, as the wild thistle stuck a sharp thorn in his hand. Antonio laughed.

"We call that plant 'Snake's Tooth,' " he said, watching Dick's face.

"Is it poisonous?"

"Oh, no, just sharp! It has big thorns, like the teeth of a snake."

"Don't I know it! I got one of those right in my finger!" Dick put his index finger in his mouth to suck it.

Prof and the other boys came up through the Sand Gate and together they climbed to the top of the hill, where the giant round towers had stood. Crumbling foundation walls spoke of great strength, as finely polished stones, pressed one against the other, formed a thick base sometimes four and five feet thick. The walls had resisted not only the ravages of time and weather, but the rage and destruction of the Spanish conquerors. Where they now stood, the wall seemed to spread out, as though in final surrender to the thousands of feet that had climbed it, crumbling it so that it formed a little ramp, inviting newcomers. Further back, around to the western side, remains of the stone wall still rose defiantly, mute reminder of solid foundations of a giant structure that had once housed enormous water towers. Dick walked on top of the wall, circling toward the west, and looking down the steep incline criss-crossed by stone breast-works where soldiers once defended their city against invaders.

Dick reached a large boulder that stuck up out of the wall like a giant irregular ball, six or eight feet high. Dick walked around it, noticed what seemed like deep cracks on one side, and, holding on with his hands, pushed his right foot into the lowest crack and climbed up. It gave him a feeling of standing on top of the world, as he walked gingerly around the big stone. Suddenly his foot slipped.

"Look out, Dick!" Antonio cried from below.

Dick waved a frantic arm to catch his balance. But his feet went out from under him and he saw the deep pit on the inside of the crumbled tower walls rising toward him with terrific speed. The next moment he felt the sharp impact of the hard ground, felt his elbow strike a pointed stone, sending a burning wire-like stab through his left arm.

"No harm done!" cried Dick, looking up into a small sea of anxious faces that peered down at him from the top of the wall. He got to his feet slowly, rubbing his elbow. He looked around, wondering how he would climb out of the wide pit, started walking along the edge. Suddenly he stopped, staring intently at the ground.

"Hey, Prof!" he called, looking up at his friends who were still watching him from above. "There's something here . . .

an entrance to something . . . a tunnel, looks like. . . ."

A hollow echo threw his voice back from the curved walls. It was like being inside a giant stone barrel. Damp moss clung to the gray stones. A lizard scampered over his foot. "Hey, what's that?" Dick wasn't sure whether it was a lizard or a snake.

"Be careful, Dick!" Prof's voice came down to him in a sort of hollow echo, that seemed to vibrate down. Dick saw Prof on top of the wall, looking in all directions as though seeking a way down into the pit.

Dick looked down at the mouth of the opening at his feet. Concealed by bushes, almost sealed off by crumbling walls, the hole showed clearly from where he stood. Thick twisted vines formed a sort of canopy over it, blocking the view of it from above. Dick unhooked his hatchet and struck the nearest branch. The hatchet blade bounced off as though he had struck a metal post. A long twig snapped violently across his face, blinding him with its stinging whiplash. Dick threw his head back, covering his face with his left hand. A cry of pain burst from his lips without his realizing it.

"Dick!" cried Prof again, "be careful!"

Blind fury sent Dick's blood racing. He gripped his hatchet tightly and swung it with all his might at the vines. The tough resilient branch quivered like a hurt animal, but did not give. The blow stung Dick's hand, brought him back from his sense-less rage. He looked up in time to see Prof jumping down from the wall into the pit. Prof landed on his feet, but the momentum of the fall threw him forward on his knees. Prof's outstretched arms protected his face from the scraggly vegetation that covered the bottom of the pit.

"Sorry, Prof," said Dick as he helped Prof to his feet. "But that twig switched across my face and made me mad!" He rubbed an angry red welt on his cheek.

Now Antonio, finding a place where the tower floor seemed to come up somewhat, jumped down, followed by Pepe and Chico who tumbled and slid down the crumbling wall feet first into the mound of dirt a few feet away from where Dick stood. They all crowded around the hidden hole in the ground, stretching to see the black opening that seemed to slant at a sharp angle under the wall on which they had stood, almost directly beneath the giant boulder from which Dick had fallen. Dick looked up quickly at that big stone, then bent his head to the left to get a better view of the black hole.

Suddenly Dick felt the earth beneath him shifting. His feet were being sucked down!

"Look out!" he cried as he tried to step back.

Prof and the others jumped back. Dick's right foot seemed caught fast, as he frantically kicked his left foot free. But his efforts only seemed to shift the sand beneath him. Suddenly, rock, sand and gravel slid from under him, sucking him feet first. Futilely he tried to grasp the vines over his head as he felt himself being catapulted into the opening, but the whole ground gave way, and a sharp oblique slope opened before his very eyes. He screamed. For one short moment he saw the outline of the yawning pit ahead, like giant jaws, deep, inky black. Instinctively he ducked as sand and gravel slashed past him. He heard the alarmed cries of his companions that reached him now muffled as though from a distance. His whole body tense, his feet outstretched, face covered with folded arms, tight hands gripping his head, he plunged down, down, at terrifying speed, over what felt like sheer rock.

The cries of his companions were drowned out as more rock, more sand sped by. Then a great shout of terror from above was followed almost instantly by a great groaning thud as the giant boulder atop the wall came crushing down and sealed the mouth of the cave through which Dick had plunged. Loose earth sped by his head; little sharp stones cut his hands, tearing at his knuckles as they sped into the blackness below. At that same instant his left foot struck a protruding ledge. The painful blow shot his leg fiercely into the pit of his stomach. But the ledge held!

Dick was trembling violently. Gingerly he spread his hands out. The face of the ledge was smooth all around him, but as he slid his hands over the rock, his fingers caught irregular little crevices on the stone surface. His left hand, just above his hip, dipped in. He explored with his fingers. The crevice opened wider, almost big enough for a foothold. Was this a step carved in the face of the rock?

He fumbled for his belt where his flashlight should have been. His heart pounded furious blows. He grabbed the familiar metal handle. The fall had dented it, and he had to jerk to get it off, yet he dared not pull too violently for fear of losing his balance. He pressed his body back fiercely against the face of the rock, moved his right foot trying to find a rest for his heel. It caught in what seemed a tiny crack, but enough to steady him. He pulled at his flashlight again. Now it was loose. His fingers trembled as he slid the little plate over the contact button.

The cave that closed all about him was scarcely more than a round tunnel opening, falling straight down into some kind of deep pit. Dick dared not shift his head to see the bottom.

"I've got to get a better foothold here," he said, half aloud. He turned off his flashlight, hooked it back on his belt. Very carefully he slid his right foot along the stone crack that had caught his heel. But suddenly the pain in his left leg shot through his whole body, and he thought for one agonizing moment he was going to be sick.

At that moment his right heel slid into some sort of opening. His foot caught hold, and instinctively he shifted his weight. Still resting his body on his right heel, he could feel with his toe that there was a flat shelf under his foot. This must be another opening, another step carved into the surface of the rock! He let the front part of his foot down. It was solid underneath!

Dick clung to the rock face, back pressed hard against the sloping cliff, his breath coming in quick gasps, his body trembling. He slid his left hand up above his head, and a little cry of triumph escaped from his trembling lips as his hand slid into still another opening. These were steps—regular, carved into the rock itself, about eighteen or twenty inches apart, one over the other.

Hanging tightly by his left hand and resting his whole weight now on his right foot, he felt with his right hand. Just above his belt, in the small of his back, was another opening! These must be double steps, like a ladder up the face of the cliff. Now if he could only turn without losing his footing, he could climb back up. He knew his friends were up there, probably digging frantically around the giant boulder that had sealed the mouth of the tunnel. If he could get back up there he could call to them.

His fingers stiffened. He felt the strain of every muscle in his left arm as he tried to swing his body around. But when his left foot touched the stone ledge which had first held him, the sharp pain that stabbed him almost sent him hurtling off his precarious perch. He bit his lips as tears of pain filled his eyes. He could not turn.

After a long moment, by shifting his left hand so as to get a better grip, he managed to unhook his flashlight with his right hand. Flashing it on again, he gulped. Immediately below his left foot he could see a flat little platform about two feet square, and below that in regular intervals like shelves in a narrow bookcase a series of small platforms that reached down into the cave, each holding some small black object, brown and dusty. By moving his eyes to the right, he could see the sheer face of the rock, blue gray in the half-light. He shifted the ray, and then could see quite clearly a series of steps carved in the face of the steep ledge. Far down, perhaps twenty-five or thirty feet, was a wider platform like a landing about four feet square. In the cramped position in which he had to hold his head he could not see beyond.

Dick pointed his light at the steps and tried to count them. He fixed the distance between them in his mind, measuring each step with half-closed eyes, trying to remember what eighteen inches looks like stretched out flat on the surface. Were these steps one foot apart? One-and-a-half feet? It didn't look like any more, but he must be sure. He couldn't take a chance now!

He snapped the flashlight off and hooked it back on his belt.

He slipped his free right hand behind him. What a relief! He hadn't realized how strained his left arm had got! Now his two arms could support him, and he could rest his right foot. His left foot was almost numb, useless. It couldn't take his weight, even for a split second. He put his right foot down again, and in the darkness felt with his right hand above his head. Yes, there was the dual opening! At least now he knew he could shift from one hand to the other, hold tight, and let his right leg down step by step. A bit of gravel swished by his head, and he ducked. It must be Prof and Antonio, digging up above!

Suddenly a choking lump thrust itself into his throat. Suppose they worked that boulder loose and it came crashing down, crushing him before he could get out of the way? Suppose . . . suppose he could get down off his perch—only to find he couldn't get out? This might be a cave straight down into the ground, a deep abandoned water well where he would drown! And that giant boulder on top sealed him off, but if loosened would crush him with tons of granite!

"I can't stay here and let it tear me off! Whatever else I do I've got to get down. And quick! There may be nothing there, but right here I am a sitting duck!"

The rough edges of the stone cut sharply into the palms of his hands. He felt a warm trickle running down his right leg. Must have cut it somehow, he thought, but can't stop for that now. A sudden frenzy seized him. He must get down! He only had his right leg and his hands. But he must get down! Get out of the way, Dick, that rock may come down any minute!

Hanging on tightly with his left hand, pressing his back against the stone ledge as far as he could, he shifted his weight on his left arm, let his right leg slide down over the face of the rock. Slowly he bent his right arm and shifted his body slightly to give his leg more reach. For a terrifying moment he thought he had missed the step, but suddenly his right heel caught. There was the step! Now if I can do that again, and again . . . steady . . . steady . . . slowly . . . another shift . . . another step . . . now shift back to the left hand . . . careful now

. . . back on the right . . . catch that heel in the next step below . . . ah, that's better . . . but how dark it is in here!

Another little stone, dislodged from above, crashed by his ear, bounced off the ledge and hit with a hollow thud below. For a moment all Dick could think of was the frantic necessity for speed, to get out from under before they get that big boulder loose! But suddenly the thud of the falling stone reached his consciousness. It had stopped. And it sounded as though it had hit hard earth!

"Hold on up there! Prof! Antonio! Stop digging!" But his voice sounded as though he was yelling inside of an earthenware crock.

One more step—and another—and another. He found he could do it more quickly now; his foot seemed to know just exactly how far down to reach. He tried to remember how many steps he had counted with his flashlight. Was it twenty? Thirty? Should he stop and look again? No, better get out of here, get off this ledge, get off! He found himself counting now—ten, fifteen, twenty. His voice was swallowed up in the vast inkiness of the cave. Thirty-five, thirty-six . . . would he ever reach bottom? Forty, forty-one—*Forty-one!* He was down. Down on solid ground!

His heart was pounding now, his temples throbbing. He swallowed hard, and he leaned his head against the rock behind him. What a relief a sigh can be! But suddenly tears welled within him, and he fought them back. Loneliness and darkness covered him. He closed his eyes, blinked off the tears. He reached for his flashlight but didn't flash it on. What if . . . what if he had just reached that stone platform he had seen from above, and this thing went on and on, deep into the earth? What do I do now? he thought. What would Dad do? Or Prof? Or Antonio? He felt totally helpless, and yet the thought of Antonio suddenly steadied him. Why Antonio? Why not his own father? Or even Prof? He could feel Antonio's arm on him, could hear Antonio's soft, precise voice.

Dick shook his head and flashed on his light. His heart leaped at the sight before him. Straight ahead, as far as his eye could see, the narrow shaft of light picked up a long narrow tunnel about as high as a man's head carved right into the solid rock. Here and there the beam picked up a sparkling reflection of quartz or mica, but otherwise the walls of the tunnel were gray, solid rock.

A tunnel! This has got to lead somewhere! And get out from under that stone up there. They must be still digging. Get out of the way!

Again Dick switched on his light, peering into the long tunnel ahead. Where did it lead to? Out on the side of the mountain? Back all the way to Cuzco? Was this the secret underground path to the Palace of the Inca?

The air . . . the air in the tunnel smells of outdoors . . . all of a sudden I can smell it cutting across the damp darkness . . . rushing at me over the hard-packed floor level. He doused his light, hooked it back on his belt. But when he tried to stand he almost crumbled under the pain. He had forgotten his useless left leg! His ankle felt like a big balloon, a balloon full of pain, burning, searing pain.

Dick steadied himself with his right hand, then slid it along the tunnel wall. He must hop on one foot, bending his knee to catch the weight of his body as he shifted forward. He started toward the other end of the tunnel. A sudden hissing under his right foot brought him up sharply, his heart pounding. In sudden alarm he grasped his flashlight again, flashed it on. He could see nothing. He decided he would carry his flashlight in his left hand, guide himself with his right hand and slide along the tunnel wall. But save that battery, Dick, you may need it! The darkness seemed deeper, blacker than ever before. But from the direction of the long tunnel ahead he could feel the fresh air. He thought he could smell the oleander that grew wild on the slopes of Sachsahuaman hill. There must be a way out!

He started forward again, listening intently between jumps. One, two, five yards. He could hear nothing. Then abruptly, and with a suddenness that sent a swift chill through him, the cave suddenly became filled with a whirring of wings and a massed sound like muffled whistling. Instinctively Dick ducked, throwing his left arm over his head. With the same motion he dropped on his right knee and flashed the light toward the whirring rat-a-tat overhead.

His eyes were frozen in fear. The entire tunnel was filled with fluttering, flying animals with thick little stubby bodies, long transparent wings spreading ten or twelve inches, and ugly, pudgy little faces that looked like miniature bulldogs. Some of the creatures clung to the walls with claw-like feet. The hissing, whistling calls were tiny snarls from dozens of silver-gray, hairy little faces like dried-up masks. Clammy wings wavered and quivered incessantly. A pungent, rank odor sank down and filled Dick's nostrils. In the blinding rays of the flashlight, which Dick was throwing from side to side as he waved his arm frantically, the creatures redoubled their hissing and their agitated whirring.

"Vampire bats!" Dick heard his own voice cry out, but it sounded as if it came from outside, from someone else. His voice reverberated from one side of the tunnel to the other, ran down until it was drowned in a hollow, mocking clack.

Suddenly the bats surged forward. Whirling with shrill and strident hisses, they fled down the tunnel. Dick thought he might faint. His mouth was dry; his body trembled all over. He dared not turn the flashlight off, even though instinct told him to save the battery. He put his head against the tunnel wall and felt the whole world spinning. Cold sweat broke out all over him.

After a few moments the bats disappeared, and the hideous noise that had transformed the tunnel into a nightmare of confusion was receding down the long opening, as though sucked out by a giant vacuum cleaner. Dick flashed the light up, then around him. He was alone again.

"I've gotta get out of here, I've got to!" he sobbed.

Suddenly he remembered having read somewhere that bats don't travel far, but congregate in numbers and seek the nearest cave to mate and hibernate. That must have been a colony. But they fled down the tunnel. That means an opening somewhere down there, an opening . . . someway out!

With new strength now Dick jumped to his feet. Ouch! Can't stand on that bum left foot, not even put it down. No matter. I'll hop on the right one, hop right down to the end of this tunnel. That's where the bats went, that's where there must be an opening, that's where this fresh air is coming from. I'm going to get out, get out of here . . .

Hopping and panting, guiding himself with his right hand as he slid along the wall, Dick made his way toward the end of the tunnel. He stopped a brief moment to catch his breath, threw the light down toward the opening at the other end. Still no daylight. The darkness that engulfed him as he flashed off his light seemed deeper every time he stopped.

Deep, dark silence again as he once more started forward. For no reason at all he started counting his hops out loud as he had done back on the face of the wall. He got up to ten, twelve, fifteen. He paused again. Still he could not see the end. Ten more, twenty. This time he stopped at forty. Nothing. The tunnel led straight ahead. Panic was returning. This might lead all the way back to Cuzco, a full two miles away! He would never make it! His right hand now was not only guiding him, but supporting him. The muscles in his right leg felt as though they had been pulled up tight and twisted. He couldn't go on much farther . . . he couldn't.

One hundred. One hundred and ten. His hand suddenly felt the curve in the wall. His heart beat faster. He stopped, and his light splashed abruptly against the wall ahead, showing a sharp turn, almost at right angles. The floor suddenly dropped steeply, to another level several feet lower, and at his feet were five narrow stone steps. Dick held his hand steady as he peered down, his nose quivered as a mouldy dampness rose to meet him.

He threw the light of his flashlight down into the round chamber-like opening ahead. Nothing! The steps just led down, deeper into the earth, but the opening which seemed to stretch out on both sides into a passageway six or seven feet wide, was empty.

Dick dropped on his knee, shifted his body around, threw his weight on his hands and with his right leg reached out for the first step, backward, like a child first learning to go downstairs.

The risers were not more than eight or ten inches high, easy for him to negotiate. When he reached the fifth step, he sat down, flashed the light on again. In front of him was a platform like a tiny balcony, but beyond, the steps started down again! The tunnel opened wider and wider.

Again the darkness. Again he turned, throwing his weight forward, reaching down with his right foot, one step after another, holding his left leg high to keep it from touching. The pain was getting worse. Another step. And another. He wasn't counting now any more, just going down, and down, and down.

Carefully he explored with his foot, felt the earth widen out. He turned, and once more sat down. At last he was at the bottom of the long stone stairway. Once again, and at right angles, the tunnel opened up; it was shorter than the one above and perhaps a little higher, but much wider. He got his bearings and turned off the flashlight, while he caught his breath. The tunnel ahead sloped very gently toward the other end, not more than thirty or forty yards away.

Dick closed his eyes, and suddenly opened them again. His heart gave a leap, almost choking him. Was—was that daylight ahead? Only a tiny little sliver . . . but it was, it was daylight! An opening ahead, and daylight!

He was trembling so he couldn't flash on his light. Finally he made the contact. The widening tunnel he had only partly seen before led directly into a wide opening, but his light could not reach far enough to show anything beyond the round mouth thirty yards away. Dick stood up, doused his light, and once more stared into the darkness. Yes! He could see that tiny crack of light, like a long ragged crack in a window pane, but enough for him to guide himself toward it, holding on to the side of the tunnel. The little crack grew bigger. Dick flashed his light.

He stood for a long moment stunned, motionless, hearing his breath come in rapid gasps. The passage had opened up wide and he was on the very edge of a large underground chamber which rounded out into an enormous circular subterranean room. Square, heavy-looking objects stood about in what seemed a planned pattern, leading toward the far end, where a huge solid chair sat against the back wall. The round shape of the room seemed to increase its size. The ceiling overhead, shaped like a dome, reached up twelve or fourteen feet high. All around the room, slightly higher than a man's head, were small niches, each holding a dried, brown mummy a foot and a half high. Long metal spears stood like sentinels against the walls. A sheet of grass matting hung over the far wall to the left. And directly opposite the matting, to Dick's right as he looked into the immense chamber, three or four small cracks let in a fading daylight.

For some minutes Dick stared at the strange underground room. It was some time before he realized that the grass matting on the left was new. How come? A new grass matting? Of course! There must be an exit somewhere!

Then I'm not trapped inside this mountain! I can get out! His little wrist compass that miraculously had not broken showed he was facing due south. That means I traveled in a great circle underneath that fort on top of this mountain! This must be facing right at Cuzco . . . there must be a way out . . . it must be here somewhere . . .

Using his flashlight now, and hopping with growing urgency across the big room, he avoided the bundles and square objects all around. He made his way to the narrow vents in the wall to the right. Again he could feel the cool air knifing in. But his heart sank as he came to them. The cracks were not more than an inch or two wide, in solid stone more than a foot thick!

The cool air sucked past him. Peering steadily, Dick could tell daylight was beginning to fade. He must have been underground almost two hours! Two hours since he was separated from his mates! Night would come quickly now. He must find that exit, he must!

"Help, outside there, help! I'm in here!" he shouted. His voice, dull and lifeless, came back at him from the solid wall.

He turned and played his flashlight into the center of the room, around the walls. His heart jumped into his mouth, stopped beating, choked him. The grass matting moved! He gulped, started breathing again, fixing the light on the grass matting at the farther side. Nothing. It was still. Was he mistaken? He kept the light beam on it. The matting hung limp, flat, and motionless.

"I'm beginning to imagine things!" Dick said. " 'Magine . . . 'magine . . ." the walls called back.

Keeping the light on the matting, Dick now made his way back toward the steps on the other side of the room. In the glow of the flashlight in his hand he noticed suddenly that his wrist watch was gone. Where?

How tired he was! The burning ache in his left leg reached all the way up to his hip, forcing him to shift his weight to his right side. As he did so, he touched the bottom step, saw that his hand was all bloody. The dust stung his raw palm. His temples throbbed. He felt giddy, and a bitter sickening lump in the pit of his stomach was tightening and screwing his insides.

And then it happened.

Far up inside the long tunnel, at first only a muffled rumbling, but gathering force and fury as it grew into a mighty roar, an ear-splitting crash filled the entire cavern. It was like an avalanche descending ruthlessly down the mountainside. The whole mountain shook, seemed to be collapsing. Splitting rock, cracking and snapping like a toy slate, rushed down into the tunnel, scraping and crumbling, dragging clouds of dust in a choking, suffocating mass. Dick jumped to his feet, but fell full on his face as his left leg crumpled under him like a soft wet rag. He felt the hard jab of his own flashlight as it poked into his ribs. He lay panting, trembling all over.

Now he was sealed in here! Prof must have got others to help dig, and they had loosened the whole mountainside, crushing the cavern and tunnels with inescapable completeness. He must find that exit down here! Retreat was impossible. But his flashlight was smashed! He didn't even feel the needle-sharp sliver of the broken lens cutting his hand.

"I've gotta get out of here! I've gotta!" he shrieked in full terror. He heard his own voice, whimpering and crying, tried to make it stop but couldn't. His own sobs shook him violently. He tried to get up on his knees, but again his left leg just folded under him, rolling him on his side. He knew he was shouting, he could hear his own voice above his hysterical sobs. He turned over on his back and gave in to despair. "No use, no use," he sobbed over and over again, "no use!"

Slowly, indistinctly at first, but insistently demanding attention, another voice came out of the darkness. New terror seized him, shook him all over. Dick held his breath, swallowed the sobs with difficulty. There it was! And it wasn't his voice!

"The young señor is hurt," it was saying, in the soft guttural sounds of an Indian talking Spanish. "The young señor must take this. He must take this," the voice repeated.

Dick felt a large hand lift his head. A cup was pressed against his swollen lips, hurting his mouth. He tried to pull away, but his head, cupped in powerful fingers, was held in place with cruel stiffness. Whatever was in that cup, it was the foulest stuff Dick had ever tasted. He fought against it, but strong fingers crushed the cup against his lips, forced the vile liquid down his throat. The room started spinning wildly. His eyes felt as though they were swimming in blinding tears. Through the growing darkness he thought he saw a large bony face close to his own, felt the breath of someone very close, heard words which had lost their meaning. Then everything went black. Dick's body went completely limp. His breathing became regular, came and went in slow measured rhythm.

He would not waken for many, many hours.

7

The Lost City of the
Mountains

Dick felt consciousness slowly returning, beginning at his head, creeping down slowly to his face, his neck, his arms. It was like being cold all over and then drinking a very hot cup of soup, having the blood start up again, with a little tingling feeling creeping over him. He moved his head, realized he was lying on a thick rug of some kind; woolly hair tickled the back of his neck. He opened his eyes—slowly, because they felt very heavy—but he could see nothing in the darkness of the room. He spread his fingers out and felt the soft wool under his hands. His left leg trembled a little as he tried to move it, as though it had been numb a long while. Somewhere around his knee—maybe it was his thigh—a muscle pulled and sent a sharp pain up his leg. He lay still, listening.

Very softly—Dick could not tell how near it was—a voice came out of the darkness. Dick felt his heart pound. He lay still, listening intently, his senses now sharpening as more and more blood coursed through him, awakening him all over. There was the soft guttural voice again.

"Huaina occari?"

Dick wasn't sure it was a human voice, or whether it was man or woman. As with a snap, his mind suddenly cleared, and he recognized with surprise the clear soft tones of a woman, repeating the question:

"Huaina occari?" Dick remembered his few lessons in Quechua and his recognition of the words was like a tonic, filling him with unexpected exhilaration. 'Huaina' meant boy, youth; 'occari' meant waking, awake. She was asking if he were awake! Should he answer? He moved his head, trying to turn it in the direction of the voice. His neck was stiff; a painful tendon pulled his head back into place. He lay very still.

Then suddenly came another voice. This one was deep, and it sounded almost like a muffled growl. A chilling dryness filled Dick's throat.

"Mana! Manarac," said the deep voice. "No, not yet."

Then suddenly it came to Dick that this second voice was not unknown to him. He had heard it before, somewhere . . . somewhere . . . but where? when? Then suddenly he knew! He could hear it again, in Spanish this time . . . "the young señor must take this . . . he must take this!" it was saying. It was the voice of the underground chamber!

"Yes, I am awake!" Dick said, loud, in English; it sounded almost like a shout. "I am awake," he repeated, speaking slowly in Spanish, for his tongue felt thick and swollen inside his mouth. "I want to be taken to Cuzco, to the Inn."

There was no answer.

"Que pasa?" cried Dick. "What's the matter? Didn't you hear me? Isn't anybody here?" He tried again to turn his head, to raise it, but his body would not lift, and painful muscles pulled him back before he even got started. From the blackness, only silence.

Dick felt suddenly panicky. There must be something wrong! He certainly had heard the voices, and the man's deep growl had sounded right over his head. His own voice, pitched high,

The ruins of the round water tower at Sachsahuaman.

Beside the walls of the fortress of Sachsahuaman an Indian plays a song on his bamboo flute to his llamas at twilight.

The Lost City of the Andes sits on the razor-edge of a high mountain surrounded by deep canyons.

The houses of the Lost City—
mud huts, thatched with straw.

Tocta, dressed for a festival.

Cuyuchi, the Keeper of the Secrets of
the Inca.

The House of Youths.

The Sundial Room.

The Lookout Tower.

"The narrow path climbed steeply alongside forbidding walls."

The summit of the fortress.

The high trapezoid window of the fortress, looking down on the terraced gardens.

"Dick stared into the deep chasm and dreamed of escape."

The canyon, two thousand feet down from the Lost City.

sounded unnatural in that deep darkness. He spoke quickly, afraid he could not get it out quickly enough.

"My father is the Ambassador from the United States. He will be very angry if you do not take me back."

Still no answer. Dick raised his voice, it was a shout now.

"Don't you understand me? *Que pasa?*" he cried. Then a sudden idea struck him. "My father will give you much money if you take me back to Cuzco," he said, trying to lower his voice, speaking now more slowly. "He will be very thankful to you. He will give you much money."

Now Dick could see, by peering intently, what seemed like a low thatched roof and over to the right—he could just barely turn his head because of those straining painful muscles pulling his neck—he could see a tiny streak of light where roof and side-wall met. It wasn't so dark in here now. If he could only turn his head the other way—oh! that neck! He felt the hot breath on his own face before he recognized the big head close to his, big round eyes intently peering into his own.

"The young señor need not be afraid," said the big face right over him, in excellent Spanish. "The young white señor has injured his foot. We will cure him and take care of him."

"My father will call the doctor—he'll fix my foot." Dick's hopes were foolishly rising. "Will you please take me to Cuzco, to the Inn?"

Suddenly the man's deep voice barked out a sharp command, now back in his own native tongue.

"*Sutti ccanchai!*" he growled. And now Dick felt the sudden movement of the woman to his right. She must have been very close, too, for he heard her breathe as she jumped to her feet. He heard the shuffling of her leather sandals as she crossed the room, heard the hard earth floor scrape as it does on leather. The woman threw back the heavy woolen blanket that hung over the doorway. Dick saw a long square of light and through it he could perceive—and for the first time suddenly smell—the weird smoke-filled grayness all around him. In spite of the pain he moved his head and quickly threw his glance about. This was a hut! A native Indian hut! Over him, directly above his head, towered the figure of a big-chested man who, straddled across Dick's body, stood now erect, feet apart, looking down at him.

"Huaina pacoma," said the deep voice, lapsing back into the Quechua tongue. Then, to insure that Dick would understand, he repeated it in Spanish. "The young white señor is my prisoner."

"Your prisoner? Why? What have I done?" Dick shouted, trying once more to move his body. He couldn't move it, could barely lift his hands.

The tall Indian was in no hurry to answer. Several long seconds went by, while Dick writhed, making desperate attempts to get to his feet. He gave up. His legs felt as though they were made of cement; cement stuck to the ground, dry, hard, impossibly heavy.

"The young señor is in my care until the Chief gives other orders," said the big native at last.

"The Chief? Say, what is this?" Dick was angry now. "What do you mean I am a prisoner? I tell you the American Embassy will get after your 'Chief' . . . You'll . . . you'll be sorry . . ."

Dick was stuttering. His body, imprisoned by its own dead weight, did not respond to his renewed effort to move. The big Indian just stood over him, like pictures of conquering enemies standing over their beaten foe. And it came to Dick that this big Indian had not been one bit scared by the mention of the American Embassy! Dick's heart beat faster.

"You dumb cluck!" he cried at last, "don't you understand what the United States means?" Dick felt despair in his own voice. He was staring up at the big face of the native. It was a dark copper-colored face, with long stringy hair framing the high cheek bones and a solid chin. Big black eyes stared intently past a long aquiline nose right into Dick's eyes. *"No comprende?"* Dick cried.

"Sí . . . sí comprendo." The native's voice rumbled, coming from deep down in his massive chest. For a moment Dick

thought he saw a faint smile cross those stony features. Then the man went on: "I understand the young señor is the son of an important foreign chief. But this is not the young señor's country. This land belongs to the Incas. This hut belongs to me. Here—I command!" There was fierce pride in the big fellow's voice, a voice that sounded almost majestic as it rounded out the words, full-bodied, deep down in the big man's throat.

Dick felt his whole body tremble. He lay still, trying to think what he should do, what he could say. And as he lay there, long moments passing over him, he felt the blood come back into his legs, felt suddenly the sharp pain in his left foot and ankle, a pain that met the returning blood head on, causing excruciating pain in his left leg above the knee. That useless left leg! Now he remembered! Even with both legs whole, and using both his arms, he would have been no match for this towering native, as impassive and solid as the rocks in the hills. And with that leg . . .

"OK," Dick said at last, "you win. Do you mind telling me why I am your prisoner?"

"The young señor was injured in the fall. We must cure him and take care of him."

"That's no reason for me to be your prisoner," Dick persisted. The tall native did not answer. Dick tried another tack.

"Where am I?"

"You are in my house. My house is your house." How noble, how very Spanish this sounded!

"And who are you?" Dick was beginning to enjoy this game of mental hide-and-seek.

"I am the Keeper of the Secrets of the Inca."

"Secrets?" Suddenly the underground chamber came back to Dick; the big square chair in the middle of the big round chamber; the lances and the spears against the curved wall, standing like sentinels of the past; the small brown mummies in the little niches all around the walls. One by one these things came into focus. Secrets? Were these the secrets of the Inca? And what *were* these secrets?

"You mean . . ." Dick did not get far. The big Indian interrupted.

"I mean that you have seen the Cave of the Inca's Chair. And you must stay with us until the wise men of the tribe decide what is to become of you."

Dick could hear his heart pounding fiercely. He lay very still, not knowing what to say. Finally the big Indian spoke again.

"The white man must not know about this cave," he said, in deliberate tones.

"But I won't say anything! I don't know anything . . . I don't even know where it is . . . I . . ."

The big native grunted, then stepped over Dick's prostrate body and swiftly walked toward the door opening. The Indian woman, wearing the wide woolen skirt and full one-piece blouse of the mountain people, sat squatting on the floor next to the door.

The man said something to the woman as he stepped outside, but he was back almost immediately. In his hand he carried a large round basket, and from the way he carried it Dick knew it must be full of something. A yellowish-gray liquid seeped through the tightly-woven wicker bottom. The woman rose to her feet as the big man returned, and together they walked back to Dick. The man put down the basket, and the next moment Dick felt the hand of the Indian slip under his left leg. Wild, piercing pain shot through his whole side as the big fellow lifted under Dick's knee. Dick felt as though some giant hand had jerked the muscles in his leg, stretching them thin like a rubber band about to burst. A red-hot needle-stab went through him, jabbing right through his leg into his stomach, making him feel sick, and weak all over.

"Hey!" Dick cried, hot tears filling his eyes.

"*Chaqui lapquer-parisca!*" said the Indian, as though to himself. Then, in Spanish, he said, "the foot is injured very bad. I will make *hampi*—I will bring the medicine."

The Indian let Dick's leg rest down on the rug again, slipping his hand out. Then, jumping to his feet like an agile athlete, the big fellow motioned to the Indian woman. Swiftly they crossed the hut, this time toward the back, and for a few agonizing seconds, while the hot burning pain in his leg gradually grew less, Dick heard the two out in what must have been the kitchen, for he heard the crackling of hot flame on new dry wood, smelled the sudden puff of fresh wood smoke, heard the hiss of big drops of water that struck the open fire. Presently the two returned, the man, as always, first; then the woman carrying a big earthenware pot between her curved arms, its handles hooked over her arms and gripping them tight. The water in the pot was steaming.

The big man came to Dick's side, knelt down by his left leg, and uttered some guttural sounds Dick could not understand. The woman set down the big round pot and stepped back a step or two, waiting. The man grunted again, and the woman bent over, reached into the big basket and pulled out what looked like a small bundle of clean white rags. Then she, too, knelt down beside Dick, and the next half hour Dick seemed to be engulfed in hot cloths, herbs, vines, steaming concoctions that came out of the big basket in never-ending variety. The first hot cloth had felt like a blast from a bursting steam pipe; but then the heat, the incense-like pungent herbs, and the unbelievably soft hands that held his leg, all seemed to bring him a queer feeling of peace. The pain was gone! He could feel the woman's hands as she peeled off one hot compress, only to wrap his leg in another, which she wrung dry over the big pot. The little dripping stream from the fresh cloth sounded like the water from a half-filled glass in the kitchen sink. But there was no pain! Dick didn't dare try moving his leg for fear the pain would come back. He just lay still and let the woman work over him, as the big man knelt, silent, waiting, his big hands hanging at his side almost touching the ground, his head bowed. Dick couldn't see his face very well, but for a moment he thought the big native must be asleep.

The woman said something, softly, under her breath. Instantly the big head jerked back, and the black eyes stared at Dick. The man raised his hands, and as the woman moved away, reached into the wicker basket. This time he came up with a big handful of soft, wet clay. He transferred this first fistful to his left hand and reached into the basket again. He slapped the two handfuls together, making one big lump. Then swiftly he molded the wet mass, patting it out into a small square platter. This he folded over Dick's ankle on the upper part of his left foot. Dick lay quite still. The cold wet clay felt good. Again the big Indian dipped his hand into the basket, again made a small sheet with both fistfuls of clay and added it to the covering on Dick's ankle. The process went on, over and over, as the man worked with a skill and swiftness that amazed Dick.

When the entire foot and ankle were covered, the Indian made a cast around Dick's leg from the shin up to the knee. Dick's leg now felt quite numb and sort of cold and clammy. The clay was beginning to harden, tightening around Dick's leg. But he could feel the blood circulating, a painless little throbbing that let him know his leg was still alive.

The big man stopped for a few moments, and silently the woman handed him a fresh rag. With this he wiped his hands clean. Then he lifted up a bundle of thin twigs the woman had placed on the floor, sorted them according to size and length and these he proceeded to press gently into the wet clay on Dick's leg, at intervals of about half an inch apart. When he had completely circled the leg, he wrapped the whole with a thin strip of cotton tape, strapping it around the leg on a slant. He tore the top end of the tape, about six inches of it, down the middle, and made a knot around Dick's leg just below the knee. Then he stood up again, and for the first time during the entire operation, he spoke to Dick.

"The bone is broken. It will take many weeks to heal. You will remain with me in my house until you are well again."

Dick didn't answer. The man had not spoken an invitation, but had made a flat pronouncement. There was nothing Dick could say. The big man spoke again, and again his voice was a deep-in-the-chest rumble.

"She will bring you some soup now."

The mention of soup brought back a flash memory of the terrible stuff he had been made to drink in the underground chamber.

"No thanks! One drink of that stuff was enough for me!"

"This not medicine, but soup," said the big Indian. The woman shuffled up to the big fellow, and passed over to him a large-size wooden cup, shaped something like a small flower vase, or a tall glass with sides that curved inward from the bottom and flanged out again toward the top, the mouth being wider than either bottom or middle. Dick noticed that the woman held the cup in both hands, as did his captor now.

"I don't want any of that stuff!" Dick was emphatic.

The Indian looked down impassively at Dick. Suddenly he lifted the cup to his own lips.

"Soup!" he said, and drank a long draught, sucking in loudly as he drank. "Soup," he repeated. Then kneeling down beside Dick, he lifted Dick's head with one hand, held the cup to his lips with the other.

Dick recognized the smell of chicken broth. Gingerly he tasted the brew. It was good! The rich chicken fat and the freshly boiled rice blended into a delicious spiced combination. He could feel the heat going down his throat, into his stomach. It revived him, gave him unexpected strength.

"More?" asked the big fellow.

Dick looked up. The big Indian who had called himself the Keeper of the Inca Secrets appeared older than Dick had thought. Walking across the room, carrying the heavy basket, he looked like an agile athlete. The big, copper-brown face, high cheek-bones and pointed, strong aquiline nose gave the native an appearance of weight, of solid stone-like massiveness. The strong pungent odor of unwashed body was especially intense as the Indian bent over him. Dick turned his head away, his nostrils quivering.

The woman returned, and Dick got a good look of her, too. She was much younger, stout and round of waist, and was barefooted, except for some crude rawhide sandals held on her feet with a thin leather strip that passed between the first two toes, wound around her ankle, then down behind her heel and into the heel of the sandal itself, where a hard knot held it in place. The woman wore a long wrap-around skirt and a high coarse blouse, and in the little light that came from the doorway Dick could see the bright red and green colors woven into them. A long silver pin, shaped like a thin letter opener, held the front part of the blouse together.

She didn't speak, but held out the curved drinking vessel for Dick. A sudden joy filled him as he discovered he could lift his head. He pulled his arms up under him, half sat up, elbows pressed hard into the thick rug under him. The big man knelt on one knee beside him.

"I will help you," he said simply, holding Dick's head in his big hand. Dick drank the second big cup of soup, relishing the spiciness of the pepper, the garlic and herbs he did not identify. He felt the big man's knee close to his face, bare, full-muscled, and noticed the knee-length woolen shorts, split a full six inches above the knee, that covered the man's thighs. The Indian was wearing dull-gold earplugs, the size of a half-dollar.

When he had finished his second cup of soup, Dick remained, half-sitting, resting on his elbows. The pain in his neck had gone. He found he could turn his head easily. The pain in his left leg was also gone. It looked distorted, that left leg, wrapped in the crude splint of twigs and vines sunk into the wet mud-like clay, like an oversized stuffed sleeve slipped over his foot and shinbone, but the pain was gone. He could distinguish the sharp smells that filled the hut, the strong acrid stench of sweat-filled woolen cloth, thin smoke of wood fire, the smell of dry hard earth, and, in spite of all, a fresh, sweet mountain air that came in through the doorway.

The woman had shuffled to the back of the hut, toward where the wood fire burned in a crude stone oven. Now she came back, in her hand a piece of what looked like a thick waffle or pancake. Silently she extended it to him, and Dick took a bite. It was good! It had a faintly sweet taste, but not the sweetness of sugar, more like honey spread on dry corn bread. He ate it eagerly. The big Indian and the woman watched him in silence.

"That was good," said Dick, looking up, first at the man, then at the woman. For the first time the muscles on her face twitched into a shy little smile. But a grunt from the big native changed them back abruptly into the stiff, expressionless stare.

"When the young señor feels strong enough, we can step outside to fill his lungs with the air from the high mountain," said the man.

Dick's heart leaped. Were they, after all, on the same mountain just outside Cuzco on which stood the remains of the big fortress? But the Indian's next words almost stopped his heart beating. It was as though the big native had read his mind.

"You will not try to escape," he said, very slowly, rolling his Spanish words in that deep voice of his. "No one can hear your voice. You are more than twenty leagues from Cuzco. And there is no road."

Dick felt himself tremble, but strangely he was not afraid. Twenty leagues might be a long distance in road-less mountains, but common sense told him that he had been brought here from inside that mountain of Sachsahuaman. Sooner or later he would find a way to escape, if Dad and Prof and the others didn't find him first. His mind ran back to that last terror-stricken moment when the avalanche had filled the tunnels in the mountain, sucking the pit of the abandoned water tower into the giant, bottomless well. Suddenly he knew he must get outdoors.

"I'm ready now," he said, trying to get to his feet. The Indian put his hands under Dick's arms, and lifted him as though he were a child. Dick found he could stand, awkwardly and stiffly, but he could put his left foot down and let it support part of the weight of his body. The Indian waited only a second, then walked ahead toward the doorway. Dick followed with half-dragging steps.

Immediately before him, the mountain plunged sharply 2,000

feet down into a deep gorge and far, far down below he could see the silver-white ribbon of the river as it wound around the mountain.

Steep, jagged cliffs on either side were joined by a knife-like ridge of granite, forming a saddle between two high, purple peaks. Scrub vegetation and gnarled, wind-twisted midget trees clung stubbornly to rocky ledges. To the right, Dick could see long, narrow terraces, held in place by stone walls, climbing one after the other, six or eight feet apart, up and up over the entire mountainside, as far as the eye could see. On the left, and on both sides of the steep saddle between the two mountains, were stone walls, walls of square buildings. Some had crude thatched roofs, but most of them were unroofed. They were built of carefully square-cut stones fitted one on top of the other. Narrow passages ran between the buildings, some filled with vines and scraggly shrubs, some empty, paved with stones that looked as if they had been worn smooth by many tramping feet. But Dick could see no one; not another soul seemed to be in all that vastness, no one beside himself and his tall captor, who stood on the edge of the narrow platform before the hut looking down into the deep ravine and across to the giant mountain on the other side.

Rising steeply behind the hut (which seemed to be a sort of caretaker's cottage at the head of a thin path that wound up the steep mountainside), Dick saw wide stone steps rising sharply to what looked like a high stone wall. It had only one queer trapezoid opening, man-high. Over the opening, a wide slab of granite formed the lintel, and two solid slabs of stone about six feet high formed the door frame. Dick could not see through this opening, but there seemed to be a crude form of roof with a short overhang toward the front; and farther back, up toward the top of the high ledge, a round stone tower rose higher than the ridge itself.

Dick looked back again at his companion. The Indian had said nothing as Dick looked across the deep ravine, and to the slopes that showed the vast semi-ruins of what must have been a large city.

"Are we all alone up here?" Dick asked. The big Indian did not answer, but instead spread out one long arm and waved it from left to right, as though indicating the frightening precipices that guarded this mountain hideaway on three sides.

"How did we get up here?" Dick tried again. Again the native did not answer. This time he pointed with a long brown finger to the zig-zag path that lost itself in the underbrush; then he pointed down the 2,000 foot drop before them, slowly raised his arm in a wide arch and ended pointing up to the sky. Dick was unable to understand his meaning.

He moved forward, to the edge of the small platform in front of the hut from which he could see far below, the wide horseshoe bend of the river as it pushed its way between these granite hills. The high mountains all around told him that here the river must bend completely around the taller of the two rock hills on which the city stood, and perhaps turn back in a complete hairpin turn, in its restless pushing toward the sea. But how far away was it? What river was that way down below in that deep ravine? In which direction was Cuzco from here? Twenty leagues, the tall Indian had said; sixty miles. But sixty miles in what direction?

Minutes passed before Dick could find his voice again. The panorama was truely awesome. Finally he spoke again.

"You live here all the time?"

The big native turned and looked at Dick for a long silent moment. Then he spoke.

"I am the Keeper of the Inca Secrets." The simple statement suddenly gained dignity by its repetition. "We watch over all his secrets."

"We? I thought we were alone up here."

"We are the last descendants of the Nobles of the Court of Atahualpa," the native said in his deep, even tones. His big head was now very high, the long black hair hung down framing his heavy face, his black eyes held Dick's with deep intensity. It came back to Dick that Prof had named the last of the reigning Incas, the king who had been tricked and captured by the Spanish, and put to death after he had paid enormous ransom in whole rooms filled with gold and precious stones. And these were his descendants? Up here in this ruined mountain hold-out?

"We are the last five hundred, sworn to keep the Inca's secrets," said the big Indian, coming one step closer to Dick. "Now you know why we cannot let you take back the story of what you have seen."

"But don't you understand . . . I come from a faraway country . . . I don't want your secrets . . . my father doesn't want your secrets. . . ."

"We know," said the big fellow, cryptically.

"Then why don't you let me go?"

"White man from a faraway country came once and took our secrets away," said the native, his eyes fixed steadily on Dick's face.

"But I'm not from that country—my father—well, he is the Ambassador from a friendly country—he's here to make friends, to help your country . . ."

"We know," repeated the big Indian.

Then abruptly, and before Dick could think of anything else to say, the tall native faced the west and raised both hands above his head. Looking straight up into the deep blue of the sky above them, he murmured soft words that Dick could not understand. Slowly the Indian put his two big hands together, and slowly he brought them down until they were on the level with his eyes. Holding both hands tightly clasped together, he made motions as though he were drinking from a cup held between his hands. His lips moved. He threw back his massive head, and the long black hair fell back over his shoulders. For a few seconds he held his head back, his eyes closed, his lips moving as though in prayer. Then he unclasped his hands, and his long, thick arms dropped to his side, where they hung like two strong branches of a sturdy tree. His eyes were still closed and his lips still moved, but no sound came from them.

Dick made no move, no noise. The sun was climbing and was now almost exactly overhead. Twice the big Indian dropped his eyes to his own feet and studied the ground with concentration; twice he threw back his head, eyes closed, arms dangling at his side. The third time he looked down, his body made no shadow on the ground beneath him. The sun had reached its zenith.

And now, with a gesture of complete humility and adoration, the big Indian dropped to his knees, bowed his head, and spreading his arms to left and right, he threw kisses to the wind with both hands, keeping his eyes fixed on the ground all the while. It was not until he saw once more the slight shadow cast by his body as the sun moved to the west, that he slowly folded his arms over his massive chest. Then he looked up at the sky again.

Awed by the noon prayer which this strong man had offered, Dick felt instinctively that he was witnessing a ritual as old as time itself. And now, as he watched the big man kneeling almost at his feet, he heard for the first time the words that rumbled from the man's big chest.

"Apu hanacpacha uyarii guacaicunas, muna maqui, Tatanchec, manai maqui." *

The Indian rocked back and forth gently as he spoke, his big head nodding in rhythm with his words. His prayer ended, he stopped his rocking and threw three more kisses to the winds with both hands, making a loud smacking noise with each kiss. Then he waved his hands toward the sky, keeping his eyes downcast. He dropped his hands again, and his long arms reached to the ground, though he was once more kneeling stiffly erect. Suddenly he straightened, rose swiftly to his feet, turned and faced Dick.

"The young white señor will live with us here in the Lost City," he said simply. "We wish you to be happy with us. Come, I will show you our city. You shall meet our Chief, Asto Huaraca."

Dick found that the packing on his leg had hardened like a plaster cast. He could use it, rather clumsily, but he felt no pain

* Lord of the Skies, listen to our tears, we kiss your hand, our Father, we kiss your hand.

at all as he limped after the big Indian. The native made no effort to help him, but led the way around the hut and toward the steep stone steps that led up to the high wall Dick had noticed before. It was evident that this big native was used to being obeyed; he didn't even once look back at Dick.

The narrow path climbed steeply up the side of the mountain. An empty aqueduct or narrow canal ran along side. Every twenty feet or so a square box-like chamber suggested a reservoir, or perhaps a crude bath-tub, made of closely-fitting square-cut stones, whose inside surface was polished finely. They were all dry now, and here and there a scraggly little plant struggled desperately to cling to life in the tiny cracks of the dry rocks. All around them was a vast silence.

When they had climbed well above the roof level of the native's hut, and some one hundred yards up the mountain side, the solid stone wall loomed like a fortress blocking further path. The trapezoid opening Dick had seen from below was much bigger than he had at first imagined; from this close distance it looked fully wide and high enough for the big man ahead to step through.

As the big Indian reached the stone threshold, he stopped. Dick thought for one brief moment that he saw something move behind the black opening. He looked again, and this time he saw that behind the wall a staircase cut right into the solid rock climbed steeply to the round tower-like building silhouetted against the sky. To his right, Dick could see again the long string of single square rooms stretching over the sharp ridge between the two mountains to the face of the lower mountain beyond. The stone buildings farther up the slope, past what looked like a huge square far off the right, seemed to be roofed with thatch tied in tight bundles.

The climbing got tougher. Dick's foot didn't hurt, but felt very heavy and very clumsy. His breath came in sharp, short puffs as the thin mountain air seemed to be fighting to keep back its meager oxygen. Yet several mountain peaks all around climbed thousands of feet higher into the sky, and thick green vegetation climbed with them, higher, higher!

The tall Indian had reached the stone wall, and there he waited patiently for Dick. Finally Dick reached the wall.

"How much more do we climb?" he gasped.

"Asto Huaraca is near-by. Cuyuchi will take you to him."

"Cuyuchi? Who's Cuyuchi?"

"I am Cuyuchi. I will take Master Deek to Asto Huaraca." The big native pronounced 'Dick' as Antonio had at first, making it sound like 'Deek.' Then suddenly it struck Dick that this big fellow had called him by his name.

"Hey! How do you know my name?" he cried, taken completely by surprise.

"We know," repeated the big native. It was the second time he had given the same cryptic answer. Then he turned, and quickly stepped through the big doorway, stooping a little as he did so to avoid the huge solid lintel. He signaled Dick to follow him.

Dick, alone in the vast emptiness of those huge mountains, with the abandoned ruins of a once great city all about him, suddenly had the feeling that a hundred pairs of eyes were watching him, though he could see no one. The brief swift thought that had crossed his mind as he saw the big Indian disappear behind the high wall . . . the thought that maybe he could make a break for it and escape . . . gave way to the grim thought that there was nowhere he could go . . . nowhere except behind the big high massive wall, as Cuyuchi had done.

Dick dragged his left foot up to the opening, tried to look in. It was all dark, except for the long flight of stone steps in the back. He lifted his left leg with his left hand to clear the high stoop, and steadied himself with his right hand against the thick stone entrance. He could feel his heart pounding fiercely as he stepped behind the high wall.

8

The Oath of Blood

Dick hobbled over the stone threshold. Not until then did he look up, and what he saw jerked him up straight. More than twenty half-naked warriors, in full war paint, carrying long spears, the two nearest him holding short-handled hatchets in their right hands, made a double row leading to a high rock-hewn throne carved right out of the mountain. A narrow canal of polished stone led down the side, gray and barren.

Seated atop the rock throne, on his head the biggest and most fantastic headdress Dick had ever seen, was an old man, shriveled and shrunken, his parched skin the color of weather-beaten leather. And standing by the old man was Cuyuchi, Dick's captor!

"Come, young white man," he said, motioning with his big hand.

Dick hesitated.

"Come!" This time it was a sharp command.

Dick's heart pounded. He glanced quickly at the long line

of savages—young, bull-chested from the high altitude, tough as rawhide. Behind him the single opening through which he had come he saw was now blocked by a powerfully built Indian, dressed in the short woolen split knee-breeches and heavy woolen poncho of the mountains, arms folded over his big chest.

Dick shuffled slowly toward the old man's throne. The young warriors, whose painted faces made them look almost like threatening animals, closed in behind him as he passed. The trap was closed!

"Chief Huaraca will speak!"

Dick stood very still. He could hear the furious thumping in his breast. He swallowed, a dry, hot swallow. He clenched his fists. The palms of his hands were wet and clammy. His knees trembled. A silly thought came to him all of a sudden; how does that old man keep that enormous head-gear of bird's feathers on his little head?

The old man mumbled something almost inaudible. The voice was high, and squeaky, and it cracked as the old man spoke. Cuyuchi bowed.

"Asto Huaraca wishes to know for whom the white youth is spying."

"Spying? Me? We were just out exploring . . . I fell in the hole . . . we were just looking . . ."

Again the cracking, squeaky voice. Again Cuyuchi's deep rumble interpreting. "Who is 'we'?"

"My teacher, my classmates. We were just looking around inside the old water tower. We didn't know anything was there!"

"But the young white man knows now!"

"I don't know anything. I'm telling you, I just fell down a hole. Then I simply walked inside the long tunnel. You know, you found me there."

A long silence followed. Dick looked around. The big rectangular room seemed to be about thirty-five or forty feet long, maybe twenty feet wide, with solid walls of stone two feet thick on three sides. In the back, the slope of the mountain made a sort of enclosure, although, as Dick had noticed before, a steep set of stone stairs led up on the right side to the high stone tower on top of the ridge. But where the old man's rock throne had been carved, a block of granite fifteen feet high stuck out from the mountain like an enormous stone fist. Overhead, long beams supported cross-poles, tied with vines; and on them bamboo reeds, grass, mats and leaves formed a thatch roof. In spite of the light from the mountain that came in the semi-open back, there was at best only half-light in the room.

The ancient's little steel-gray eyes were focused intently on Dick. Suddenly the old chieftain didn't look old any more; or perhaps ageless. He looks like a mummy, Dick thought.

Cuyuchi's deep rumbling voice brought Dick's thoughts back sharply.

"Huaraca wishes to know for whom you spy!"

"I tell you I am not a spy! Honest! I don't know anything about this. We weren't looking for anything in particular."

"No! You were searching for Inca gold."

"No, we weren't! We didn't know there was anything there."

"But you were looking for it."

"We weren't looking for anything, we were just looking. Don't you understand?"

"*Silencio!* Enough!" Cuyuchi waved his big right hand for silence.

The old man, with the agility of a wild-cat, jumped to his feet. No longer a short, mummified body, but tall and very straight, almost as tall as Cuyuchi! His headdress made him look even taller. The sun struck the short hatchet the old man carried in his hand, causing it to shine like pure gold.

"*Huac cuti, maimanta jamunqui—imatarur anqui!*"

"Huaraca asks again, where do you come from? What are you doing here?" Cuyuchi's voice, translating, rose high like the old man's.

"I told you we were just out for a walk. I fell in a hole. That's all I know."

The old man waved an imperious hand. The signal was unmistakable.

"Pusai pitapis yurac huaina. Guacaichai! Aiquii macchuchi!"
"Huaraca orders young white man to prison hut. He orders us to watch him. If white youth try to escape, he will be punished!"

Four powerful hands now seized Dick under his arms, whirled him around, and, half-carrying him, whisked him to the doorway. Once here, they thrust him through the opening, and Dick almost fell on the other side. He hopped twice on his right leg to get his balance. The stolid, thick-chested big Indian who had earlier blocked the doorway stood outside, silently watching him. He made no effort to help Dick, but waited until Dick had regained his equilibrium. Then without changing expression, without moving a single muscle in his face, he stared at Dick. "Come!" he said in Spanish. Then he turned, sure that Dick would follow. This big fellow, then, would be his guard!

Silently, his left leg suddenly very heavy, Dick followed the bull-chested native down the steep path. The guard waited at the corner of the hut for Dick to catch up to him, let Dick go ahead to the doorway. The Indian woman who had brought Dick his food was waiting there, her big round face just staring.

"Feed him his food when the sun sinks beyond the peak." The guard spoke in labored Spanish so Dick could understand. The woman nodded and stepped aside to let Dick enter. But she did not drop the heavy blanket over the door opening as Dick slowly walked back toward his rug on the other side of the hut. There was still enough daylight for him to see the low, narrow clay benches along the wall to the right which served as beds for the natives. His own thick rug was on the bare clay floor, and on one end of the narrow clay bench a pile of neatly folded woolen blankets made a little square tower. A stone shelf projecting from the wall above the bench held a stone idol, half-fish, half-rounded body like that of a tiger, or a cat. The eyes were two green stones the size of small marbles. Dick could still smell the chicken soup and the wisps of gray wood smoke that clung everywhere.

Dick sat down heavily on his floor rug. He felt lonely and rather sorry for himself. What were Prof, and his father, doing? How could he possibly get word to them where he was? He didn't even know himself!

From the dark corners of the square hut, from behind the open doorway, even from above he felt silent black eyes staring at him. But he could see no one, not even the woman who seemed to have melted into the shadows behind the stone fireplace in the far corner.

Suddenly the woman appeared, as though from nowhere. "Your dinner," she said in Spanish, handing him a round wooden plate. Dick recognized the little mountain potatoes, smothered in reddish-brown sauce; he could smell the spices; and the pieces of brown meat, square-cut, also covered with the peppery-smelling sauce, were steaming. There were no vegetables.

Suddenly he was very thirsty; his throat felt as though it were burning from the highly-spiced food. He remembered that in all the time he had been here, he had not seen a single drop of water! His stomach was now jumping, his throat felt on fire.

"*Agua!*" he cried, and again, "*agua!*"

The woman reappeared almost immediately, bringing him a wooden cup, shaped something like an hour-glass.

"*Gracias!*" he said, attempting to smile. But the Indian woman's face was expressionless, her brown eyes, her deep brown skin and her jet black hair making an indistinct whole in the growing darkness.

"*No mas,*" Dick said, pushing the plate toward her, "no more."

She took the plate in silence. Then she extended her left hand with a large piece of the same semi-sweet corn bread. He ate this hungrily; then he drank the rest of the water. The woman took the wooden cup from Dick, and went back into the shadows of the hut.

He got up awkwardly and walked slowly toward the door. He stepped through the doorway. The shadows of the gathering twilight had already thrown the ravine before the hut into blackness. The treetops on the rim of the mountain opposite still clung to the last yellow half-light, and the huge rock ledge that rose steeply into the growing night seemed almost purple. A cool breeze brushed past him as he looked down into the almost black abyss.

Even in the swiftly gathering darkness he could see the path, zig-zagging down the mountain to the river. He couldn't see it all, and here and there shrubs and small gnarled trees cut it off entirely; and as it reached down into the gorge, it disappeared entirely into the darkness. Instinctively Dick's hand went to his belt. His hunting knife was still there!

Slowly, Dick walked around the hut. He looked all around but could see no people anywhere. Where was the guard? Watching him perhaps from behind one of those big boulders to the left? Then he had an idea. There's one sure way of finding out if people are near: start a fire!

He picked up some dry twigs, reached up and grabbed a handful of straw from the thatch roof. He laid the straws down, formed a little teepee with the twigs around it. His water-proof match box was still intact, still full. Quickly he struck a match, lit the straw with it. The red and yellow flame shot through the dry twigs like a miniature chimney.

Nothing happened. Dick threw some more straw on the fire. It blazed higher with a furious little spurt. Still no voice was raised, no one came.

Apparently not afraid of signal fires, thought Dick; or else these signals were not the ones the Indians used! More likely, Cuyuchi had been right when he had said no one would hear him up here in the mountains. But the little fire felt good as the cold mountain draft swept past him down into the deep ravine.

Dick added more twigs, the flame flared up again. In the sudden light he saw the big round boulders to the left, the little square hut where he was a prisoner, the narrow little path that led up to the stone wall and tower high above to the back. Dick watched the little fire dim down, rubbing his hands over the fading warmth. When it was almost out he kicked loose dirt and sand over it. The embers hissed in protest as they drowned in the dust and sand.

Slowly he walked back to the front of the adobe hut. As he approached he thought he saw the blanket over the doorway move just an inch. Maybe not. It was almost dark, so he couldn't really tell. Might as well go inside and wait until morning. Even if he wasn't being watched now, he couldn't try getting down into the deep ravine.

Dick dropped heavily on his thick rug. Drowsiness spread over him like a warm sheet. From far down in the deep ravine he could hear the restless muffled river.

Suddenly he sat bolt upright. It was pitch dark. Even the little embers from the wood stove had died out. He didn't know how long he had been asleep, but he was sure someone, something, had touched him. He peered hard into the darkness, but he could neither hear nor see anything. Nothing, nothing but the faraway rumble of the river and the wind that blew through the bundles of dry grass on the thatch roof, wheezing and whining as it found here and there a little crack through which it could squeeze, as though trying to come in out of the cold.

Then from back in the hut somewhere he was sure he heard a slight hissing that was not the wind. Dick reached for his knife; its hard handle gave him new confidence. Slowly he drew it from its sheath, listening, and waiting.

Then came the voice, very softly, not even a real whisper, more like the gentle murmur of a person speaking in his sleep. But it was a woman's voice!

"Be patient," said the voice, and now it sounded quite nearby, "Tocta Cuca will help you."

"Who are you?" demanded Dick, not loud, but finding it hard to suppress his voice.

"Shhhhhhhhhh! Do not speak. Be patient. Tocta Cuca will help you, but I cannot do it yet. Be patient . . ."

Dick thought he heard the rustle of skirts in the darkness, or maybe just a naked foot scraping over the hard clay floor. His heart was thumping furiously. Cold sweat broke out on his forehead. He held his knife point out and upward, and gripped the handle tighter. Was someone trying to get him to escape so they could kill him? 'Ley de Fuga,' they called it, 'the law of flight.' The prisoner was trying to escape, so the guard shot him. Finish. Just like that. Afterward the guard tells the judge, and is commended for his watchfulness. All very legal. But if he did try to escape, where would he go? How far away was Lima from here?

Lima! The thought of the big, white, beautiful city brought tears welling inside. Lima! What was Dad doing? And Mom? He swallowed hard, felt the choking wetness in his throat. He waited. There were no further sounds. Gradually he felt his heart beat more slowly. His temples stopped throbbing. His eyes cleared. Had he been dreaming?

Dick dropped back on his rug, and for a few long minutes just lay there, listening. But gradually sleep overcame him again. The last thing he remembered was putting the knife back in its sheath.

In spite of the darkness inside the hut he knew it was morning because from somewhere came the crow of a rooster. Back home in Indiana that meant sunrise! A new day, new light, new hope.

Dick quickly rose to his feet. He would go outside and look for that path he had seen last night. Turning toward the doorway, he was startled to find the Indian woman almost in front of him, not two feet away, her round expressionless face looming out of the darkness.

"Your breakfast," she said in the monotone she had used before. Without a word Dick took the wooden plate and cup she handed him, and the woman disappeared again into the shadows.

He tried to recall the voice that had come to him during the night. It had been soft, and had spoken a very clear sing-song Spanish, not a monotone like this one. He looked around, could see nothing. But from under the woven rug across the doorway, Dick could see a faint line of light that told him it was, indeed, day, and the sun was coming up. He dropped on the blanket he had just folded, using it like a seat, and tasted his breakfast. The broth, made of spiced corn and herbs, smelled like dried laurel leaves and sage. The corn bread was crisp, hot, and tasting of honey. Dick ate every crumb of it, washed it all down with the hot, thick broth. He set the plate down on the ground, and slowly got up on his feet again. It was awkward walking, but he felt no pain, no pain of any kind. But could he walk far with that cast? Could he try to run down the mountain side? One of those swift arrows could cut him down from behind, or a poison dart, deadly accurate, right through his neck, like a bird brought down in flight.

"It won't be my feet that get me out of this," thought Dick. Dad always said that it was thinking that separated civilized man from the savage, thinking and using your head. How old do you have to be before you can really think and plan?

"The young white man come with me!" commanded a voice almost beside him. Dick jumped. "Where did you come from?" he demanded.

The big heavyset Indian guard did not answer, but walked toward the doorway. Before he reached it, the Indian woman lifted the woolen rug, then the rawhide. The fresh morning air rushed in.

"The young white man come with me," repeated the big native. It was the bull-chested guard who had blocked the way in the doorway yesterday.

"Where are we going?" asked Dick, stopping at the doorway.

"Chief Huaraca has called you," the jailer replied. And he turned, as Cuyuchi had done yesterday, walking swiftly toward the back of the hut, toward that narrow path that led up to the high stone wall. He, too, expected to be followed!

Dick thought the path was narrower, steeper than it had been the day before. He dragged his left foot as he tried to follow the native who had climbed ahead. When the jailer reached the high wall, he waited, watching Dick puff and struggle up the narrow path. When Dick was only a few feet away, the big native passed quickly through the stone opening.

The old Chieftain on his stone throne across the big room seemed even more shrunken than on the day before. He was not wearing his plumed hat. His hair was a dirty gray, matted over his shrunken head, and in the early morning light which slanted in through the wide opening at the back the old man looked as though his skin were made of brown, weathered leather.

Once more Cuyuchi was standing by the old man. He looked almost as brown as the old man himself, but his skin was smooth with the vigor of youth and health.

Dick looked from one to the other. Only the big bull-chested guard, who had stayed respectfully by the open doorway, and the old Chieftain and Cuyuchi, besides Dick, were in the room which seemed inordinately large and empty, without yesterday's painted warriors.

"Huaraca wishes to know if young white man know the white man's cure for snakebite." Cuyuchi's deep rumble spoke more quickly than before, a note of anxiety in his voice.

So that was it! They were going to throw him into a snake-pit, and torture him!

Dick looked quickly around. Might as well make a dash for freedom, be killed outright. Snakebite! But the squat, bull-chested guard stood, arms folded on his chest, watching Dick intently. Dick turned to Cuyuchi and the old man.

"Snakebite?" he asked, and his voice shook a little. "Why?"

"Huaraca has beautiful grandchild, bitten by a snake this morning. The medicine man is away with a sick family over the hills. He will not be back until the sun makes shadows in the valley. Huaraca fears that may be too late."

A deep and thankful sigh came from deep inside of him as Dick's mind suddenly cleared.

"Snakebite, you say? How long ago?"

"When the sun touched the mountain tops. The child was alone."

"Quick, Cuyuchi, there's no time to lose! Where is he?" Dick was not trembling.

Cuyuchi looked at Dick as though trying to pierce through him. His deep dark eyes squinted, his mouth was a thin tight slit across his face. Then he spoke.

"It is a small she-child. Here!"

Cuyuchi walked swiftly toward the back of the throne. For the first time Dick noticed the narrow passage between the granite block and the wall. Cuyuchi slipped sideways into the narrow opening, as the old man turned in his big throne, watching. Dick followed, as quickly as he could, dragging his left leg a little.

Behind the wall was a large square chamber made of white stone. A low thatch roof closed it in completely, except for two small openings on the farthest wall, small narrow quadrilateral trapezoids, like the doorway in the high stone wall, but smaller and narrower. The rumble of the river, two thousand feet below, came up faintly, and through the window openings Dick could see the tree tops on the other mountain side far across the deep canyon.

In the center of the white room a crib made of slender bamboo stakes with a woven, basket-like bottom covered with a rich vicuña rug, held the body of a small child. The little arms hung through the crib sides, limp and listless. As Dick reached the crib, he stepped back in astonishment: the child's skin was milk-white, and long blonde curls fell all around the little head! Her face was fever-red. Her eyes were closed. Only the lips moved, and through them came the soft groan of half-conscious pain.

On the right side of the crib, her back to the window openings so that the light fell across her bowed head, knelt a white woman close to the wall. Her dress was that of the mountain natives, but her hair was brown-blond, her skin was unmistakably white. She rocked back and forth silently, watching Dick with big, wide eyes that spoke the age-old concern of a mother for her child.

"We need hot water and clean bandages," Dick said, almost mechanically. "Do you have any disinfectant?" he asked.

"Disinfectant?" Cuyuchi's deep voice betrayed anxiety, but he did not understand.

"No, of course not, not up here!" Dick was thinking fast. "Build a fire here, and bring hot water, lots of boiling water!"

Cuyuchi turned to the woman near the wall.

"Tocta Cuca, hot water!" he commanded. The woman jumped to her feet and disappeared to the rear.

Tocta Cuca! Where had he heard that name before? That voice out of the darkness, whispering! It hadn't been a dream! But . . . this woman . . . Tocta Cuca?

Now she was coming back, holding in both her arms a steaming earthenware jar. Dick turned quickly to Cuyuchi.

"We need a small fire here," he said. Then: "Where was she bitten?"

"Here." The tall Indian bent down and pointed to the child's leg. Even in that half-light Dick could see the nasty black spots, the ugly swelling. The child whimpered as Dick touched the distended skin softly. Cuyuchi dropped on his knees and quickly made a small fire. Dick didn't even notice what the Indian used to light the fire, for now he could see quite plainly where the fangs had struck. Already the swelling was moving up the little leg, showing red and angry under the child's white skin.

Tocta Cuca, almost running, returned with some fine cotton bandages. She held them gently in her hand as she watched Dick swiftly tie one bandage under the child's knee, and another one a few inches lower on the little calf, but above the fang marks. The child's vein stood out, very blue. He loosened the bandage a tiny bit. Then he drew his knife. Tocta screamed. Cuyuchi raised his arm, and in that raised hand Dick caught the flash of a long thin dagger!

"No, no Cuyuchi," Dick called. "I'm only sterilizing this—

look—like this—I burn the point of my knife—we have to open this swelling on her leg . . ."

Tocta dropped on her knees beside the child and clutched the child's hand hysterically. Cuyuchi brought his hand down slowly, but watched Dick intently, as he held the tip end of his knife in the little fire, waved it in the air to cool it, passed it through the flame again.

"God help me!" he murmured to himself. "This has got to work!"

Quickly now, his hands trembling a little, he washed the fang marks with boiling hot water, made an X-shaped cut over each mark. The child uttered a muffled little cry. Tocta grasped the little hand convulsively and kissed it. The child's eyes were closed. Dick dropped the knife, bent over the child and put his lips to the cuts. He sucked, first one, then the other. He spit out the poisoned blood. He sucked again. And again. Suck, then spit out. The swelling went down a little. He sucked again.

Half an hour later, great beads of perspiration on his forehead, Dick straightened up. He was shaking all over. The earth was hard as stone under his knees. He dropped his head in his hands.

Suddenly a wild hope struck him, chilled him at the same time. Maybe he could trade! Bargain with these savages—the child's life for his freedom!

"I have a magic powder but I will not use it unless you set me free!"

Dick stared into the big bony face of Cuyuchi. The Indian's eyes, black, piercing, stared into Dick's eyes.

"Only Chief Huaraca can make such a promise," said the big Indian in his deep, rumbling voice.

"Then take me to him. I'll talk to him!" Dick's voice was high with excitement.

Cuyuchi did not move. He stared at Dick with intense, black eyes. "You would let this child die?" he asked after a long moment.

Dick looked down at the little girl. She stirred, moaned. Dick caught the mother's eyes, brown, soft, pleading. Tocta looked deeply into Dick's eyes; her lips trembled, but she said nothing. The child opened her little blue eyes. Pain—or was it a smile?— twisted her little lips.

Dick was on his knees again.

"Cuyuchi—did you save my kit, that little canvas bag I carried on my back when you found me? There's a small tin cylinder in that kit. That's the powder, Cuyuchi!"

The big Indian nodded, grunted something to the guard by the door. Instantly the big-chested fellow disappeared behind the white wall. They all waited in silence.

After what seemed an intolerably long time, the big guard reappeared. He had Dick's kit in his hands! Dick tore the adhesive tape off the top of the tin cylinder and sprinkled the sulpha powder on the open cut.

Cuyuchi was standing, tall and erect, by the child's crib, his big black eyes ferreted on Dick's hands. He watched, unmoving, as Dick sprinkled the powder, hesitated, closed the little tin cylinder again. The adhesive tape had got twisted, would not stick on the cylinder top again. Dick tried to untwist it, but finally gave it up. He looked up quickly, half embarrassed, to find both Cuyuchi and Tocta staring at him.

Dick's hands were trembling. His face, hot and sweaty, felt almost on fire. But the child's leg looked less angry; the black spots around the wound had almost disappeared.

"That's one of the new wonder-drugs," said Dick, addressing the big man who towered over him. "That will keep infection away."

Cuyuchi looked down at the child. The little girl smiled. Her eyelids were heavy, but the fever seemed to be less. Cuyuchi stared at the child for some moments, then abruptly turned and went back behind the opening in the wall. He motioned the guard to follow.

Now the woman let go of the child's hand, moved swiftly to Dick's side.

"God bless you, Dick," she said, and Dick instantly recognized the soft voice of the night before. "Tocta will help you. Be patient. I will help you!"

Quickly she moved away, as though in panic. Dick was left alone with the child in the bamboo and wicker crib. He listened to the child's breathing. It was almost regular, even. The child slept.

A great weariness overcame Dick. Slowly he slumped down on the bare floor. The big white room, now catching the growing sunlight outside, seemed even whiter. The rumble of the river far down in the canyon made muffled drumming noises. But in the big room nothing stirred.

Once more Dick dropped his head in his hands, arms aching as though they would drop off from sheer weariness. His head, too, felt heavy and a little giddy. Dick thought for a moment he was going to faint, he felt so weak. He wanted to cry, and couldn't. His throat was choked up; his lips were dry. Then he felt a giant tear slide slowly down his cheek, curve over the cheekbone, stop for an instant at the corner of his mouth. He tried to spit it off, but by this time more and more tears were streaming down his face. Dick dropped his arms to his side, and his head sunk deep. He didn't know that his shoulders were jerking with big sobs; but he felt better suddenly.

The child did not move. She was sleeping very quietly.

9

The Feast of the Purification

DICK HAD NEVER SLEPT MORE SOUNDLY IN HIS LIFE. HE had a hard time awakening, even though he could feel the shaking hand on his shoulder long before he actually opened his eyes. He opened them and closed them several times before he recognized the voice, and heard what it was saying. Cuyuchi was shaking him.

"The white señor will come with me," he repeated.

"Eh? What? . . . Oh, it's you, Cuyuchi! Where am I going now?" Dick tried to shake the sleep out of his head. His muscles were stiff from sleeping on the clay floor, even though his sleeping rug was thick and soft.

"We are going to the Plaza, where the people dance the Dance of Purification."

"But why do I have to go? I can't dance . . ." Dick was still half-asleep.

"This is the day of the Feast of Purification. We will go down to the river after the dance and wash away all the sins." Cuyuchi's voice, though deep and throaty, was gentler than Dick had ever heard it.

"Down to the river?" Dick said, his spirits rising suddenly. The river!

"Acachu the guard will stay with the young white man while Cuyuchi marches with his people." Cuyuchi was looking steadily at Dick as he spoke.

"Oh, but I want to come down to the river, too! I want to see the festival!" Dick's voice rose high as he protested.

"The young white man will not try to escape?" Cuyuchi's face was almost smiling, Dick thought. Was he being sarcastic, or did he actually think there was a chance? Had this inscrutable native read his thoughts?

"How could I?" Dick said quickly, but he felt that his answer was weak and unconvincing.

"The young white man will not try to escape?" repeated Cuyuchi, this time with a serious frown as he stared at Dick.

Before Dick could make an answer, the bull-chested guard, whose name he had just heard was Acachu, stepped through the doorway. As he lifted the woolen rug, a flood of sunshine and cool air rushed in, and Dick realized, with surprise, that the day was already quite advanced—nine o'clock, surely, maybe even ten.

"Acachu will guard you while I march with my people," said Cuyuchi again, almost sadly.

"Please let me come and see the festival!" Dick's voice was pleading now. "I . . . I can't run away . . . with this leg . . . I don't know where to go . . . I promise."

Cuyuchi looked at him in silence. Then he turned to the bull-chested guard.

"*Guacaichai!*" he said gruffly. "Watch him closely!" Acachu nodded his big black head. "*Guacaichai!*" he echoed, and stepped to Dick's side.

Cuyuchi stepped outside. Acachu lifted a silent hand and pointed to the doorway. Dick looked at his guard for a moment, then turned and walked into the sunshine and fresh air. He took several deep breaths as he stepped outside, squinting in the bright mountain sunlight. His lungs felt good with the clean air.

From the high ridge, beyond the round tower above the wall, there came loud shouting and singing. Dick walked around the hut as fast as he could, caught a glimpse of Cuyuchi, who had already climbed the steep path to the stone wall and was about to disappear behind it. Without waiting to be coaxed, Dick started climbing. The long night sleep had rested him; his leg, though clumsy, did not ache, and he found he could make surprisingly fast time up the steep path.

Once up to the wall, Dick passed through the wide opening, lifting his mud cast high over the threshold. The wide throne room where he had first met the Chieftain Huaraca was empty. But from behind the round tower Dick could hear louder and louder the shouts and cries of several hundred voices. He crossed the wide room and started climbing the long stairway.

Stepping up with his right foot, Dick soon evolved a certain rhythm for climbing and he found his breath quickening steadily as he climbed. But in spite of the exertion, he was not puffing when he reached the top. He had not turned back, but he could hear the steady measured step of Acachu right behind him. At the top, Dick stopped.

"Through the tower?" he asked, as Acachu reached his side.

"No—this way." Acachu pointed, with his left hand this time, and Dick saw a smooth, wide path that skirted the base of the tower. At this point the tower walls, made of solid blocks of stone, looked three or four feet thick. The walls inclined slightly inward as they rose, and Dick noted several openings near the top, shaped like all their openings in trapezoid form but almost man-high and wide enough to permit a man to stand in them. Look-out posts, thought Dick. This must be the look-out tower!

From the other side of the tower the shouting was now almost deafening. Dick walked as fast as he could and suddenly stood still.

On the other side of the high tower, and dropping steeply away from the little platform on which he stood, Dick could see a wide flat plateau that stretched out several hundred feet. It ended abruptly, and at the edge the mountain fell off sharply into a deep gorge on the other side of the ridge. The river, which Dick had seen from his hut, made a wide horse-shoe turn, circling the two mountain peaks on three sides, leaving deep jungle ravines which fell almost perpendicularly from the high ridge on which the tower stood. The plaza was the only wide space in the saddle connecting the two rock mountains, spreading out like an unfolded saddlebag. An infinite number of square stone rooms, some with gabled-end walls, most of them unroofed, clung to the steep and narrow ridge between the two mountains. But to the left of the plaza, and rising a full two stories above it, a long barracks-like building, its roof covered with new thatch, formed a solid stone wall against the west, facing the purple mountains and jagged peaks that rose higher and higher as they stretched, as far as the eye could see, toward the everlasting snows of the giant Mount Vilcanota. Dick's heart leaped as he recognized the faraway peak. It was from this mountain volcano, Prof had told him, that the original Inca tribe had spread, northward and westward, conquering the other tribes and eventually establishing the great Empire of the Incas in the sacred valley of the Cuzco.

Now he knew at least where he was! This might be, as Cuyuchi had said, twenty leagues away from Cuzco, but Dick knew that those sixty miles lay due south. And that river that roared and growled through the deep gorges as it carved its way through granite on its restless and determined way to the sea, was the mighty Urubamba, fed by countless mountain streams that swelled the tiny spring beneath the frozen masses of the giant volcano, making it the longest and the greatest of all rivers save the mighty Amazon itself into which it poured its icy waters a thousand miles downstream.

But Dick had little time to contemplate the awesome sight before him, for from the great square below the Outlook Tower now rose a mighty shout. Hundreds of young men, in full war paint, rushed from the high building to the left, and the populace which had previously filled the square pushed back to the far edges. Now the young men leaped, and danced, and chanted, carrying a long garland of colored woolen tufts, strung together into an endless chain. Weaving and shouting, they crossed the square. On the right, so close to the edge that it seemed to Dick it would topple over into the deep ravine, a high stone platform had been erected. On top of the platform Dick could see the wizened leathery form of Huaraca, the Chieftain.

From far down the long narrow valley there came the distant rumble of thunder. Big black clouds climbed menacingly toward them, hanging low above the jagged mountains, wet, heavy, threatening. But the dancing went on, and no one paid any attention to the clouds.

When the dancing youths reached the high platform, they stopped and quickly formed a giant phalanx before their chieftain to the north of the square. A sudden hush fell upon the multitude. The youths dropped on one knee, heads bowed, and on the outer fringes of the great square, men and women did likewise. Where the mountains had but a few seconds before echoed and re-echoed the great shouting and screaming, now came only the hissing of the black clouds that sped by overhead, crashing into the mountains, filling the valley and the lower peaks with a chill dampness.

Dick looked quickly at the big-chested guard who had stood beside him throughout the ceremony. "What happens now?" he asked.

"Young white man look!" commanded the big Indian, pointing to a little square building almost immediately beneath them, at the foot of the tower itself. Dick leaned over and looked down, and almost at the same instant a tremendous roar filled the entire valley. A tall, straight figure, dressed in long flowing surplice covered with gold and silver threads from which hung an infinite number of colored bird feathers—red, green, purple, yellow, black and some colors Dick had never seen before—marched out of the small square building. He marched at the head of a double column, which now emerged, also wearing long flowing surplices, but these were not so ornate, although their long embroidered woolen robes made fantastic patterns of color as they slowly marched toward the high platform and their Chief Huaraca.

"The High Priest!" said Acachu, as if in answer to Dick's unspoken wonderment. "And those are the lesser priests who will assist him in the Festival of Purification. For Huaraca has decreed that all must give thanks to the Great God Viracocha, Maker of All Things, for the life he has given back to his granddaughter, his little Miskqui."

Something in the way the High Priest walked, the way he held his head, suddenly drew Dick's attention. He could not be sure, because from this distance he could not see the High Priest's face, but suddenly he was sure . . . this must be . . . but how could it be?

"Is that Cuyuchi?" he asked, pointing.

Acachu stood very straight and looked at Dick for a long moment before he answered. There was great pride in his voice when he finally spoke.

"Cuyuchi is son of Chief Huaraca. Cuyuchi is High Priest of the Lost City, chief guardian of the Secrets of the Inca!"

"Cuyuchi is Huaraca's son?" Dick found it hard to put together all these baffling relations.

"Cuyuchi is father of Miskqui," answered the guard. The sun shone full on the big Indian's face, giving its copper-color a clear metallic sheen. The big guard turned away from Dick, his eyes staring off into space across the deep canyon, across the valley and the high mountains beyond. Dick had seen that same look on Antonio's face that morning—oh, so long ago!—in the mountain village of Ayacucho.

Cuyuchi the father of Miskqui! Father of that blonde white little girl! It couldn't be! Then Cuyuchi must be the husband of that white woman, of Tocta Cuca! Dick's head was swimming.

"I don't understand . . . !" Dick was cut short by the imperious raising of the guard's hand.

"*Silencio!*" cried the Indian. Then, pointing, he added, "Look! The parade to the river starts!"

Slowly the High Priest led his small army of Lesser Priests past the high platform on which Huaraca sat. They bowed as they passed their Chieftain, and Cuyuchi, at the head, chanted in deep, sonorous tones. Moaning echoes from the other priests were followed by answering echoes from the young warriors, who were still kneeling on one knee at the north end of the square. Slowly Cuyuchi led the parade, then made an abrupt turn to the right after he passed the high platform, and seemed to disappear at its base. Dick walked to the far end of the terrace on which he had been standing, and saw, for the first time, that a path led down the mountain on the other side of Huaraca's platform. And as the priests passed, the young warriors rose, and slowly followed the priests down the steep path.

When all the young warriors had left the square, the populace pushed forward once again and filled the open space before their Chieftain. The men bowed, holding their hands outstretched before them. Then they, too, formed into two long lines and solemnly followed the priests and the warriors. Last came the women. They burst into a high chant, and from down deep in the canyon the voices of the men who were already far down below joined them. The last of the black clouds that had come up suddenly from the far-off hills was chased across the valley and over the mountains; the sun shone in all its glory and filled the giant square with brilliance and warmth. Then the women, too, formed into two lines and followed their men down the mountainside.

Now in that giant square the shrunken body of Chief Huaraca was left alone, atop the high platform. The rhythmic chanting of the people as they marched down the long hill grew fainter. Only the sun, Giver of Light and Life, looked down upon the now empty square. Dick felt his whole body tremble. He stood very still, and for several long minutes neither he nor his guard moved. Then the guard spoke.

"Come," he said, and his voice was almost as deep as Cuyuchi's, "we go down now to Huaraca."

The guard walked ahead and Dick followed, not saying a word. The terrace above the big square came to an abrupt end, and a long, steep stone stairway, almost as steep as a ladder, led straight down to the square below. It must be forty or fifty feet, Dick thought. He climbed down as he would have down a ladder, face toward the wall, like the guard who went ahead. Dick found the slight incline in the staircase helpful, and was glad especially because his left leg felt awkward and big. But he had no difficulty getting down. The bull-chested guard was waiting for him at the bottom of the ladder. Dick noticed the evenly matched square flagstones that covered the entire square, each set tightly against the next, not the least crack opening between them. Yet Dick could see no mortar or cement. How did they do it? he wondered as he followed the big guard toward the high platform.

Once before the Chieftain, Acachu bowed and fell on both knees before Huaraca. Dick wondered if he was expected to do same. But while he hesitated, he heard the high, nasal voice of the old Chieftain.

"Cuyuchi tells me you prayed to the white man's God for my grandchild," he said, speaking for the first time in Spanish. Dick's astonishment grew. This old man could speak Spanish all the time, but had chosen to speak in Quechua before, allowing Cuyuchi to interpret!

"Yes, yes, I prayed for Miskqui," said Dick, when he finally found his voice.

"Miskqui!" The old man suddenly stood up, and again Dick was struck by the tall thin figure that seemed to shrink and shrivel into a little bundle when the old man was sitting!

"Miskqui!" repeated the old man. Dick had been told that meant "little drop of honey," the old man's pet name for his grandchild. "You have saved my Miskqui's life. Huaraca will not forget."

Dick's heart was suddenly pumping. "Then you'll set me

free?" he cried, looking up at the old man who was still standing.

Now the old man looked down, and Dick thought that for a moment he actually saw pain and regret in the old man's eyes.

"No, that I cannot do," he said, bending down low to speak to Dick. "That I cannot do," he repeated, more slowly. "The wise men of the tribe have spoken. The young white man must stay with us here in the Lost City."

Now the old man waved a long, thin arm, and from the small square building that had housed the priests came four tall, strong natives. One of them carried what looked like a litter, two long poles on which was stretched a finely woven blanket. The first man climbed nimbly up the side of the high platform, and the other one passed the litter up to him. Then the second man, too, jumped up, and the two of them lifted old Huaraca on to the blanket. With infinite care, as though they were handling something precious and very fragile, they lifted the blanket over the side of the platform, and the two tall natives below reached up to seize it in firm, strong hands, arms outstretched. They held it thus aloft until the first two had jumped down again, and the four of them turned swiftly and started for the path that led down into the deep river canyon, carrying Huaraca's litter shoulder-high.

When the native guard pointed a silent finger, Dick followed the four stalwarts as they carried their Chieftain down the steep path. Dick had to stop from time to time to catch his breath, and to rest his leg, which grew heavier as he descended. The guard was very patient, made no move to pass Dick, but waited with him, impassive, unsmiling. When Dick would start up again, the native did also. The old chieftain had been carried to the water's edge when Dick finally reached the bottom. No one seemed to be noticing Dick at all; all eyes were on the old Chieftain, who was now seated on a wide stone, on which low arm rests had been carved. The old man held on to these, his hands trembling a little. The priests made a semi-circle to the left; the young painted warriors made a wider, deeper half-circle to the right; and before him, in long lines three deep—the men on one side, the women on the other—the people whom Dick had seen dancing in the square now formed a long tunnel leading right down to the river.

The mighty Urubamba River, which roared and foamed as it sped through the rock gorge below the prison hut where Dick was held, here curved wide, making a flat, grassy platform, green and damp. Now held in the arms of the four carriers who had brought him down the mountainside, Huaraca was carried through the silent lines. Men and women bowed as he was carried past, straightening up immediately again, and from their throats came a low, guttural chant, monotonous and repetitive, as though men and women alike were moaning one word over and over again. A round flat stone at the very edge of the river, but rising two feet or so above the water's edge, was carefully brushed by a youth with a small broom of twigs and grass. Then the old Chieftain was gently placed on this stone, facing the river.

Now came a loud shout, and Cuyuchi, once more at the head of the column of priests, moved swiftly through the long line of chanting men and women. The other priests joined him.

"Sickness! Disaster! Unhappiness! Danger! Go from these shores, never to return!" Cuyuchi's deep voice shouted, and the chorus of male voices answered. Again Cuyuchi shouted, and this time only the women answered. "Sickness! Disaster! Unhappiness! Danger! Leave these shores!"

"Never to return!" cried Cuyuchi.

"Never to return!" echoed the multitude. Dick noticed that the women joined in a low moaning prayer, subdued and plaintive.

Now Cuyuchi, standing in the cold river up to his knees, his brilliant gold and silver surplice floating gracefully around him like a giant leaf on the calm water, held up his hands toward the sky. In his right hand he held a tall thin vessel of gold; in his left, a similar vessel, but of silver. Slowly he lowered his hands, and as they reached the level of his chest, he suddenly turned his wrists. A thick white foaming liquid poured out of them, splashed into the placid water of the river.

"Out with the devils! Out with the sins!" Cuyuchi's deep, sonorous voice filled the canyon with its roar. The women shrieked, and fell upon their knees, rocking down deep, hitting their hands with their heads. The men raised their right arms, and the young warriors who had marched to the water's edge raised their long spears into the air.

"Out with the devils! Out with the sins!" they cried in unison.

While Cuyuchi stood in the water, the lesser priests, then the warriors, then the men, singly, came down to the river's edge, bowed, and each in turn received from Cuyuchi a few drops of water dipped up from the spot where the two vessels had emptied their white foaming contents. As they approached, and as Cuyuchi anointed each in turn first with the golden vessel then with the one of silver, each man bowed and repeated the soft chant that came from Cuyuchi's lips—until the last man in the tribe had been anointed. The women, who had been joined by a large group of silent, wide-eyed children that seemed to spring up from behind the rocks and the bushes by the river, all joined in low, plaintive song.

The men now walked, single file, past their old Chieftain, and took their places, one beside the other, on the river bank. When the last of them had passed before Cuyuchi, the High Priest, turned, bowed to Huaraca and dipped his arms low into the river waters. This was the signal, and all the men did likewise. The women and children pushed their faces down unto their hands, flat on the ground.

"Oh, Viracocha! Maker of All Things! Wash away all sins!" Cuyuchi's voice rose in a mighty shout.

The young warriors suddenly broke into a wild dance, swinging their long spears above their heads, shouting, jumping, wildly gesticulating, as the older men formed a wide circle on the grassy flat of the river bend. Stiff-legged, knees pumping in high kicks, left arm stiff at their side, right arm held high, long spears pointing to the sun now almost directly overhead, the young men jumped, shouting their song of thanksgiving. For several minutes they leaped, more and more excited. Suddenly they stopped, stood absolutely silent. The sun was high and straight overhead.

Slowly, majestically, Huaraca rose. From the folds of his great cloak he drew a long strand of painted straw, brilliant in red and green, and shining in the clear sunlight. With measured steps he walked to the river's edge, dipped the straw into the water, and lifted his eyes upward. All others dropped upon their knees, bowing, murmuring, moaning.

"Cleanse all these my people of sin, Oh Great Sun God Viracocha, Father of Incas, Father of Life!" The old man's high crackling voice trembled as he raised it, the only sound that could be heard in that vast valley. "Creator of Miracles, Great without Measure, multiply my people. Let the little ones grow big, make their bodies strong and clean!"

And now, from the top of the high ridge, from the very edge of the giant plaza, came a mighty shout, as two tall youths raised high a small golden chair. The multitude below jumped to its feet, and a thundering shout echoed from the hills all around. The two youths started down the long path, and Dick, who had stood all the while some fifty or sixty feet back from the crowd saw that the two youths carried something in this golden chair —a small dark brown object which took shape as they neared the great throng by the river. Suddenly Dick recognized it: a mummy! The mummy of their ancestors! Shrunken, leathery skin stretched tight over a skeleton whose knees had been pulled up to its chest, arms folded over, hugging the knees, the whole making a bundle not more than thirty inches high, skull bones showing through the tight and dry skin. In place of eyes, and filling the eye sockets, were two giant emeralds that shone and sparkled as the sun hit them.

As the youths with their precious burden reached the assembled multitude, men, women and children threw themselves upon the grass, face down; all save Cuyuchi, the High Priest,

and Huaraca, the Chieftain; and Acachu, who watched Dick
intently. Cuyuchi had dropped on one knee. Huaraca lifted
both arms, shaking and trembling, toward the skies; and the
two young men brought the mummy of their ancestor and
placed it at the feet of their chieftain. Then, they, too, threw
themselves prostrate before it and their chief.

"*Apo, Aya hatun!*" crackled the thin voice of Huaraca, "oh
great and powerful Dead One. *Apu Punchao!* Oh Radiant Master! *Arpay, Ayrihuarcitua!* Great Master, Great Sun, Great Giver
of Life! We offer thee sacrifices and dances. Cleanse away our
sins. Cleanse our bodies, Great Sun God!"

And now Cuyuchi, too, had prostrated himself before the
mummy, so that in all that great multitude only three bodies
were not cast down in humble adoration—Huaraca, whose father's mummy was by his side; Dick, the young white man
whose heart was filled with awe; and Acachu, whose eyes never
left Dick for a single instant.

"Cleanse all my people of sin, oh Viracocha!" cried the shrill
cackling voice of old Huaraca. "Make my people strong, make
my people brave, make my people clean!"

"Brave! Strong! Clean!" echoed the hills about them, as hundreds of voices shouted the words.

The procession started back up the hill, the priests leading,
then the painted young warriors, the older men, and last the
women and the children. When they had all gone, the four
litter-bearers came for Huaraca, and carried him up the hill. It
was not until they were well on their way up that Acachu
spoke to Dick.

"Many years ago the tribe of the Chancas came down this
river in rafts and attacked the Inca cities. They were defeated
with much bloodshed and their leader, their curaca, was changed
to stone. That is the stone Huaraca sat on." He had spoken
slowly, as though conscious of the fact he was using a tongue
other than his own.

But Dick was suddenly alert. Rafts! And the Chancas had
come from far down stream, so this river must be navigable.

They had attacked Cuzco and the other Inca cities. This river must lead to Cuzco!

"Have you ever gone down the river in a raft?" asked Dick, his heart racing within him.

"Raft? No, young white man, not raft. But at the Festival of the Sun, the great Intip Raymi, all young men of the village race in canoes below the tunnel falls. The young white man will be all well by then, will be able to race with our young men in canoe."

The Festival of the Sun? That was the third week of June, at winter solstice, a full six months away! I'll never see that Intip Raymi up here, Dick thought, never! Six months! Surely Dad will find me, or Prof, or the Government, or somebody! Six months!

And now Acachu pointed to the top of the ridge, where the people were once more gathering in the giant plaza.

"We go back now," he said, and started up the steep path. Dick followed, finding the climbing much harder than he had thought. The steep narrow path, hard-trodden by the hundreds of feet that day, was slick and slippery. Here and there a small pebble rolled under his foot and once or twice Dick stumbled, forcing him to grab wildly for the nearest bush to keep from falling.

"It is well to watch where you step, white man. There are many snakes." Acachu had been watching.

"Snakes?" cried Dick, unable to keep back the sudden alarm.

"But they do not like you either," the bull-chested Indian assured him. Dick looked up quickly to catch the Indian's look, but it was the same impassive, unsmiling stare of always.

They resumed their climb. It would be some stunt to 'run away' on this path, thought Dick. But he watched the path intently, not so much because of the warning the guard had given him, but to fix in his mind every turn, every incline. "Just in case," he thought, but his hopes were slim indeed.

By the time he reached the top of the ridge and the entrance to the large square, Dick was puffing and sweating. He thought how welcome that bed-rug would be in the hut, how welcome, too, the quiet cool darkness after all this shouting and commotion.

But at the top of the path a young warrior, still in full paint and with a long lance in his hand, was waiting.

"Huaraca say young white man come!"

"What's the trouble?" Dick asked, looking up annoyed.

"Huaraca say young white man come."

"But what's wrong? Why can't I just lie down and rest?"

"Miskqui! She sick again. Medicine man say young white man blow evil spirit in Miskqui. Huaraca say young white man come!"

Fever! That must mean infection from the wound! He was sure he had sucked out the poison . . . but the Medicine Man . . . was he jealous? Had he done something to get Dick in trouble?

Dick found himself hurrying after the young native, in spite of his weariness. Silent faces stared at him as he pushed forward across the plaza. The young native led to the terrace above the square, on the side of the Lookout Tower.

"Where is she?" gasped Dick, trying to keep up with the young warrior.

"In White Room," he called back, without slowing down.

Dick climbed the steep stone ladder from the square to the Tower. The young native had already disappeared behind the curve of the tower. Dick followed as quickly as he could, and saw the young warrior waiting at the bottom of the stone stairway leading from the tower to the Throne Room. Acachu, Dick discovered, was right behind him. Half-hopping, half-jumping, Dick hobbled down the stone steps, reached the large Throne Room. It was empty. But the young painted native who had brought him here pointed with his spear to the passage behind the throne.

Dick squeezed through the tight passage and stopped short. Beside the crib stood Huaraca, Cuyuchi, Tocta Cuca and a tiny little hunch-back, brown and parched-skinned, grotesquely dressed in some sort of feathered cloak, and wearing on his head a wooden mask resembling roaring tiger jaws. Dick noticed especially that the tiny little man had very long arms that hung down like spider legs, skinny, covered with black hair. His gnarled and twisted little body reminded Dick of a giant tarantula.

"I am Moncoy, Medicine Man!" The deepness of his voice startled Dick, for somehow he had expected a squeaky whine.

"Young white man make like medicine man, not medicine man!" he accused.

"But I only gave her first aid . . . I sucked out the poison . . . I . . ." Dick was walking toward the crib as he spoke.

Miskqui lay on the golden-brown vicuña rug as she had before. Tocta knelt by the crib, holding the little girl's hand, swaying slightly back and forth as though in prayer. Huaraca trembled as he peered at Dick through half-closed eyes, then shifted his little ferret eyes to the Medicine Man, back to Dick.

"*Jatun honccoi!*" crackled the old man, "*Huacmanta! Allyachi ucta!*"

Cuyuchi's deep voice came almost immediately, translating. "The great illness returns. Cure her!" His voice, too, cracked, almost echoing the old man's shrieks. The old man, now screaming, repeated, "*Allyachi ucta!* Cure her!"

The child tried to smile at the sight of her white friend. Her fever-swollen eyes and lips hurt. She whimpered, but tried to lift her hand to Dick. Dick knelt down, gently took her little arm. It was burning with fever!

"What happened?" cried Dick, looking from one to the other in the group. "She was fine only a few hours ago!"

It was Cuyuchi who answered, and his voice was steady now, his eyes black and intense.

"She became ill by the river. Moncoy has told Huaraca that young white man has blown evil spirit into child."

"But I gave her white man's medicine . . . you saw that, Cuyuchi . . . I put a little powder on her wound to keep it clean . . . !"

"Mancoy says young white man blew evil spirit into she-child. He says young white man prayed to Evil White Spirit to enter body of little Miskqui."

"Oh, no, Cuyuchi! You certainly don't believe that! You saw what I did . . . Tocta, you tell them! You were here!"

"*Silencio!* Huaraca says you must call out Evil White Spirit, you must cure little Miskqui!"

Dick looked around in despair. Then he saw, for the first time, that others had come into the White Room. Six young warriors, naked but for their loin cloths, had taken their places, one in each corner of the room, one by the windows, one by the door. They were armed with long spears, and each one had a long wooden dagger hanging from a leather thong around his waist. The daggers' handles were covered with leopard skin. These were the Tiger Men, the Blood Avengers!

"Cuyuchi! Tell them I only tried to help! Tell them I didn't hurt Miskqui! I . . . I love this little girl . . . tell them, Cuyuchi!" Dick's voice was high, almost panicky.

"Huaraca says young white man must cure her!"

Dick felt the cold sweat pour out all over him. He looked down at the sick child. He tried to remember the times his sister had been sick. Then he remembered the time they had played in the yard and he had accidentally kicked her in the leg with a dirty shoe. That night his mother had spent many anxious hours with hot compresses until finally the infection had gone down.

Slowly Dick lifted the little girl's leg. An ugly red-rimmed spot about the size of a quarter seemed to pulsate with the little girl's heart beats. Blood poison!

"The hot water again, Tocta, lots of boiling hot water!" he cried.

Then suddenly Dick heard a long, low moaning incantation that seemed to come from nowhere, yet filled the room. He turned, and caught sight of Mancoy, the spider-like hunch-back Medicine Man, jumping like a tarantula, circling the crib, bowing, groaning, moaning. Every so often he stopped, his soft-

sandalled feet making no noise at all as he simply pumped his
feet up and down, as with his long spidery arms he would
reach down into two green cotton bags that hung over his shoulders and come up with fistfuls of dry leaves and herbs. These
he would pile on the floor on either side of the crib, adding to
them from time to time as again he stopped his gyrations. The
leaves were coca leaves, from which cocaine is extracted. A
poultice of hot steaming coca leaves would draw the poison, and
the cocaine might deaden the pain.

"Where is that hot water, Tocta? Quick!"

She brought a deep earthenware dish, steaming. She passed
clean white cotton bandages to Dick, knelt down beside him by
the crib. When Dick dipped the bandages into the water, he
jerked his hand out, burned. Tocta took the bandages from him,
dipped them into the steaming crock, unmindful of the heat.

Dick spread the white bandages at the foot of the crib and
filled them with coca leaves. He twisted the ends and dipped
the poultice into the hot water again. An acrid stinging smell
struck him as he bent over. He pulled out the poultice, swung
it gently to get the steam out, laid it on the child's leg.

A shriek of pain escaped the little girl's lips. Dick shuddered
and lifted the hot poultice up for a second. Then he put it
down again. The child whimpered. He motioned to Tocta to
prepare another one, took it from her as soon as it was ready.
He gave her the cold one, motioning to her to dip it back into
the water again. Over and over again. After a while, he held the
hot poultice off for a few seconds. The little leg was red from
the heat, but the brown spot seemed to be shrinking, concen-
trating in one little puffed spot and swelling upward.

Dick looked up and caught Cuyuchi's unmoving eyes fixed
on him. The big Indian, hands behind his back, was just staring. The Medicine Man, now still and crouched at the lower
end of the crib, was mumbling something to himself. Huaraca
had withdrawn to the back end of the room, shrunken into a
little bundle of despair. The young warriors in the four corners

and by the window and door stood straight and still, staring straight ahead. Dick, holding the last poultice in his hand, addressed Cuyuchi.

"We may need your knife this time, Cuyuchi," he said. "You better clean it and burn the end. This may break open . . . I hope it does . . . but we may need a lot more hot water."

Dick didn't wait for Cuyuchi to move, but he noticed that the big Indian dropped to his knees, and again started a little fire on the floor of the White Room. Afterward Dick wished he had watched what the big native used; it looked like a small wad of cotton, but he wasn't sure. Dick had returned to the poultices, and was glad when Tocta silently left, carrying the earthenware dish with her. She soon returned, the water steaming in the dish.

The sun went down behind the purple mountains. Dick's arms ached as he changed bandages, one after the other, allowing a little longer between changes now, giving Tocta full chance to remake them as they came apart. Once or twice she rose silently and brought in fresh hot water from somewhere to the rear. Once or twice the Medicine Man dropped additional coca leaves on a little pile by Dick's knee. No one spoke. The little girl had stopped moaning, now lay quite still in her crib. It seemed to Dick that ages had passed. Somewhere in the back of the room someone lighted a torch, stuck it in the stone wall.

Dick lifted the poultice from the child's leg mechanically, turning to get the fresh one from Tocta. In midair, Dick stopped, his hand and stared at the wet cotton bandages. They were red, and yellowish . . . the infection had burst . . . the infected blood had started to run!

Quickly he bent over the little girl and put his ear to her lips. The child was breathing, breathing regularly!

"Oh, God, thank you!" The words jumped out of Dick's mouth, and he didn't know whether they were loud or soft. "She's sleeping, Tocta," he said.

The woman nodded, said nothing.

"Now some fresh clean bandages." His arms ached, the hard ground felt like stone under his knees. He looked up at Cuyuchi.

"We won't need your knife, Cuyuchi," he said.

Suddenly the Medicine Man started his jumping again. Once he raised his spidery arm high above his head and shook his hand violently in the air; then he stopped abruptly again, crouching and trembling all over at the foot of the crib. His lips moved, and Dick could just barely hear a low moaning sound. Deep shadows filled the big room. Dick could hardly see anyone, even Cuyuchi's tall body close by was blurred in the growing darkness.

"Do you still have my kit, Cuyuchi?" he asked . . . "You know, that canvas bag?"

Cuyuchi produced it from somewhere. Dick felt inside with his right hand for the little bottle of tincture of merthiolate. Thank God for Prof's methodical caution!

It must have been near midnight. Through the window opening Dick could see the new moon, and the brilliant mountain stars in the blue-blackness of the sky. The child stirred. Tocta gasped. Summoned by a grunt from Cuyuchi one of the warriors brought a torch. Dick bent over the child, the little bottle of disinfectant in his hand.

Slowly Dick pulled out the stopper with the glass applicator. His right hand trembled as he slowly spread the reddish liquid over the spot.

Little beads of sweat stood out on the child's forehead. Dick mopped them softly with the cotton bandages in his left hand, silently passed them over to Tocta, took fresh ones from her. He felt very clumsy as he bent over with great gentleness and bandaged the little girl's leg. The child did not even move. She was sound asleep.

"Bring the blankets, Tocta," Dick heard his own weary voice. "The fever is broken, we must keep her warm."

And now Cuyuchi moved away from the crib, toward his father who still crouched by the wall, on what looked like a low leather hassock. Cuyuchi murmured something to the old man.

"*Checa?*" cried the crackling old voice.

"*Checa;* yes, it is true. The child sleeps now, Huaraca. The fever devil is gone."

The old man bowed his head. Slumped over the hassock, he looked more like the mummy that had been carried down to the river that morning. Dick could see the long, jumping shadows of the torch fall across the tall figure of Cuyuchi, light silently and nervously on the old man, move swiftly back again into the darkness. For a moment it seemed as though the old man was dead!

But then his voice suddenly sounded, in that high crackling whine Dick had heard before. Only this time there seemed very little command in it, it was slow, almost soft.

"The young white man shall rest," it said, speaking now in Spanish again. "On the morrow take him down to the river and wash away his sins. Then bring him to me. I wish to speak to him . . . tomorrow."

Dick thought he was going to collapse. His eyes burned, his head was giddy, his stomach was empty and choked. A soft hand pressed his arm. Dick fought to steady himself. He heard Tocta's soft voice very close to his ear.

"Come, you must sleep now," it said.

Dick didn't know how he got down to his prison hut. He dropped on the thick woolen rug. The smell of raw wool, recently wet, assailed his nostrils as his head hit the rug, but just for an instant. Dick was already asleep.

10

Initiated

THE SUN WAS ALREADY HIGH IN THE SKY WHEN CUYUCHI called him. Dick had slept right through, scarcely moving from where he had dropped the night before. He felt stiff, and his neck hurt as he moved it.

"Do I have to get up?" Dick asked sleepily.

"It is time to go to the river."

Dick slowly rose to his feet. Cuyuchi, dressed in the ceremonial robes of the day before, stood before him. There was Acachu, the guard, and the woman who had brought him his meals. The rug over the door had been lifted, and bright sunlight filled the square opening.

"Come!" Cuyuchi's voice was steady, calm. His arms, folded over his huge chest held up the fringes of the multi-colored surplice. His long black hair hung straight, a single strand of red-colored band over his forehead. Cuyuchi turned, and walked across the hut to the doorway. Dick followed.

Outside, two young painted warriors waited. They bowed as Cuyuchi emerged, fell in behind Dick as the little procession started up the long steep walk to the tower, down the stone ladder, across the wide square, and down the mountainside.

Except for the crowds, and the other priests who were not there, the ceremony was the same, taking much less time because only Dick was anointed. Cuyuchi sang, and the two young warriors answered. Cuyuchi held aloft the two vessels, the gold and the silver cups, emptied their white contents into the river, dipped up a few drops with which he wet Dick's hair. Then Cuyuchi motioned Dick to kneel, and sang a soft, low chant. The two young warriors answered. They all stood up. Cuyuchi, without another word, turned and started up the hill again. Dick followed, and after him came the two warriors. The ceremony was over.

At the top of the Plaza Acachu awaited their return. It was he who escorted Dick up the ladder and back into the Throne Room. The old Chieftain was alone on the stone throne.

"The young white man will have the freedom of the city," said the old man, talking in his high, nasal voice, and once more speaking Spanish. "When he is well again, he shall prepare with our village youths."

"Prepare for what?" Dick asked, puzzled.

"For the war games." The old man was looking very intently at Dick with those little ferret eyes.

"War games?" The exclamation was out before Dick could check it. Then this old man did mean to keep him here! The war games would come at the Festival of the Sun, six months away!

The old man waved his long thin arm. Instantly Acachu took Dick by the arm. In the doorway Cuyuchi, now back in his mountain clothes and split-knee breeches, stood waiting. For the first time in all these weeks Dick saw the trace of a smile on the big Indian's face.

"Master Dick may come and go as he pleases. Acachu will always be nearby, but Chief Huaraca wishes young white man to have freedom of the Lost City."

But Dick soon found that there were, after all, only a few

places where he could go: the high wall, the Lookout Tower, the White Room beyond the Throne Room, and, of course, his prison hut. Once he started down the stone ladder into the giant square, but Acachu stopped him.

"When young white man all well, he may join other youths. Soon now," he said. But he had blocked the way.

Long dreary days followed, one after the other. Dick found more and more companionship with Tocta, and her little Miskqui. Sometimes old Huaraca was in the White Room, watching, saying little. Other times Acachu took the old man's place, silent and unsmiling. Cuyuchi, too, came into the room, solicitous over the child but rarely speaking. Occasionally he interpreted for the old man when the chieftain spoke in Quechua, but more often he just watched while Dick played with the child. They were, however, never alone.

But the growing attachment between the child and the young white captive did not escape the sharp eyes of Cuyuchi, nor the old man's. Tocta, too, noticed it, and seemed pleased.

"My little one loves the young man from the north," she said one afternoon, as Dick was giving the little girl a piggy-back. The sound of steady rain beat on the thatch roof. Cold, wet air came in sheets through the ever-open windows. Tocta's voice sounded strained and formal, but her eyes were soft as though she were trying to say something to Dick her voice did not say. Dick looked quickly at the woman, then looked around the room. Cuyuchi stood, arms folded, in the far corner, apparently lost in thought. "But he is listening," Dick thought. Was Tocta trying to warn him? That afternoon he went back to his prison hut, an uneasy feeling giving him a sense of unreality.

The next morning, before Dick had a chance to get up and wash his face in the cold water the Indian woman brought him, Cuyuchi appeared.

"We will uncover the young white man's leg," he said.

Acachu took his place in the doorway, watching. The Indian woman—Dick had learned that her name was Cheterni— brought in a shallow wicker basket, some clean white cloths, a small stone shaped like an orange. This Cuyuchi took in his cupped right hand, and gently but firmly tapped the cast on Dick's leg. Starting at the top, he gradually worked down, on the outside of the leg, then around the foot. Dick noticed that the tapping, although it did not hurt, was strong enough to crack the cast. Then Cuyuchi, dropping the stone, took the cast in both his hands and pulled. It came off, exposing Dick's white, bleached leg, his foot wrinkled where the cast had hardened over the skin.

"The young white man will move his foot," said Cuyuchi, rising. Dick moved his toes, wiggled his foot up and down. It was healed! And it felt so light, now that the heavy cast was off. The blood came rushing back into it, and where a moment before the air had seemed cold on the newly exposed skin, now a warm tingling filled the leg, the foot.

Chaterni silently slipped back into the far corner of the hut, and returned with an earthenware pan full of warm water. With infinite care she lifted Dick's left foot and proceeded to wash it as though she were bathing a child. She used no soap, but her soft fingers gently rubbed the leg. Dick was surprised to feel how good the water felt.

"The young white man may wish to go to river this morning for bath," said Cuyuchi, as the woman was drying Dick's foot.

"Tocta send this," added the big Indian, as Dick looked up.

Dick took a sponge-like plant from Cuyuchi's outstretched hand, and recognized the dried fruit of the *pashte* tree. Dick had seen the natives use it in Lima. When wet, this fruit gave off a sort of soapsuds, and when the dry fruit was used for bathing or washing, it was like a soapy sponge.

Acachu followed Dick down to the river below the erstwhile prison hut. The path was very steep, making many sharp hairpin turns as it zig-zagged down the mountain slope. But as they neared the water, Acachu suddenly turned his back to Dick and swiftly walked up-river, leaving Dick alone.

A wild thought seized Dick as he stood in the cold water. Around the bend of the mountain he could hear the roar of the swift current, and then the splash of the river tumbling over big boulders into the deep canyon. Why not make a dash for it—now?

Acachu had disappeared. Dick looked up to the other side of the river. Only yesterday he had seen from high up on the ridge a slow-moving native leading two llamas down the steep mountain path. There must be houses somewhere nearby, and people. Could he find them? Would they help him if he did? Would they take him back to Cuzco?

These and other thoughts crowded into his mind as he suddenly jumped out of the water and ran for his clothes. They were dirty, plainly showing the wear and dirt of constant day-and-night use. But they were all he had. His heart beat faster and faster as he pulled and strained to get the clothes on. "I'll follow the river bend behind the hill. I'll get across the river somehow, and up the other side of this mountain. There must be a path of some kind. I saw the native and his llamas on that path. I'll find it . . . it must be there. . . ."

Dick picked up his hunting knife, jerkingly hooked it on his belt. Then he reached down for his shoes. His hand froze on the leather. The sun cast a short thick shadow across his boot.

"The young white man hurries?" Acachu looked down imperturbably, arms folded over his big bull-chest. His beady black eyes were steady. His lips did not smile.

"I . . . I was cold." Dick was aware his voice sounded scared.

"Yes, it is not good to wash all the body at one time."

Dick was trembling as he followed Acachu up the steep path. Neither of them spoke. It had started to rain again by the time they reached the top of the ridge. Dick shivered with cold.

When he reached his prison hut again, he was surprised to find a small bundle of clothes: a crude shirt, like a poncho; woolen shorts of rough cross weave; and fresh new cotton underwear, crudely cut but clean.

There was no one in the hut. The rain came down steadily. Realizing he had never actually seen the cooking oven, Dick now walked over to the far corner of the hut. The little wood fire that burned almost day and night smoked, as always, but the warmth was welcome. No one was there, and Dick decided quickly he would change his clothes, put on the dry ones. It was only a matter of seconds to drop off the wet garments and put on the dry ones. The lower part of his legs felt cold in the damp air with the rough mountain shorts, but the rest of him was surprisingly warm. In his bare feet, Dick walked around the room. It gave him a feeling of pleasure to scrape his feet on the hard-packed clay floor as he had seen the natives do when they walked.

But when Dick returned to the fireplace to pick up his other clothes, he was startled to find that everything except his knife, his match box and his shoes, was gone!

Dick whirled, peered intently into the darkness behind the stone oven. It was then that he noticed for the first time the thick woolen blanket that hung in the corner, making a sort of triangular closet three or four feet deep.

"Who is in there?" Dick cried, staring fixedly at the woolen blanket. He thought he saw it move an inch or two, then bulge out as someone pushed against it. Dick grabbed the handle of his knife, held it hard, waist-high.

Then suddenly the blanket was lifted and Tocta stepped out from behind it!

"Tocta! What are you doing here?"

"The young white man's clothes will be washed, and will be returned to him when the sun has dried them," she said. Again the formal voice and something in the way she pronounced the stiff words, warned Dick. He turned quickly. In the doorway stood Acachu, rain pouring off his thick woolen poncho and wide-brimmed straw hat.

Making a little bundle of Dick's clothes, Tocta crooked them under her arm, and went through the doorway into the rain.

Dick slowly pulled his heavy woolen socks on, then his shoes. Acachu simply stood in the doorway, oblivious of the rain, and said nothing.

"Where did these clothes come from?" Dick said finally.

Acachu answered immediately. "Tocta make them," he said evenly. Then he added quickly, "Tocta and Miskqui."

"Miskqui?" repeated Dick.

"Ah, yes, the little one learns to weave like all girls of the tribe. Some day she will make all the clothes for her grand-father. And for her father."

"You mean Cuyuchi?"

"Yes, Cuyuchi!"

The words struck Dick like a whip-lash. Then it was true, the child was Cuyuchi's daughter! And Tocta was Cuyuchi's wife. But why? Why had this white girl married the son of a chief-tain, this Indian who lived in the past and hid far up in the mountains in the ruins of a city that had been destroyed hun-dreds of years ago?

Dick was still trying to imagine some solution when the girl suddenly reappeared in the doorway beside Acachu. The rain had let off somewhat, as it did so frequently up there in the mountains, and now a few thin lines of blue showed in the sky where the sun was trying to come out. Dick knew that this rainy season would soon be over, and he would be able to go out into the sun again. But if he had been surprised by the reappearance of Tocta, he was even more surprised at her words when she spoke.

"Asto Huaraca bids the young white man to break bread with him at sun-down," she said simply.

Her eyes did not meet Dick's, for she held them cast down. But Dick could see the roundness of her cheeks, the white skin with just a faint glow of color in them; the small, even mouth and bright red lips that needed no artificial color. Her hands which held the woolen shawl folded over in front of her as it dropped from her head and shoulders were small and very white against the dark color of the shawl. Beside the bull-chested Indian, this white girl looked tiny and fragile.

"Me? Asto Huaraca?"

"Yes. At sun-down," the girl repeated. "In the White Room."

Dick looked across the ravine before the hut, saw the glistening drops of rain clinging to the bushes and the trees on the
slopes of the mountain across the deep canyon, sparkling like
little pieces of glass as the sun came out and struck them with
long slanting rays. In another two hours, Dick thought, it will
be dusk; then I report for my command performance, dinner
with the Chief!

But the Chief was not alone when Dick arrived. The big cotton torches had already been lit, and they stuck out of the holes
in the stone wall like big candles on a slant. In the center of
the White Room two split logs supported by short stumps on
either end made a crude table. Chief Huaraca sat on the leather
hassock. Cuyuchi, cross-legged, sat on the floor at one end. Little
Miskqui, on a low wooden bench just big enough to hold her,
sat between her grandfather and her father. On the other side,
two tall youths, each wearing the mountain short breeches slit at
the knee, and red and green poncho-like shirts that hung loosely
over their broad shoulders, stood waiting, very straight; and at
the other end of the crude table, opposite Cuyuchi, sat an old
man Dick had not seen before. Acachu, who had accompanied
Dick to the White Room, immediately withdrew. Dick walked
slowly across the White Room toward the table and bowed his
head as he approached.

"Good evening, Señor," he said. He stood still, waiting. Cuyuchi motioned Dick to the side of the two other youths. The old
Chieftain's voice, high and nasal, spoke in Quechua. Cuyuchi
translated.

"Chief Huaraca bids the young white man welcome to his
table. Chief Huaraca wishes the Señor Dick to know Hatun,
the *Amauta,* the teacher who will teach Señor Dick the customs
of our tribe; and Chaqui and Yutu, who will be Señor Dick's
companions in the House of Youths. They both know the
Spanish tongue."

Now Cuyuchi was standing, as were the old man introduced
as Hatun, the teacher; and all four, Cuyuchi, Hatun and the
two youths, bowed to Huaraca, then turned and bowed to Dick.

Instinctively, Dick bowed back to them; then, because they waited and seemed to hesitate, Dick bowed to Huaraca. The Chieftain's wrinkled, leathery old face broke out in an unexpected smile. He made a little halting bow. They all sat down.

The young men next to Dick crossed their legs, pulling their knees up somewhat. He tried sitting that way and discovered to his surprise that it was not at all uncomfortable. Little Miskqui, wide-eyed, had watched the whole proceedings without making a sound.

Tocta served the dinner, which was the strangest Dick had ever eaten. Tiny little potatoes, covered with spicy cheese sauce. River fish, broiled, smothered in spices. Raw onions and raw fruits—oranges, apples, sour-sap, one or two others Dick did not recognize. And when this was over, Tocta brought in three golden cups filled with white, frothing liquid.

"We will now drink the ceremonial *acca*," said Cuyuchi, standing. The two youths had already jumped to their feet. The old teacher also got up, and Dick followed. Only Huaraca and little Miskqui remained seated.

With great solemnity, Cuyuchi passed the first cup to the old Chieftain. Huaraca took it in both trembling hands, held it tightly between them. Next Cuyuchi gave Dick a cup. Dick glanced quickly at the old man opposite him, and held his cup between his two hands, imitating the chieftain. Cuyuchi took the third cup, and holding it high over his head in both hands, mumbled something Dick could not understand. Cuyuchi then brought the cup down slowly, intoning a thin whining chant, and brought the cup to his lips. Slowly he drank from the cup, leaving about half of the contents. Then he put his cup down on the split log that served as table.

Now it was Huaraca's turn, and the old man lifted the cup above his head, then chanting softly like Cuyuchi had done, drank from his cup while all the others watched. Then he, too, put his cup down.

Dick knew it was his turn, but he didn't know what to do.

He looked at Cuyuchi, but it was Hatun, the teacher, who spoke.

"*Atun—Apa—Huallpi!*" he said, and once more Dick was surprised by the deep vigorous sound of the man's voice, as he had been when the Medicine Man had spoken. Then, speaking Spanish, the teacher added: "The Father-Teacher of all the Skies will give his flower to the youths that they may be strong and brave in serving him."

"*Atun—Apa—huallpi!*" repeated the teacher once more in Quechua. "*Atun—Apa—huallpi,*" echoed Cuyuchi. The old Chieftain nodded. Then the teacher spoke to Dick.

"The young white man will drink," he said evenly.

Dick drank, leaving as he had seen the others do, half of the contents in his cup.

"*Atun—Apa—huallpi!*" cackled the old man. Then, very slowly, the old Chieftain raised his cup, tipped it, and emptied it on the rough table from which they had eaten. Cuyuchi did likewise. They waited. Dick tipped his cup and emptied it on the rough surface.

But even as he did so, Dick caught sight of Tocta, standing rigidly by the back wall, staring. Her eyes seemed full of fear as she peered intently at Dick. Her hand trembled as she clasped it to her mouth as though to stifle a cry. The torch on the wall threw a weird dancing shadow across her face. Then she was gone.

Cuyuchi was speaking. "Huaraca wishes young white man to train with the young warriors of our village and prepare for the initiation," he said.

"Initiation? I don't understand . . ."

"Huaraca wishes to honor the young white man for his service in saving the life of little Miskqui. Young Señor Dick will be made a knight in our tribe. But he must train, and he must learn a great deal before then. He must be strong and brave. He must learn to win in the war games. He will live in the House of Youths until the initiation."

A knight of this Indian tribe! But I don't want to be an Indian knight, thought Dick, in this or any other tribe! I want to go home, to Dad, and Mom . . . there must be some way I can get out of here . . . some way out of this ruined, abandoned city of long ago. . . .

Suddenly it flashed through Dick's mind that he had seen the Medicine Man go north along the ridge, and come back three or four days later from the same direction. The path led straight up the hill, past the cemetery and over the other side of the mountain. There must be a way out! Maybe . . . maybe I can hide in the cemetery, Dick thought . . . maybe I can . . . and the vision of a dwarfed little figure he had often seen at the entrance of the cemetery. Was that the Aya—Camayoc— the guardian of the dead? Could Dick get past him?

"The young white man hesitates?" It was Cuyuchi's deep voice, and it sounded angry.

"Oh, no, no!" Dick brought himself back from his thoughts, and a guilty feeling rushed the blood up to his face. "I was . . . I was only thinking."

"Huaraca grants great honor to white youth!" Again Cuyuchi's voice sounded angry, accusing.

"Oh, yes, I know. I understand. What must I do?"

"Tomorrow morning when the sun first touches the crown of the Vilcañota, the young white man will join the other youths in the House of Preparation on the hill."

So that big snow-covered mountain to the north was the Vilcañota! Mother of Snows, sacred Knot of Inca valleys! Dick was right. That path past the cemetery led to the valley of the Vilcañota. That way the Incas had marched in their conquest of the great empire. That way lay——freedom!

Dick scarcely knew how he got back to his prison hut. Huaraca had said something, then Cuyuchi, and then all of them had stepped through the throne room and the teacher and the two youths had climbed back toward the tower. Acachu had been waiting and had led Dick back to the hut. Once there,

Dick threw himself on the rug and lay staring into the darkness. The picture of that cemetery high up on the ridge kept coming back, again and again. That must be the way out . . . it must be . . .

He must have been asleep. A soft hand touched him, startled him. He bolted upright.

"Who's there?" his voice shook.

"Shhh . . . do not speak, Dick!"

That was Tocta's voice! How did she get here?

"You must not let them induct you into the tribe, Dick!" Her voice, eager, full of anxiety, was however scarcely above a whisper. "They will make a slave of you, as they have me . . . you will be a prisoner . . . forever!"

"But Tocta. . . ."

"No, be quiet, Dick! I must speak very fast. I have tricked Cheterni to leave you, but she will return soon. My father and my mother were English missionaries. But when they tried to leave . . . my father was killed. A swift arrow from the hills at sundown—no one knew who did it. My mother was brought back here, treated with great kindness, but not allowed to leave. Soon I was born. My mother lived only a short time after, and I was left alone. They have treated me well, as you know . . . but I am a prisoner!"

"But Cuyuchi?" Dick couldn't finish his own question.

"Yes, he is my husband by command of Huaraca. And Miskqui is our daughter. So I must stay . . . and my lips are forever sealed!" There was an anguish in the muffled whisper. "But you must not stay, Dick! I will help you get away!"

"But how, Tocta, how can you help me?"

"When the full moon brings an end to the festivals and the dancing, when the youths are taken into the tribe, I will bring you a token."

A slight rustling by the door, a soft foot scraping on the hard clay floor outside told them someone was coming. Tocta clapped a small hand over Dick's mouth, and silently slithered away.

Dick was surprised at the strength in the small hand, the tenseness in the smooth fingers. "Good night, Dick," she whispered very softly.

Dick lay back on his rug, listening. His body was trembling all over, and he fought to control himself. He scarcely breathed. Presently he heard two soft female voices from somewhere in the back of the hut, then a soft shuffling of sandalled feet as they came toward him.

Silhouetted against the starlit sky was the lumpy figure of Cheterni. She was carrying a large water jar, and the way she held it suggested it was empty. That must mean she was on her way to the water fountain some distance back. Now was his chance!

Dick felt for his belt. Yes, his knife was there. Silently he rolled over on his right side, still favoring his left leg. He got to his knees, watching the doorway.

Dick stood up, took one step, and his heart stopped beating as his foot came in contact with some large form, like a body on the ground. Slowly he pulled his knife from its sheath, ready to strike. Keeping his eyes on the doorway, with the faint silhouette of the sky marking the square opening of the door, he reached down and touched the shape. In spite of himself, a deep sigh of relief escaped his lips. It was a bed-rug, rolled up.

He stepped around it, walking now a little faster. Once outside, he would cross swiftly to the steep zig-zag path that led into the ravine, to the river bed two thousand feet below. He would hide until he could make his way across the river, up the other side of the mountain where he had seen the native and his llamas.

Dick reached the doorway, still clutching his knife in his right hand. Suddenly he froze.

"It will not be morning for two hours yet." The steady voice of Acachu came like a slap across the face. Instinctively Dick put his right hand behind him, hiding the knife.

"The white youth can sleep another two hours."

Dick turned silently back into the hut. He sheathed his knife, jerking the sheath on its belt-hook.

Two hours!

No more sleep tonight. Two hours! Or two eternities.

Dick sank down on his rug again. The inside of his hands felt wet and cold.

In two hours more he would join the other youths in the tribe, and start training to become one of them. A prisoner. A slave. An Indian knight.

"I've got to get out of here . . . I've got to . . . I've . . . got . . . to . . . get . . . out . . . of . . . here . . ."

He gritted his teeth, doubled his fist tight, bent his head forward as he stared at the square opening and the fading starlight of the night. Already a faint gray blurred the stars. Not much more than an hour now. The jagged rim of the big mountain . . . I can almost see it outlined . . . it is almost morning . . . *the* morning . . .

11

The Golden Earpiece

PROMPTLY WITH THE FIRST LIGHT, AS THOUGH BROUGHT by the sun itself, Acachu appeared in the doorway.

"We go now," he said simply.

Dick got up and followed him. He knew the path well now, up to the wall, across the Throne Room, up the long flight of stone steps, around the Lookout Tower, down the stone ladder, into the Square. At the edge of the giant Plaza, Chaqui and Yutu were waiting—his tutor-companions! They both looked very tall, taller than Dick by half a head, and their muscles stood out like sculped bulges on their arms and legs. These were the lads who were going to teach him the war games: wrestling, running, jumping, fighting with the lance. They looked as though they could do all of that, and more.

Dick felt suddenly very small. How about boxing, he thought. But of course they don't box up here. No, just wrestling, and running. And the lances, the long, sharp lances made of tough chonta wood, the same wood from which they made their daggers.

Dick looked at his two companions. They were polite, but there was little warmth in their eyes. Their faces were unsmiling. Look at Chaqui! How serious he was. Not much more than fifteen, thought Dick, maybe sixteen. His own age. Back home they would be thinking of baseball and football, and camping in sleeping bags on warm summer nights. But here they were thinking of war games. "Must be strong, and brave," the old Indian had said. "Strong, and brave." But not happy, or carefree. This was serious business.

In the doorway of the big two-storied house Cuyuchi was waiting, his brilliant feather head dress sitting on him like a colored crown. He motioned to the three boys as they approached. Acachu had disappeared.

"You will dress with the clothes that have been prepared for you," he said, his Spanish sounding, for the first time, guttural. "You will leave those shoes and wear the sandals instead. We march when the sun reaches the doorway."

Cuyuchi stepped aside, and Chaqui led the way. Dick followed. Yutu brought up the rear. They walked briskly into a large square room. Everywhere Dick noted signs of recent occupancy, but there was no one else in the vast room. Chaqui went to the far wall, where near a window opening Dick found a neat pile of new, coarse-woven woolen clothes, exactly like those Chaqui and Yutu wore. There were no stockings, but for his feet a pair of exquisitely woven sandals, soft and golden, fitting his feet as though they had been measured for them. The fine yellow straw woven in strands and held together with soft woolen thread was the color of gold; the warm-feeling soft sole was made of tightly knit vicuña wool. Mothers and sisters of the youths had worked for weeks making them. Cuyuchi, standing nearby, watched as Dick put his on.

"Tocta and little Miskqui made them," he said slowly. "The young white man does not have his family here." His black eyes held Dick's. Was this big Indian telling him something, warning him? Did he know of Tocta's visit of the night before?

Dick was surprised to see how lithe his own body looked in

those clothes. They made him look more like the Indian boys;
his own muscles stood out, reassuring him. Maybe these "games"
wouldn't be so uneven after all.

The sun struck the large opening in the wall opposite, flooding the room with golden light. Dick was startled to discover
that the door-jamb through which he had entered was covered
with a thin sheet of gold-colored metal that reflected the rays
of the sun, shooting the light in every direction. No one spoke.
But Cuyuchi now turned, and followed by Chaqui, moved toward the door. Yutu motioned to Dick to follow, then closed
in behind Dick.

It was a strange little single-file procession that crossed the
giant, deserted square. Dick had the feeling he was being
watched, but he could see no one. They crossed to the other
side of the square, where a few days before the high stone
platform had held old Huaraca. The platform was gone. And
to the right, on the other side from the path that led down into
the ravine, a smooth, narrow path followed the ridge up toward
the round stone mountain ahead. The path led straight up the
ridge, past ruins of square one-room houses, unroofed, abandoned. But where the path reached the wide slope of the mountain, it suddenly made a wide turn to the left and there, hidden
in the fold of the mountain itself, Dick saw an immense
quadrangular building made all of white stone, its thatched
roof shining yellow and new in the early morning sunlight.
Spaced at regular intervals were small trapezoid window openings, half-way up the wall, more than head high. The thatch
roof overhang protected them from rain, but otherwise they
were open and exposed. Wide, solid granite slabs formed a
massive stairway to the big door opening almost in the exact
center of the building.

"The House of Youths," said Cuyuchi, pointing. "Here you
will live with the other youths until you are ready."

Cuyuchi turned abruptly, and swiftly made his way back
over the path along the narrow ridge. Dick noticed with sinking
feeling how quickly the tall man seemed to grow smaller,
realized that they must have come a much longer distance than

he had thought. He dipped down just before he reached the plaza, and then was lost from view. Not until then did Chaqui speak.

"White brother come with us now." He spoke slowly, his Spanish a little stiff and formal, but his voice was friendly. It was serious business, this job they had to do. Dick followed Chaqui into the big stone building.

Dick was swallowed up into strenuous training activities that left him little time to feel either tired or sorry for himself. From early morning until sundown, with only three regular inter- ruptions for meals that were served to them as they stood in long rows outside their big building, Dick, Chaqui, Yutu and some fifty other youths trained, marched, wrestled, ran, jumped. The first day or two Dick thought he could not last until sun- down; he was too exhausted even to eat, just dropped on the thick vicuña rug Chaqui had told him was his 'bed,' and slept. Chaqui slept on the rug to his right, Yutu to his left. And down the long wall to the right and to the left, and all around the big square room, other rugs held the tired bodies of other youths, who marched in after supper at sun-down, dropped on their respective rugs, and slept. Sleep, get up, march, eat, wrestle, run, march, eat, jump, run, wrestle, march, eat, sleep.

Day after day, as his muscles grew hard and his tension grew less, Dick found himself enjoying it in spite of himself. Once or twice he had been able to pin Chaqui's broad shoulders on the hard ground when they wrestled. No soft mats here, just plain hard-trodden clay that hurt and burned when you scraped on it. The training went on and on.

It must have been three, maybe four weeks, before one after- noon a very tall, very wiry man—Dick guessed him to be about thirty—brought a long, chonta-wood lance, trimmed with soft fur where the hand held it. With soft guttural exclamations which meant nothing to Dick, the warrior proceeded to dem- onstrate the art of dodging, piercing, throwing the lance, close-in fighting, long-range fighting. The movements of his lithe body were beautiful to watch.

Realizing this teacher was talking Quechua, Dick wished he

had learned the language. "I'll have to learn it, if I stay here long enough," he thought. Then the very thought of it, that he might have to stay here long enough to learn it, sent a panicky stab all through him.

He was startled when the tall warrior suddenly stopped in front of him, thrust the long lance into his hands, uttered some gruff, guttural command, and stepped back.

"You must show what you have learned," said Chaqui.

"Me?" Dick's voice was full of sudden alarm. "I don't know anything about this!" The long lance suddenly felt very top-heavy.

"White youth *must!*" Chaqui's impassive eyes met and held Dick's.

Dick tried to push, to jerk back, to thrust forward, to step aside, as he had seen the lean soldier do. He tripped, caught himself, the long lance dropped to the ground, bounced, made a strange, almost metallic *ping* as it struck.

Dick expected a chorus of derisive laughter, but not a sound came from the half a hundred young men who simply stood staring at him, forming a large square. Awkwardly Dick picked the lance up, tried to balance it in his hand, only to have the heavy front end dip, unbalanced.

Without another word, the tall instructor stepped forward, took the lance from Dick's hands, motioned him back into line again. Once more he demonstrated, and the agile way in which the tall Indian jumped, side-stepped, rammed, pulled back and finally pierced an imaginary fallen foe was so realistic that sweat broke out on Dick's forehead. Dick gritted his teeth. "The next time," he thought, "I'll just jab, and pull, and jump . . . I'll jump aside like he does it . . ."

More days, more weeks—only now instead of the afternoon running and wrestling, the boys were instructed in lance work. Three more instructors appeared. They broke up the group into four smaller groups, and intensive instruction followed, sometimes with big shields made of straw to protect their bodies. Day after day they trained, and Dick felt a warm glow one evening when, coming in from their simple but spiced and filling meal, Chaqui stopped while they were taking their sandals off and said:

"White brother learns lance work fast. It is good . . ."

At last came the day when Chaqui, standing very straight, his eyes shining, looked at Dick as they prepared to march for their noon meal.

"Young white brother is ready," he said, with evident pride. "Tomorrow the war games start!"

The sun rose brilliantly, rimming the jagged mountain tops to the east with bright gold. All the boys had been up for some time, and now with the first light of the Great Day they were ready.

Chaqui fell alongside of Dick as they stepped outside the House of Youths, and together they took their place in the long double line. The lance instructor was already there, dressed in loose-fitting red woolen poncho and knee breeches slit at the knee. He looked very tall, and very happy.

At a signal the march started toward the giant square. When they came to the foot of the wide steps in front of the House of Youths they took their shirts off, and once more fell into single file as they marched in easy rhythm along the narrow ridge.

Great shouts greeted their arrival at the giant square. All the older men of the tribe, all the women, all the girls over fifteen—everyone in the entire Lost City was there, men on one side, women and girls on the other. Here and there a youth, about the age of those in the training group, looked wistfully and sometimes sullenly as the youths marched around the square, heads held high, muscles rippling, eagerness giving springiness to their step as the multitude shouted their greeting. The high stone platform had been erected again, but this time on the north end of the square, in front of the two storied building. Old Huaraca was perched on top, his little shriveled head bobbing with the giant headdress of wire and feathers. Dick heard Chaqui's voice close behind him.

"Don't forget—when we reach Huaraca on the third turn, you kneel. You do not look at Huaraca. Your head is bowed until he orders us to stand."

"I won't forget."

"And do not cry when the men hit you. It is to make you strong. It is to make you a man. Do not show weakness, like a child."

"I won't forget."

"And do not touch your head when it is shaved. No one may touch that until Cuyuchi puts on the oil."

"I won't forget!"

The double column made its third triumphant turn around the square. The brown, proud youths who headed the column walked five steps beyond Huaraca's platform, and stood rigidly waiting. The others came up from behind, stopped. The crowds were now hushed. A deep voice called out a single word. As one, the fifty youths turned, forming a half circle before the ancient chief. Their eyes were down-cast. Another deep command. The youths all dropped to their knees, arms straight down, heads bowed.

A deep silence rose from the canyons all around them and engulfed them in awed stillness. Old Huaraca got to his feet, lifting his thin body into the air. Then came his high, cackling nasal voice as he exhorted the youths before him:

"Be strong, as I have been strong! Be brave, as I have been brave! Whatsoever virtues I have, take them, and be like me!"

"Be strong! Be brave!" The rising chorus of men's voices shouted the words, and the mountains around them threw them back in stony echo, "Be strong! Be brave!"

Again the old man's cackling, high-pitched voice rose above the silence.

"Rise, and be strong! Rise and be brave! Rise, and be like Huaraca!"

At these words the fifty youths jumped to their feet, an exultant shout in their throats. Dick's own voice mingled with that of Chaqui, of Yutu beside him, of the others in front of the old Chieftain.

"Yes, we will be brave! Yes, we will be strong!" they shouted.

"Be brave! Be strong!" came the roared chorus from the men. "Brave! Strong!" echoed the granite mountains.

And now the youths, single file, once more marched around the giant square, past the women on the left, past the men on the right, and now past the old chieftain who stood erect atop the stone platform. Cuyuchi climbed the platform and stood beside his father and watched as the youths passed before the high platform. Suddenly the women pushed back, and the older men ran, shouting and jumping, to form a giant circle around the inner edges of the square and enclose the youths. Each man held a stick or a leather thong in his hands, waving it and shouting.

"Be brave! Be strong!" they cried, as the youths, now trotting in double time, passed in front. Viciously the older men lashed at their legs, their backs, their arms. Dick felt the stinging of the whiplash; red, angry welts swelled his legs and his arms. He bit his lips to stifle the cry that almost choked him. "Be brave"—*slash!* "Be strong"—*swish!* A big bull-chested figure loomed ahead of Dick and for a split second he saw the tight skin over Acachu's high cheek bones, saw the bared teeth, heard the rasping fierce cry. Acachu's arm swung twice, twice caught Dick around the back with stinging, burning lashes.

"You grinning, silly ape!" The cry stuck in his throat. Dick bit his teeth, swallowed hard. "I'll get you for that Acachu, I'll get you!" But again his voice died in his throat. He doubled his fists harder. "Be brave! Be strong!"

As the walls of the big barracks echoed the words, the shouting blurred into one long howl. Each word meant another slashing, stinging whiplash.

Just as Dick thought he couldn't take another blow, when every muscle ached and cried out, the shouting suddenly stopped. The silence was deafening by contrast. Dick trembled, but was relieved to see that Chaqui just ahead was trembling too—and bleeding, as he himself was.

The crowd parted. The youths stood still, making a wide circle inside the square. And now from the two-storied building

at the end of the square came a long, low moaning sing-song as
the High Priest appeared, holding before him a big golden
disk in the shape of the Sun God. Ten lesser priests followed,
two by two, and then five boys, heads shaven clean. Each held
one strand of a long leather rope, at the end of which came a
jet-black llama nervously turning to right and to left.

The women on the far side broke into a high-pitched song,
the triumphal song of *Taqui Huari,* the song of The Sacrificial
Dance.

"Oh Sun! Thou who art in strength and health, shine on
these brave new knights! Keep them brave! And keep them
strong!"

A long string of red, and green and blue woolen tufts strung
together into a giant chain, was suddenly pulled from the
crowd as a hundred young men and a hundred young women
now took hold. The women were on one side, alternating with
the men on the other, so that the women's left hands were on
the chain while the men's right hands held it a little higher.
Like the windings of a giant snake, the dancers wove in and out
the circle, pausing a few seconds before the old chieftain, then
weaving in and out again as they danced around the square.
Three times they did this; then they dropped the chain, and
fifteen maidens in gaily colored skirts and big full blouses
rushed forward, picked up the chain, and folded it over and
over. The women parted as the girls carried the chain away.

"Now comes the *acca,*" said Chaqui, almost under his breath.
"You will take your jar to Cuyuchi."

"Why Cuyuchi?" asked Dick.

"He stands for your father."

Girls in multicolored dresses appeared in the doorway of the
high barracks, each bearing a small jar. The one who gave her
jar to Dick did not look up, but shyly and quickly retreated as
soon as Dick took it from her. Dick saw that the other youths
walked solemnly toward the crowd of men, each singling out
one man to whom to present his jar. He walked to Cuyuchi,
who stood in full regalia at the foot of the chief's platform.

Cuyuchi accepted the jar, but in contrast to the other men, scarcely touched his lips to it. He set down the jar and lifted his arm high.

"To the mountain!" he cried.

"To the mountain! To the mountain!"

All the youths began running in full pack along the steep, narrow mountain path with its sharp stones.

"Don't be the last one, white youth!"

Dick's chest was bursting. The thin mountain air choked and hurt inside of him.

"I can't—run . . . any . . . faster. . . . !" he panted.

"They will beat you! They will all beat you if you fall behind!"

Dick saw them coming, those men who had slashed at them in the square, Acachu was in the lead, swinging his stick, shouting. Dick's legs felt as though they would drop off.

"They'll beat you!" shouted Yutu in his ear. "Run!"

From somewhere Dick found the strength to run, scarcely a yard or two ahead of the howling pack. He tripped, felt the strong hand of Chaqui hold him, pull him up.

When they reached the foot of the high mountain, Chaqui's face broke into a broad smile.

"They didn't catch you!" he said. He was proud that this white youth who had been given him to train had learned enough. Dick couldn't even answer.

The same maidens who had brought the sacred drink now carried newly woven poncho-shirts for each of the youths, and close behind them came another group of girls who brought them luncheon. The shy girl with the downcast eyes who served Dick also put some soothing salve on his back as she helped him on with the shirt.

The food consisted of cold boiled potatoes; a small piece of venison, smothered in spices and also cold; and a small square of corn bread. No liquid of any kind. Most of the youths stood about; some, however, sat on the rocks. Chaqui and Dick sat together, and presently a third youth joined them.

"I have drawn you for the match this afternoon," he said.

It was Quilaki, the tallest of all the Indian lads who had been in training. At no time during all the weeks of training had he shown the least friendship for Dick. His manner had been sullen, even antagonistic at times, and once during the brief rest period when Dick had walked over to where Quilaki was talking with a small group, they had all suddenly become silent and simply stared at Dick. Dick knew that Quilaki spoke Spanish, but the resentful Indian youth had never spoken a single word to him other than in Quechua, and then only when he had to. But this time he spoke in Spanish. The muscles in his arms and legs rippled with eagerness.

"They will shave your head and give you your padded suit up by the sundial rock," Quilaki said.

"Padded suit? You haven't got one on!"

Quilaki stared at Dick, his eyes narrowing into little black slits. His lips curled.

"I refused a padded suit when I was told you were my opponent!"

Dick jumped to his feet, his fists clenched and his legs apart, and stood very close to Quilaki.

"Oh, yeah?" cried Dick, "so that's it, is it?"

Dick walked swiftly back to where Cuyuchi and several of the other priests were shaving the heads of the youths. Dick had to wait his turn, but when Cuyuchi noticed him he motioned Dick to come. Cuyuchi's long flat knife was made of wood, but along the edge, pressed tightly in place, was a thin strip of polished bronze, sharpened to the keenness of a razor blade. He spread a salve that smelled like rancid lard on Dick's head, and deftly shaved off all the hair. Then Cuyuchi dipped his hand into a small silver jar and rubbed some sort of oil over Dick's shaven head.

"The padded suits are over there," said Cuyuchi, pointing.

"I don't need a padded suit," Dick said, looking steadily into Cuyuchi's black eyes. "I'll fight him just like this!"

The crowds separated into groups, making a small ring about

twenty feet square, where the youths were to meet in the Game of the Shields. Boys were paired off, given the choice of putting on padded suits, and allowed their choice of shields and weapons. The disk-shaped shields were of thick straw wound tightly in circles from the center and tied together with thin wire. They bulged outward slightly, and a handle of tough cotton belting on the inside allowed the left arm to hold and maneuver the shield. For weapons, there were short thick sticks, about a foot long, one end polished smooth for the hand, the other holding long rawhide thongs. At the end of each thong was a little metal ball. The youths could also choose the "long whip," which was a wooden handle about an inch thick and two feet long, at the end of which there were six or eight short leather strips made of rawhide, each with its own little ball. Dick noticed that Quilaki already held the "long whip" in his hand, waiting.

"Take the short whip," whispered Chaqui.

Dick saw friendship in his companion's eyes. He chose the short handled whip, and picked up a grass shield that smelled of new wet hay.

Wearing only the knee-breeches and sandals, they clashed in the middle of the square, their bodies glistening in the afternoon sun. Dick saw the swift movement of his foe, but was too late to dodge the blow. The leather straps slashed across his back, the knot cutting deep. Then the savage rush of the tall Indian's body, the shock of a hundred and sixty pounds of bone and muscle. Dick tried to sidestep, lost his balance, went down. The young native jumped on him, slashing, beating, yelling. Dick ducked his head behind his shield, but caught the full blow of the whip on his shoulder. A spurt of blood wet his arm. A shout of triumph shook the ground.

"*Hurac Huaina! Hurac Huaina!* The white youth is down, he is down!"

Desperately Dick turned over, rolling with the shield. Quilaki's rawhide stung his bare legs. He pulled his knee forward and leaped to his feet, swinging out wildly with his own whip.

The thongs twirled with swift fury around the young Indian's legs. Dick gave a furious pull, to free the whip and strike again. Again, hit him again! Blindly now, scarcely seeing more than the jumping form before him, Dick struck, pulled back, struck again. Quilaki cried out in pain. The next instant Dick caught a full blow on his shoulder and back.

Both boys were bleeding, panting. For a second they faced each other. Quilaki's coppery skin glistened purple with sweat. Then they rushed at each other, clashing full force, shield against shield, and Dick saw Quilaki's body hurtle past as the tall Indian lost his footing and sprawled full length on the ground. Dick turned swiftly, whip lifted.

Quilaki made a desperate effort to dodge the lash he knew was coming, and as he did so, he turned his face up. Never had Dick seen such hatred in anyone's eyes. Quilaki's face, twisted in defiance, was swelling like a misshapen balloon; the corner of his mouth was torn and bleeding.

For a moment Dick stood over his foe, his whip poised. Then slowly he dropped his arm, turned, and pushed his way through the silent group of natives. The men who had watched the fight opened a small path for him and stared as he went by. Dick walked to where his poncho-shirt lay, and put it on, leaving his whip and his shield on the ground. Then he slowly walked up the long mountain path toward the House of Youths.

Finally he reached the stone house where he had lived these many weeks. It was empty. He made his way toward the wall where his bed-rug was, and dropped on his knees. He heard his own sobs, tried to stifle them. It was as though they belonged to someone else. It wasn't himself at all. He felt no pain, just rage, and fury, and a strange sort of humiliation.

Hot bitter tears rolled down his cheeks. "Blast them, blast them all, I want to get out of here!" he sobbed.

Chaqui's voice startled him. "Huaraca wishes you to come to receive your arms," he said. His eyes were bright with pride for his white brother.

"Now?" Dick got to his feet.

"Now," said Chaqui. He turned and led the way back to the giant square. Huaraca was standing before the stone platform. The silent crowd had formed a respectful half-circle before their chief. At his side stood Cuyuchi, holding something in his hand. Chaqui stepped back to let Dick pass.

"You kneel down first. Huaraca will now knight you," he said.

The other youths detached themselves from the crowd and pressed forward toward the old chieftain. Last came Quilaki, his face distorted hideously.

A long blast from the giant sea-conch was followed by a blood-curdling shout from the crowd.

"*Tupac Yauri! Yurac huaina! Tupac Yauri!*" The young white youth was now a full-fledged warrior of the tribe!

Huaraca, walking very slowly, a silver staff in his wrinkled hand, approached Dick. When only a step away, Huaraca stopped. First he touched Dick's forehead, then his right shoulder, then his left shoulder, then placed the silver staff lightly on Dick's shaven head.

"*Huanacauri. Atun-apa-huallpi.* Oh Father, oh Creator, Father Sun, Thunder and Lightning. Make these youths strong and brave. Accept them now, oh Huanacauri!"

The Chieftain raised his left hand, and the golden cup he held shone in the sunlight. "*Atun-apa-huallpi!*" the old man repeated. In the entire multitude there was not a sound. "*Atun-Apa-huallpi! Tupac Hauri!*"

"*Tupac Yauri!*" The hills reverberated with the shout from hundreds of throats.

"I give you now the arms of men, of warriors, and of knights!"

Cuyuchi came forward and extended his arms to Huaraca. One by one Huaraca took the weapons and insignia.

"Rise, young man, and receive your weapons of manhood."

He presented Dick with the staff of solid silver and a small hatchet of gold. And as other young knights stepped up, more staffs, more hatchets were brought forward. According to his rank, and also whether he had won or lost his final match, each received arms of silver, of gold or of bronze. With each gift, the same tapping.

As they moved back toward the high building, Dick noticed that a small stone seat flanked by two stone falcons had been brought out.

"Your ears will be pierced now for the golden ear-plugs," whispered Chaqui joining Dick in the march toward the Falcon Seat.

"My ears? pierced?" Dick's voice was high with alarm.

"It will not hurt. They pack it well with coca leaves. It is only a small opening. Later they will make it bigger."

Chaqui was right, it didn't hurt. A priest held a long, sharp quill made of bamboo in his right hand. He spread the earlobe, and while another priest pressed a wet pack of coca leaves to the back of the ear, the sharp quill made a puncture, like a hypodermic needle. Suddenly Dick's ear felt big, and numb, but it did not hurt.

Huaraca sat on the Falcon Seat, and as the youths were released by the priests, they passed before the old Chieftain, who presented each of them with a pair of earplugs the size of a silver dollar, symbolically holding one plug to each ear. Not all the plugs were of gold, Dick saw, but his were bright yellow and shone in the afternoon sun.

"The young white man is now a Knight," cackled the old chief.

Suddenly everybody was shouting. Dick looked up and saw Cuyuchi watching him with impassive intensity. At last Cuyuchi spoke.

"You will wear those golden earplugs at the Feast of Intip Raymi," he said. Dick shuddered.

The Intip Raymi! The Festival of the Sun, at the end of summer, still a full three months away! I won't be here, I can't be here! Dick thought. Dad has got to find me, or Prof! Three more months! No! No!

12

Escape!

Dɪᴄᴋ ᴡᴀs sᴛᴀɴᴅɪɴɢ ᴏɴ ᴛʜᴇ ᴡɪᴅᴇ sᴛᴏɴᴇ sᴛᴇᴘs ʟᴇᴀᴅɪɴɢ to the House of Youths when he saw Quilaki coming. He wondered whether this meant more trouble, whether Quilaki still bore a grudge because of his defeat in the Game of the Shields.

"I should like to speak to the white youth alone," said Quilaki. His face still showed the effects of the beating he had taken.

"What about?"

"I should like to speak to him alone."

Quilaki did not stop, but kept on going up the hill to the Sundial Chamber atop the high ridge. The long shadow on the west side of the giant stone disk said it was still early for noon. In spite of his weeks of training and living up here in the high altitude, Dick found his breath still coming fast when he climbed.

"The white youth is not happy here," said Quilaki as Dick reached the summit of the ridge. "Perhaps he would like to get away, return to his own people."

"What?" Dick couldn't believe his own ears.

Here far above the ruins of the city, the plaza below looked small and cramped. Only the wind heard the two talking, the everlasting wind that blew day and night on top of the mountain.

"Quilaki wishes to know if white youth wishes to go back to his own people."

"Is this some sort of a trap?"

"A trap? No! Quilaki wishes to help white youth leave the Lost City."

"But why? Why should I believe you?"

The silence that followed was broken only by the wind's hu-eeeeh, hu-eeeeh!

"Why should you help me get away?" Dick insisted.

Another silence. They stared at each other across the round stone dial. Dick could see no friendship in the black eyes of the Indian youth. Then why this offer of help?

"Because Quilaki wishes to see white youth away from here. Far away!" Quilaki spit the words out through clenched teeth.

"Because I beat you yesterday?"

"Quilaki does not care for himself. But evil things have happened in our village since the white youth arrived. We wish to see him go."

"We?" repeated Dick, "who is 'we'?"

"I do. Quilaki."

"And why should I care what you want me to do?"

"I am Cuyuchi's son. Some day I will be Chief. I do not want white youth in our tribe. I wish him to go!"

"Cuyuchi's son? How can that be? You're not Tocta's. . . ."

"Tocta is second wife. She is not principal wife."

"Now I begin to see! But how do I know I can trust you?"

"You wish to go away. I wish to help you."

"How do I know I can trust you?" Dick repeated.

Another silent battle with the eyes. The wind whined around the sundial . . . hu-eeeeh . . . hu-eeeeh.

"The white youth does not believe Quilaki?" asked the tall Indian at last.

"Frankly, no."

"Will he believe this?" Quilaki opened his right hand, displaying a golden pin, six inches long, one end shaped like a miniature image of the sun.

"That's Tocta's pin!" exclaimed Dick.

"Yes, this *topu* belongs to Tocta. Now does young white man believe?"

"Did she send you?" asked Dick, his voice rising with hope in spite of his attempt to control it.

But the Indian only shrugged his shoulders.

"I don't understand . . . but that's Tocta's pin, all right."

"Then let us stop talking like old women! The moon will not rise for many hours after sundown tonight. When the city sleeps, we will get young white youth away."

Dick's heart was pounding. He swallowed hard. Tocta's words came back to him then, on the whining of the everlasting wind. "On the full of the moon I will send you a token," she had said. This was the night of the full moon.

"The white youth is afraid?"

"No, I am not! Go on, I'm listening!"

The plan was simple enough. After the guard had blown the giant conch to signal silence in the House of Youths, Dick and Quilaki would climb over the low parapet guarding the precipice to the south of the big house, slide swiftly down the steep embankment. There were no houses there, no guards because of the steep precipice.

"But if it's so steep, how can we get down . . . in the dark?"

"I know the secret path. I will go ahead of you." Quilaki's voice was full of contempt.

Dick thought hard. Why not? If these savages meant to harm him, they could have done it much earlier. If he was caught fleeing, Quilaki would be involved, might even lose his status as heir to the chief. Surely Quilaki would not risk that lightly.

"Where do we go?" asked Dick.

"To the river."

"What am I supposed to do then? Swim?" Dick asked.

"There is a raft at the wide bend of the river. The river flows north and travels with great calm."

"How far?"

"For many leagues."

"Are you coming with me?"

"The white youth travels alone!" Quilaki's voice almost trembled as he answered.

"But how can I make the raft travel fast . . . your people have dug-out canoes and will catch me as soon as you give the alarm."

"The boats are all being repaired. They are all out of the water above the falls. The young men are cleaning the boats. They cannot go into the water now."

"How do I know you are telling the truth?"

"See for yourself, white youth!" Quilaki pointed a long, strong finger down into the deep ravine. Far down by the river Dick could see a group of men working on the boats, scraping them, filling in the cracks. Below the rushing falls was a white balsa raft made of four logs tied together. There seemed to be some sort of shelter on it.

"How fast can I travel alone on that raft?"

"Who knows?" Quilaki's black eyes bored into Dick's. "The white youth will have poles, and two oars. He can go as fast as he wishes. He can guide the raft in midstream and travel with the fast current."

"But how can I steer at night? There are big rocks in the middle of that river, I saw them!"

"White youth will watch for them," said Quilaki. He turned and started down the narrow path.

"When the city sleeps, before the white of the moon," he said, moving quickly down the steep path with the graceful, gliding motion of a trained mountain climber.

Dick sat down on the great sundial and looked about him.

The landscape looked peaceful in the morning sun. Down deep in the canyon he could hear the rumble of the river as it wound around the mountain and started its northward flow. Wild rugged cliffs guarded the city on three sides, terrifying and forbidding.

It would take a secret path to get out of this. One false step, and a drop of a thousand feet straight down over the face of the cliff! Dick's heart jumped into his mouth as he looked. A path? there? He couldn't see it.

By the time Dick got back to the House of Youths he was shaking all over. It wasn't even mid-morning, and he would have to wait until dark. What would he do until then? What about his clothes? These soft sandals wouldn't hold out for two miles! Rocks, heavy brush, rough, tough going. Would he have to travel—barefoot?

At noon he joined the others in the line-up for luncheon, wondering whether his companions could guess his excitement. One more meal after this. Where would he eat tomorrow?

The sun finally went down. Darkness shut down, swift and complete. But it would still be an hour more before the guard blew the giant conch. How long after that would he have to wait for the signal from Quilaki?

Dick thanked his lucky stars that his rug was at the far end of the room, close to the wall and the wide window opening. Quilaki had mentioned that window opening, bigger than the rest. It would be easy to climb through it in silence. But again his uneasy feeling about Quilaki came back. If Quilaki didn't mean it, what was he up to?

Another disquieting thought assailed Dick. Quilaki knew a secret path. Who else knew it? Cuyuchi? Acachu? The thought of Acachu hiding somewhere in the darkness, waiting to stick a long silent blade in him, sent shivers up Dick's back.

Everyone in the big House of Youths was silent. From either side Dick could hear the regular breathing of his companions as they slept. Dick turned toward the wall, facing the opening just a foot or two above his head. It was inky black outside, but away up in the high dome Dick could see the stars twinkling in the early night. What was there on the other side of that black opening? Escape? A trap? Would he be able to find that secret path and follow it in the deep darkness? And what about that raft? Could he float it free into the middle of the stream, keep it there? Where would it take him?

Try as hard as he would, Dick could not shake the image of Acachu's face, teeth bared, waiting, waiting for him. But what would happen if he did not take the chance?

What was that? Someone at the window? The wind?

"Shhhh . . . white youth. Come."

Dick was instantly alert. The sound came again—a voice, whispering.

"Come, and make no noise!"

Silently Dick glided on his hands and knees toward the window opening. He thought the pounding of his heart must surely awaken Chaqui, or Yutu, lying nearby. He listened. Silence. The two companions slept. He was at the window. He raised one hand, pulled himself up, pushed the upper part of his body out. He raised one knee, swung his leg out, pulled the other knee to the window sill. One more motion, then he would be out. It was only a few feet to the ground; he had measured that many times that afternoon with his eyes. His sandalled feet made no noise as he dropped to the narrow platform outside the House of Youths.

The hand that clamped on his mouth was strong. But it was not Quilaki's!

"Shhhhhh! Be quiet, white youth!" It was Tocta's voice!

"Listen! They have set traps for you. I heard them talking. Deep man-traps, with sharp lances sticking up from the bottom. You do not see the hole in the darkness, you fall in. The tips of the lances are dipped in poison. Do you understand? You must not follow Quilaki down the path!"

"But . . . but . . ."

"No, do not speak. Pretend to follow him. He will come

soon. But at the foot of the cliff, by the stone ladder, there is a cave. On the right of the cliff, understand? I will be there. Shhhhh . . . he comes!"

Dick pressed his body against the wall of the House of Youths. His hands shook, his teeth were close to chattering. One of these two, Quilaki or Tocta, was lying. But which one? Or both?

"Ready, white youth?" The voice startled him, although it was barely a whisper. It was Quilaki!

"Yes, yes, I am ready."

"Then follow me."

Strange how Dick's eyes could see, even in the dark of night, even when it was pitch dark. Quilaki's body shone with a faint gleam. He reached the low protecting wall, hoisted himself over it.

Dick, following closely, cleared the wall. The narrow path that slid down the other side dropped abruptly. Quilaki was crouching, and traveling fast. Dick quickened his own step to keep up, leaning toward the left to keep his balance against the mountain. On the right side of the path was the sheer drop, down the face of the cliff, a thousand, maybe two thousand feet.

Dick tried to hurry, but he remembered he must watch where he was going—put one foot in front of the other, make sure each foot was on solid ground before he stepped. Then he saw Quilaki glide around a big boulder and disappear from sight.

Was that the first trap?

At the side of the boulder the ledge dropped sharply perhaps fifteen feet. A ladder of vines and twigs hung down. Quikali was almost down. But down where? Dick descended the ladder backward, feeling carefully each rung. He felt the ground while still hanging on the ladder, scraped the little platform all around with his toe. It was perhaps two feet wide, not big, but solid and wide enough to stand upon. Where was Quilaki?

Dick stood still, waiting, listening. He peered into the darkness, looking for the greenish gleam of Quilaki's body, caught a glimpse of it some yards below. Quilaki's voice came up to him out of the darkness.

"Come down this ledge. There are holes for you to hold on, to put your feet in. When you reach bottom, turn left. The path goes down more slowly there."

Dick could not tell how far below Quilaki stood, but he could see there was a sharp drop ahead. He stooped, holding one hand on the twig ladder, and felt with the other for the face of the ledge. He found the first hole. Still holding on the last rung of the ladder, Dick tried that first hole, searched for the next one with his free foot, found it. Slowly he let himself down, leaning forward as far as he could to keep his balance. He felt for the next hole, and the next. His fingers were stiff and taut as he made his slow, careful progress down the cliff. Suddenly it came to him.

The cliff!

"At the foot of the cliff! At the foot of the cliff, turn right," Tocta had said. But Quilaki said "turn left"!

The wind swept up from the cold canyon and went right through his clothes, chilling him, whining past his ears, hissing as it scraped up the face of the rock.

"Pssst! This way! Do not go left! Stand there!"

It was a voice . . . but from where? Quickly Dick looked down the mountainside, saw the greenish light of Quilaki's crouched body moving swiftly to the left forty or fifty yards ahead. Dick could barely see it, and then only because of the sulphur-like gleam. To the right was a sheer drop. "To the right," said the voice from nearby. "To the left," Quilaki had said. Was this the end?

Then the voice came again.

"Reach around this sharp edge. There is a stone you can catch like a handle. Take hold tight and swing. The cave is on the other side."

That was Tocta's voice! Even though barely more than a

hissing whisper, the sounds were hers. Dick was trembling, undecided. Then he heard her again.

"Dick! Do not lose more time! Come!"

Dick reached around the sharp stone edge, waving his hand first sideways, then up and down. A hand seized his wrist, guided his fingers to a long stone pin carved in the rock. Dick grasped it tight, pulled down to test it. It held.

It's now or never, he thought. If God wants me to live, I'll make it. If not . . .

Dick took tight hold, then swung his body loose. For a moment he hung by his left hand alone, his feet dangling, his whole body suspended high over that bottomless abyss. He waved his feet frantically, trying to find some landing place. Nothing, nothing but empty space below! Then something, someone, gripped his swinging foot and pulled it. The next instant Dick felt hard rock under him. He swung his body forward, and the hand that had guided his foot seized his free arm. Then he saw Tocta.

"You are safe now, Dick."

The sound of her voice, speaking softly, calling him "Dick" instead of "the white youth," the hard solid earth beneath his feet—these sent a wave of confidence through him.

She took him by the hand. "Come this way. The cave is long and deep, and inside we can make light. It cannot be seen."

He followed, his heart pounding, mounting curiosity replacing the stark fear he had felt before.

"How do we get out of here, Tocta?" he asked as she led him down the long narrow passage.

"You will see. Do not be afraid. We have a friend who will help."

"A *friend?*"

"Yes, do not be afraid."

The deep cave turned as it went into the mountain. The mountain seemed to fold over it, shutting it out completely.

Suddenly the whole inside sprang into view, as Tocta snapped

on a small flashlight. Dick thought he saw at the far end of
the cave, where a long black crack opened obliquely to the
right, a shadow as though something had moved.

"Who is in here with us, Tocta?" Dick was suddenly alarmed,
suspicious.

She evaded a direct answer. "You can rest now, Dick," she
said. "Here are your clothes. You may have this flashlight, also.
And your shoes. But tonight you must sleep, so you can travel
fast when light comes again."

"But didn't I see somebody down there at the other end?
Turn the light down there, Tocta, I want to see . . ."

"It is a friend, Dick." She did not turn on the light.

"Tocta, is this a trick?" Dick's voice shook.

"A trick? Oh, no! You saved my child, Dick. I want to save
you."

"Then who is it down there?"

A long silence followed. Then she said: "It is the Medicine
Man."

"The Medicine Man! That spidery hunchback? Why did you
bring him here?"

"He is helping me. He promised to help me always, as my
father helped him. I asked him to help."

"But can you trust him, Tocta?"

"I trust him completely," she answered, her voice very calm.
"He owes his life to my father. He owes it to me."

"Then he is going to show me the way out?" Dick suddenly
remembered how the spidery little man shuffled in and out of
the Lost City, past the silent cemetery.

"Yes, but not tonight. Not tonight," she repeated. "Tomorrow,
when light will make traveling easy, he will come and show
you."

"And you, Tocta?" Dick asked.

"I am going back now to my house."

"Do I stay here alone tonight?"

"Yes, for the night. You are safe, Dick," she said very seriously. "You can sleep and rest. Tomorrow he will come for you."

"How can I ever thank you, pay you back?"

"When you return to your own people, be kind to old Huaraca and his people. They are not evil. But they have sworn to keep their secrets from the white people. Do not betray their honor, Dick."

"You're pleading for them? Don't you want to be free?"

"No, I belong here now, Dick. It is too late for me to leave. My child belongs here. And I understand how they feel— Huaraca, Cuyuchi, and the rest. But you belong . . . to other people, Dick. People I once belonged to, too. You must return."

"What will Huaraca do to you? And Cuyuchi?"

"Nothing. They are not evil, Dick," she repeated solemnly. "It is their honor and their glory. But sooner or later their secret must be found. Only do not betray them, Dick."

"I promise, Tocta."

"God travel with you, Dick! And remember Miskqui when you are back home with your own mother and father . . . with your own people. But do not be sorry for us—for me and for Miskqui. Cuyuchi is a good father and a good husband."

"Husband, Tocta. What about Quilaki?"

"You do not understand, because their customs are so different from yours. But I am his wife, and Miskqui is his child. And we are both safe. I must go now," she added quickly. "Rest well, and God be with you on the morrow."

"And with you too, Tocta!"

In the light of the flashlight Dick watched as she crossed the deep cave and disappeared behind the black crack down below. He held the light on for a moment longer, then snapped it off. On an impulse, he snapped it on quickly again. Everything was still. He was alone. A thick woolen rug lay at his feet. Dick was surprised to feel big wet tears on his cheeks. He sank down on the rug. He suddenly felt very tired, so very, very tired . . .

The cool stillness of the night reached in and soothed him. His head sank into the soft wool. He wondered whether he should flash on the light again, just to make sure, but his hand lay still.

13

Rescued!

OUT OF THE DARKNESS, DICK HEARD A SOFT VOICE.

"Come, it is time. The sun will soon be over the hill."

He sat up abruptly, and reached for his flashlight. He snapped it on, directing it at the spot from which the sound had come.

It was Mancoy, the grotesque little Medicine Man.

"You are still not out of danger, white man," he said, speaking very slowly. His Spanish was clear and correct.

"You will take me to my father?" Dick asked, jumping to his feet.

"No, young white man. But I will show you the way out. You must reach your people yourself."

"Can I trust you?" Dick was tearing off the Indian clothes he had worn, putting his own back on again. They had been washed clean and they smelled of the sweet sunshine. They had been mended, too, where they had been torn.

"Tocta has told you," the little hunchback answered. "I have given my word to Tocta."

"When do we start?"

"Now. As soon as white youth is ready. Soon the sun will fill this canyon. We must be down by the river before that."

"The river?" Dick's voice betrayed his alarm.

"Yes, but we will cross it, go up the other side. Come, I will show you."

Dick flashed the light on once, saw the crack at the other end of the cave. Mancoy was already slipping through it, sideways. A little gray light seemed to slant in, barely visible.

"Follow me and walk carefully," the spidery old man said as soon as Dick had squeezed through the crack. A few yards away there was a wider opening in the side of the mountain. "When we come out of the cave, the path goes down steeply, but there are low bushes that will hide you. Keep down, but travel fast."

The twisted little old man held up his hand for silence as he went through the opening. He was back almost instantly. He waved Dick to come, but put one long skinny finger to his lips in sign of silence. The little hunchback body crouched even lower.

Just outside the entrance to the cave was a long, narrow ledge, looking down a thousand feet into the deep river gorge. Jungle vines clung tenaciously in scraggly patches, here and there making little islands of green. Twisted small chonta trees, wind blown and bent from the everlasting wind, stood out like little sentinels in the green patches. A thin, almost invisible zig-zag line followed the contours of the mountain slope, lost itself in the vegetation down below. Mancoy was already gliding, tarantula-like, moving his hairy arms and legs like snakes. Dick took a deep breath and followed, crouching, careful to keep his balance. A giant rat scampered over his foot, startled him out of his balance. When he recovered it, Mancoy was far ahead. Dick hastened to catch up.

They had gone a hundred yards or so when Mancoy stopped. The sky was beginning to get some light, the rim of the jagged mountain to the right and across the deep ravine was outlined faintly in growing yellow, silhouetted against the receding darkness. One by one the stars faded into the gray-blue of the morning. Old Mancoy waited for Dick to reach his side; then holding up a finger, pointed across the gorge.

"Can you see the little hut on the other mountain slope?" he whispered.

Dick peered intently. He could see nothing except the dense jungle vegetation, almost black in that early dawn. "I don't see anything but woods," he said at last, keeping his voice down.

"You see no smoke across the valley?"

Dick looked again. There it was! A thin little ribbon of smoke, rising straight up.

"Is that it? Half way up on the other side?"

"Yes, that is where we are going. We must reach there before noon, and I must get back to the village before I am missed."

The little hunchback turned and started down the path again. The brush was higher here, and Dick found he could walk almost erect. The muscles behind his knees ached from the crouching position; the small of his back hurt too. But he kept his head down, eyes front, watching Mancoy. The old man seemed to slip down with incredible ease, although Dick found the going rough and tiring.

Ten minutes, half an hour, an hour. The sun was now on top of the ridge, must have reached the Sundial Chamber. Dick could remember how the long shadows from the round upright stone reached out to the very edge of the disk, indicating the length of the day, slowly receding as the sun mounted higher and higher, until there was no shadow at all. "The needle captures the Sun," Chaqui had explained. Was that only a few weeks ago? Or years?

Dick suddenly felt hungry.

"Do we get anything to eat?" he asked as they reached another little green patch where the Medicine Man had stopped.

"Only this," said the little hunchback, handing Dick a piece of fresh corn bread. "But soon we shall reach the hut, and you will find much food."

The old man was already moving again. Dick followed. The little path twisted and turned, lost itself under the bushes, came out again. Dick could hear the loud rumbling of the river, knew they must be getting closer although he could not see it.

Suddenly the old man stopped, held up his hand. Dick waited, motionless while the old man, crouching low, glided very slowly forward.

Mancoy vanished into the thick bushes, then reappeared, waving to Dick to follow. And suddenly there was the river. At this point it traveled swiftly, and to his right Dick could hear the roar of the waterfall. This must be below the bend, then, close to where he had sighted the raft!

"Is that a waterfall?" he whispered to the old man.

"Yes, the tunnel falls. We are below them. Stay low, be quiet, and be careful."

The roar of the river grew louder. The ground went up sharply, and big stones formed a sort of wild natural steps. The old man climbed, motioning for Dick to follow.

Where they emerged from the bushes at the top, a natural arch of rock spread before them. The river went through it, dropping ten or fifteen feet, then sped on.

"We cross here," said the old man, keeping his voice very low and pointing to the stone arch before them. He moved silently forward.

The river made a deafening noise through that stone tunnel, crashing angrily on the lower side. The old man was already on the hollow rock, the spray from the river splashing over him.

"Come, white man, it is the only way," he said, seeing Dick hesitate.

Dick slipped on the wet rock, held his breath, reached down to grab with both hands. Frothing, churning angry mountain waters roared around the bend, rushed in wild fury at the narrow granite arch through which they had made a funnel-like hole. The sucking of the waters made a furious hissing as they sped through the opening, throwing up spray around and over them. The banks were soggy from the constant spray, and the giant rock, covered with glistening drops that shone and sparkled like diamonds in the morning light, was slippery.

"Step with great care. Turn your face down the river." The Medicine Man was already on top of the arch.

"Down river?" Dick could see the crashing foam below, could hear the splashing water hit before it spread out at the spot where they had reached the river bank.

"The river sometimes climbs high and splashes with fury," the old man said. "You would be blinded if it hit your face."

The water seemed to gather fury as Dick climbed the arch. Angry whirlpools twisted and churned, then scattered, joined again the rushing stream as it catapulted through the tunnel deep in the jungle ravine. The spray was cold; the rock was slippery. Dick moved very slowly, crawling on hands and knees.

"Turn your face away!" cried the old man.

But Dick was too late. A thin blanket of water stung him like ten thousand needles as it caught him on the side of his face. For a second he thought he was being swept off. Long, thin arms grasped him, held him while the fury of the water splashed over him.

"Get down flat! Keep your face away from the river! Come now before another wave hits. We must reach the other side before it comes again. Hurry, young white man!" Old Mancoy's voice, deep and anxious, reached him through the roar of the river.

Dick was shaking violently. His teeth chattered. His hands felt numb in the cold wetness. His knees hurt deeply as he crawled over the wet and slippery rock, inch by inch, trying desperately to hurry, to get off that slippery death trap. Now he reached the top, started down the other side. Ten more feet, eight, five. The rock suddenly broadened into a large flat platform. Mancoy was already there. Dick clawed at the edge, lifted his aching body to the top. Gratefully he stretched out, panting.

"The difficult part is over. But you must not lie here, you may be seen!" Mancoy's voice, in spite of the warning, sounded relieved.

Dick got up on his hands and knees again. He rose to a semi-crouch, followed Mancoy into the nearest clump of bushes on the other side of the river.

"You can rest now. But not long. We must reach the hut before noon."

Dick took deep breaths, trying to steady the pounding in his chest. Breathing was easier down here than on top of the ridge. The memory of that ridge, of the Throne Room, the White Room, the House of Youths, flooded through his mind, gave him a sudden panic, urged him on.

"Let's go, Mancoy!" he gasped. "I'm all right!"

The little hunchback turned quickly and started climbing through the thick brush. The path was barely visible; it was obvious that it was not used much.

The mountain slope rose gradually. Tough high grass with blades as sharp as knives grew between the bushes. Mancoy knew exactly where to step to avoid them. Dick tried to step in the same spots, but he felt the sharp edges cut his flesh, and blood trickle down his leg. Impatiently Mancoy waved to Dick. The sun was climbing higher. It might be eight, maybe nine o'clock. Only three hours to noon. Then what?

They climbed steadily. The tall bushes hid them now completely, and Dick welcomed being able to walk upright. Where the mountainside was steep, the little path zig-zagged sharply. They made good time. Once Mancoy stopped, waited for Dick to catch up.

"Puma," he said, pointing down. In the soft sand at his feet Dick could see plainly the big paw print.

The older man read his fears. "No danger," he said, evenly. "It is only a stray cat. They do not often come up here."

"Once is all it takes," said Dick quickly.

"She will not trouble you."

"How do you know it's a she?"

"It is a mother lion, hunting for wild pig."

Again they started climbing, steadily upward. The river lay far behind now, like a horrible nightmare that still bothers but

no longer scares you. Dick turned once or twice to see if he
could spot any signs of that mother puma. There was nothing,
no sign of life besides old Mancoy and himself. It was getting
hot.

It must have been close to noon when they reached the bam-
boo-walled hut. Although it was deserted, Dick noticed a fire
burning in one corner, the smoke rising up through the thatch
roof. A large earthenware pot boiled over square-cut rocks. He
could not identify the smell, but his lungs filled with the welcome fragrance of food. His stomach muscles ached, and he felt
a deep hollow inside.

"We will eat and rest for a short while. Then I must leave."
Mancoy had dropped to the ground, and was sitting cross-
legged in a grotesque shape.

"What do I do then? How do I get out of this jungle?"

"When Mancoy shall have been gone one hour, Piqui Chiqui
will come to take you to the village. It will be dark when you
arrive. He will take you to the house of the soldiers. They will
use the talking wires."

"Piqui Chiqui? Who is he? How will I know him?" Dick
could not completely hide his new anxiety.

"You know him well. You have seen him often. Piqui Chiqui
—lives by the cemetery in The Lost City."

"You mean . . . that dwarf?" Dick's mind raced back to the
many times he had seen the little man, quietly guarding the
stone walled entrance to the ancient cemetery atop the hill.

"Yes—he is a friend, too. He owes much to Tocta. And to
Mancoy. He will help the young white man."

It was too late to retreat now! Dick must trust him . . . and
Piqui Chiqui. A sudden thought struck him.

"Is there anything I can do for you, Mancoy? I owe you . . ."

"Yessss!" Mancoy interrupted, and his voice sounded almost
vicious. "You can remember Tocta's words: Do not betray
Huaraca and his people!"

"I promise, Mancoy—word of honor," Dick said.

"Word of honor!" echoed the old man. His voice was very deep.

"Yes, Mancoy, word of honor. I will not betray Huaraca!"

"It is good. Mancoy believes the young white man." Their eyes met in a long silent pledge. Then Mancoy spoke.

"Come, let us eat."

From the bamboo poles that formed the rear wall of the hut he unhooked two wooden dishes shaped like plates but deeper. Rough wooden spoons hung nearby. Mancoy took two of these. Then he dipped into the earthenware pot over the fire, bringing out big lumps of meat and the inevitable marble-like potatoes.

"What is this, Mancoy? It smells delicious!" Dick's mouth was watering.

"It is *visac*."

"And what is that . . . in the white man's language?"

The medicine man did not answer immediately. He ate in silence for a few moments, and Dick did likewise. It tasted as good as it smelled, with a rich, wild game taste. Dick finished what was on his plate.

"May I take some more?" he asked. The old man nodded. Dick filled his plate again, found something that looked like cabbage leaf in the stew. Dick looked at the living yellow leaf, dropped it back into the pot, took only the meat and potatoes. The old man had finished his food before Dick finished his second helping.

"Did you like *visac*?" he asked. Dick thought the smile on the wizened old face made it look almost friendly.

"Yes, very much!"

"Those are mountain rats!"

A great lump leaped into Dick's mouth.

"Oh, no!" he cried, staring at Mancoy. The old man returned his look, his little black eyes dancing.

"I ate them also," he reminded Dick.

Then suddenly Mancoy jumped to his feet, crossed the hut and looked out of the doorway. The sunlight trickled through the bamboo walls in long thin slats showing the twig-twisted vines that held the sticks together.

"Mancoy leaves how," he said solemnly. The smile was gone, his face was serious as he turned back to Dick. "The warmth of the Great Inti surround the white youth. The hand of Mama Quilla take him safely to his people."

"Thank you, Mancoy." Dick felt the solemnity of the moment. "The white youth will not forget his promise," he said.

The old man, moving swiftly, passed through the doorway. Dick was alone. He felt an overwhelming sense of alarm. The stillness of the hut was overpowering. He ran to the doorway and looked out, but he could see nothing beyond the white heat of the morning sun beating down on the jungle around him.

A sudden panic seized him, made him tremble all over. Was this part of the scheme? To be brought up here where . . . where the mountain lions would attack him . . . where no one would ever find him? Why had he ever trusted the spidery Medicine Man? And Tocta?

The thought of Tocta brought him a little reassurance. She couldn't betray him! She couldn't be in on this! She had helped him, had warned him. Or had she?

Dick walked back slowly into the hut, sat down, cross-legged as he had learned to do. "About an hour after I am gone," Mancoy had said.

Dick waited. The silence grew deeper, more lonesome. The fire under the big earthenware pot burned down, but the thin column of smoke that rose from it still climbed up through the thatch roof. Dick watched it for a few moments, he didn't know how long. The wood coals died down, then went out. Only a little smoke remained.

Suddenly Dick jumped. A small dark shadow in the doorway startled him. He hadn't heard a sound.

"This is Piqui Chiqui." The voice was thin, the body like that of a small boy; but the face was wrinkled like an old man's. His small eyes darted over Dick, taking in every detail of Dick's clothes. Dick instinctively gripped the handle of the hunting knife. Piqui Chiqui's eyes widened.

"I do not come to harm the white youth," he said. "I come to show him the way to the town."

"How far away is the town?"

"*Curarac min.* It is far away. Five, maybe six hours."

"Can we reach it tonight? Before the sun goes down?" Dick suddenly felt panicky at the thought of another night alone in this jungle fastness.

"*Allin tuta* . . . not until the dark. But not very dark. The young white man will sleep in bed tonight."

"What do I give you for pay, when we get there?" Dick was watching the small beedy little eyes of Piqui Chiqui. The little old wrinkled face broke into a smile. Silently he pointed to Dick's knife.

"My knife? You want this knife?"

The native's beady little eyes were shining with excitement.

"Young white master keep knife until we reach village," he said slowly. "Then he give knife to Piqui Chiqui."

The queer little native reached down and lifted two small round baskets, tied together with a thin leather strap. He slung these over his shoulder, waved a small brown hand.

"Come, we go now," he said.

On the other side of the little hut there was a narrow path winding up the mountainside. It was not as steep as the one they had climbed that morning, but Dick felt again the growing altitude and his breath came in shorter gasps as they climbed. After about a half hour Dick felt dizzy.

"Stop a moment!" Dick cried. "I've got to rest and catch my breath," said Dick.

The little guide waited. Dick let the air out loudly through his mouth, breathed again. "I'm all right now, let's go," he said after several deep breaths.

They started up again, up, always up. The climb was steady, to the north. A ridge like a smooth Western saddle loomed dark green in the distance between two mountains.

"We cross the mountains there," said the little man, pointing. "On the other side is the village. Three days' journey from the city. The white man's city."

"What city?" asked Dick, his pulse quickening.

"Cuzco!" It was plain that even after these long centuries of conquest and occupation by the white man, the city of Cuzco still was the proud and ancient Holy City of the Incas to the natives.

They resumed their long climb. The going got easier, but the saddle-pass did not seem to come nearer.

The sinking sun had already darkened the mountain with green-black shadows when they finally reached the ridge between the peaks. Below them, stretching as far as the eye could see, Dick saw a rich green valley, gently sloping northwestward. Stunted stands of corn told of man's labor, even this high up in the mountains. Nestled among the giant trees in the full bloom of late summer, lay a little toy village with pink and light green painted houses crouching under yellow thatch roofs. One lone, long building rose two stories high. Dick's heart pounded furiously at the sight.

"That is the House of the Soldiers," he said. "The Captain and his soldiers live there. We go there now."

A new urge pushed Dick forward. Once or twice he stepped on his guide's heels.

"It is a long walk, do not tire yourself," the little gnome warned. Dick felt the impatience that pulled at him like a rope. But though they walked faster now, the land seemed to go away from him; and the village lay still far away as the sun gradually lengthened its shadows then suddenly disappeared behind the big mountain. Twilight changed into swift night.

Dick suddenly felt very weary. His knees ached; the back of his neck felt stiff and cold. A chill wind swept up the long valley, made him shiver. One or two early stars appeared in the sky, shy little lanterns far, far away.

"Soon now we reach the village," the guide said. "Then Piqui Chiqui go back. Young white man not tell the Captain about Piqui Chiqui?" His voice sounded anxious.

"I won't tell him about you, Piqui Chiqui." Dick's voice was trembling. Soon now! Soon he would talk to the Captain, the soldiers! They would use the talking wires, would 'phone his father! Soon, soon. . . .

"Young white master give Piqui Chiqui knife now?"

"Oh, sure, I am sorry! I had forgotten!" Dick pulled the knife out of the sheath, unhooked the leather sheath, passed both of them to the little man in front of him. "I wish I could give you more," he said, "lots more."

"Piqui Chiqui is content," said the little man. His little eyes looked greedily but happily at the knife. "I hide this in my house," he said.

Then he looked up at Dick. He pointed into the growing darkness, to the yellow lights in the big House of the Soldiers where light bulbs hanging from the ceiling broke the blackness of the walls.

"*Allin punchaita consunqui,*" he said, almost under his breath.

"*Jinallatac consunqui,*" Dick answered. "May He be with you, too."

The greeting—'God go with you'—and the proper answer he had learned in the House of Youths.

Dick was alone once more. The little path widened at the edge of the town into a narrow little unpaved street, lined on both sides with adobe huts, thatched roofs hanging low, protecting the dwellings, keeping out the chill and the dew. A dog barked loudly, and Dick jumped. But the dog only came to the edge of the road, a mangy, scraggly little animal, just warning. Dick walked faster. The big long building at the other end of town formed one closed side of the village plaza. More lights came on. The House of the Soldiers. That's where the Captain was . . . the Captain who could use the talking wires . . . Dick was running now, sweat beaded on his forehead . . . his feet felt like leaden weights . . .

The startled barefoot soldier at the door jumped to his feet as Dick stumbled into him.

"*Alto!*" he cried, trying to bring his gun up.

"Take me to your captain, quick!"

"Who wants to see my captain?" The soldier now was alert, suspicious.

"Stop talking. Take me to the Captain!" Dick's voice was a high shrill cry.

"Who calls the Captain?" A deep voice called down from the low balcony that ran the length of the building on the second floor.

"Captain! It's me! Dick Collins! The son of the United States Ambassador! Quick! Phone my father!"

"Collins? Richard Collins?" The Captain's voice now was even more excited than Dick's. "*Santa Madre! Muchachos!* The telephone! Call the *Señor Embajador!*"

Heavy boots sounded on the wooden stairs. Lights went up all around.

Dick staggered past the barefoot guard, past the heavy wooden door and into the big square room. An officer behind the little table at the other end jumped to his feet. The heavy footsteps pounded on the stairway, came nearer. Dick felt the thick warm air strike his face, saw the running figure come toward him. The room spun.

Two strong arms grasped him under his shoulders. Dick tried to focus his eyes on the big round face.

"Young Meester Collins!" The Captain's voice, high with excitement, filled the room. "Come! The telephone!"

Dick's legs sagged as he let the Captain lead him to the table. More men ran in, pointing, babbling in excited half-Spanish, half-Indian dialect.

"The son of the Meester *Embajador!* The young Yankee!"

Dick heard the excited voice barking orders into the telephone. The long, agonizing wait.

"*Sí! Sí! Sí, Señor! Señor Embajador! Sí, Señor, aquí está Deek! Sí, sí, Deek! Sí, Señor, su hijo! En Torontoy! Sí, Señor!*"

"Dad! Dad!" Dick's voice choked, "yes, Dad, it's me, it's Dick!"

He couldn't hear what his father answered. It sounded something like "Thank God!" But Dick wasn't sure.

14

The Golden Throne of the Incas

THE LITTLE ARMY JEEP, DRIVEN BY A DARK SKINNED YOUNG
soldier who deftly turned and twisted the wheel as the machine
followed the narrow mountain road along the river, jumped as
though it shared the eagerness of its occupants. Dick, and the
Captain, facing each other in the back of the Jeep, held on
tight to the iron bars alongside the seats. The young sergeant,
with fixed bayonet, who rode alongside the driver, seemed intent
on the road ahead. The dust was choking, and the hard springs
jolted and shook as the Jeep sped over the rough road.

"It will only be a few hours now," said the Captain. His
round face, his light skin, his deep forehead showed mixed
Indian and Spanish blood. He had a thin black moustache,
trimmed neatly, and his teeth were the color of polished ivory.
He smiled easily; in fact, he had not stopped smiling since they
had started that morning, after another long telephone call.

"Your parents are flying to Cuzco," said the Captain. "We
will meet them there!"

And now they were on their way to Cuzco, Dick thought. Dad! Mom! Can't this thing go any faster?

At noon they stopped in a little mountain town. A soldier opened a wooden housing by the road, revealing a gasoline pump, filled the Jeep's tank, and the extra five-gallon can strapped in back. Dick could not eat the food they offered him, but drank a cup of corn soup. His mind flew back to another day when he had awakened to a cup of hot corn soup, thick and spicy. How long ago was that?

"Let's get going, Captain!"

"The plane from Lima will not reach Cuzco until afternoon," said the Captain, but he was smiling. "We will be there before it lands."

But they weren't. For when the noisy, speeding Jeep, horn blowing to warn startled populace out of the way, roared down the long steep road into the Plaza San Francisco in Cuzco, great crowds had already gathered before the Cuzco Inn. Soldiers and police were holding back the crowds as they pushed forward, and great excitement filled the streets and the plaza beyond. The Jeep, in spite of its loud horn, had to slow down, then stop, half a block away.

On the top of the steps leading to the wide mahogany-framed doors stood Dad, and Mom, and Dorothy, and Prof, and Antonio, and one or two very dignified looking officials, all staring at the Jeep. Mom and Dorothy were waving wildly, shouting, screaming above the hubbub of the crowd.

Dick jumped out of the Jeep, and with the Captain running interference for him, pushed his way through the crowd.

"Mom! Dad!" he shouted over and over again. His eyes filled with tears, and his throat kept swallowing thick, choking lumps that rose again and again.

Then . . . then . . . oh, the soft warmness of his mother's arms, the soft sweet perfume that was Mom! "Dick! Dick!" she cried, "my boy, my boy!"

Dick clung to his mother. "Mom! Mom! Mom!"

Finally his father's voice reached him. "Hey! I'm here too, remember?"

Dick now flung himself into his father's arms, felt the strong bear hug almost crush him. His whole body shook with violent sobs; his arms felt like wet rags, his knees sagged. He could feel his father's heart beat against his.

Dick didn't know how they got back up the stairs and into the inn. Vaguely he heard the shouting of the crowd, the sharp commands of the police and the soldiers. Dorothy ran along side, touching Dick.

"Hi, Sis!" Dick said, noticing her for the first time.

"Hi, Dickie!" she said through her tears.

The doors of the inn closed mercifully behind them. In the high lobby a fire of split eucalyptus sent out a warm fragrance. The hotel manager in his stiff-shirted tuxedo was waving his arms in excited orders as the *mozos* brought big platters of food. More people crowded in, and then Dick caught Prof's round, wide eyes beaming on him.

"Prof!" Dick grasped the outstretched hand. He couldn't say anything more. But he saw Antonio come forward, and Dick gave him his left hand, as Prof clung on the other. The three friends stared at one another. Prof's lips moved several times before he finally made a noise. His thick, choked voice was barely more than a croak.

"Are you all right, Dick?" he asked at last.

"Swell . . . now!"

"What do you want first, Dick?" His father's practical voice made Dick turn.

"Gee, Dad, a bath! A hot bath and clean clothes!"

At the opposite end of the lobby, two graceful white marble staircases rose on either side, leading to the second floor. Mr. Collins dropped an arm over Dick's shoulder, led him toward the stairs.

"Can you make it on foot, Dick?" he asked.

"I can walk all the way back to Lima!" Dick cried. Mom and

Sis joined them as they walked up the stairs. From the second floor Dick saw Prof and Antonio staring up at him.

"I'll be down in a little while," Dick called down. "Don't go away."

"Not much chance of that," answered Prof, smiling. Antonio said nothing, just looked at his young friend from the north.

It was long past sundown before the last of the visiting officials, police and army officers, and the editor of the *Cuzco Sun*, left the little hotel. Dick felt very tired. He had answered innumerable questions, but had steadfastly refused to give the names of his captors, or to say anything about them.

"I gave my word of honor, Dad, that I wouldn't," he said. "My word of honor, Dad!"

"I won't press you, son, not today," his father answered. "Dr. Ortega is arriving tomorrow in the President's plane. The President is sending it to take us all back to Lima. You must get some rest."

Sleep! In a bed!

"I could sleep a week!" said Dick as they reached the room that had been set aside for him.

"Sleep as long as you want to," said his father, "Dr. Ortega's plane will leave Lima around eight and should be here around ten. That will give you a long rest."

But the church bells the next morning at six o'clock, church bells ringing—in deep tones, in high tones, in muffled tones, in sharp clear tones—clanging out into the early morning, shook the walls of the little inn.

"Oh, no! Not that!" Dick sat up in bed. But his heart was too full this morning to feel resentment. He felt rested, his lungs filled with the cool mountain air that sweeps down off the high hills around Cuzco. From down the corridor came the smells of fresh strong coffee, mingled with crisp wood smoke. A dog barked. A rooster greeted the morning with high imperious crow. A woman's voice, sounding high in the patio, called out a cheery morning greeting.

Dick got up quickly, went into the bathroom off his room. How good the toothpaste tasted! Three months—or was it four —he hadn't brushed his teeth. He brushed them twice now, pressing the tube until the paste spilled over the end of the toothbrush. A little thick glob fell with a splash on the hard tile floor. Dick rubbed it with his slipper, smiling.

"I'll squirt as much of you as I want to," he said out loud, "there!"

"Home!" he thought as he started to dress. "We'll be home tonight. That's where I'll sleep! I'll sleep a week!"

His father and mother were already up and waiting. There was a shine in his father's eyes as he greeted him outside his door, shaking hands, man to man. Mom was . . . well, Mom. She kissed him, and again Dick smelled that warm perfume he associated with his mother. They walked down the white marble stairs together.

In the dining room they were soon joined by Prof and Antonio. They did not speak much, beyond a cheerful good morning, as though content with the joy of just being together again. It was Dorothy's turn to chatter excitedly all through breakfast. Dick drank three cups of hot coffee, couldn't seem to get enough.

"Stop your chattering and finish your breakfast," said Mr. Collins finally. "The plane will be here soon. We must be ready."

Crowds of excited people surrounded the hotel, talking in little groups, pointing, looking up expectantly as Dick and his father came to the door—and turned back as they saw the multitude of people outside.

"We'll wait inside," said Mr. Collins. "Feel like talking, Dick?"

"You mean about . . . about those people in the mountain, Dad?"

"Yes, Son."

"No, Dad, I don't. I gave my promise."

Father and son looked at each other steadily. There was pride in Mr. Collins' eyes as they met Dick's steady gaze.

"OK, son," he said finally, dropping a friendly hand on Dick's knee. The little lobby was filling with people who walked quietly and respectfully, keeping as much distance as they could between them and the Ambassador from the big United States of the North, as father talked to son.

A shout from outside the hotel doors warned them of the approach of the government officials. Not only Dr. Ortega, but the Minister of Education, and the Minister of Foreign Relations, sent by the President himself, to escort Dick and his family back to Lima in the President's big four-motored plane.

"There will be a parade in Lima, starting at the Limatambo airport!" Dr. Ortega was shaking Dick's hand warmly.

"A parade!"

"It was arranged two days ago, as soon as we heard the good news," Dr. Ortega went on. "You are a national hero now, Dick!"

"A hero? Me? How come?"

"Haven't you told him?" asked Dr. Ortega, looking at the Ambassador.

"No," answered Dick's father, smiling. "We thought you would rather tell him on the way back to Lima, Dr. Ortega."

"If you will allow me to sit with him, then, on the way back?" said Dr. Ortega.

"Mrs. Collins and I will let you have him for the two hours," said Mr. Collins, a wide grin on his face. "Won't we, Mother?"

Dr. Ortega grasped Dick's arm, led him through the lobby toward the door.

"Come," he said, "the President's plane is waiting."

The crowd broke into loud shouting and clapping as Dick emerged from the hotel, Dr. Ortega by his side. At the top of the wide steps they stopped for one short moment, while Dr. Ortega waved his hand to the crowd. Dick waved also, and the crowd shouted its approval.

The narrow little cobblestone street was lined with waving, shouting, clapping people. Dick waved again and again as the big car slowly pushed its way through the crowds the police could not keep back. A young boy broke through and slapped the car with his open hand.

"Viva el gringito!" he cried.

"Viva!" shouted the crowd.

The big four-motored plane was already waiting, like a giant sky-bird poised for flight.

"Come with me to the first seat, Dick," said Dr. Ortega. "I have much to tell you."

The plane shuddered and started its quick, impatient run down the cement runway.

"We will fly over Sacsahuaman," Dr. Ortega said, tightening his seat belt. "You must look out the window and see what you can see."

Dick stared down. Almost directly beneath them were the vast stone works, the big field, and to the right, the round foundation of the abandoned water tower. Only now Dick could see great numbers of people there, great mounds of earth piled high all around, tractors, jeeps, digging equipment. The workers on the ground waved as the plane swooped low in greeting. Dick turned to Dr. Ortega.

"When you disappeared down there, we started digging," said Dr. Ortega. "Professor Bentley gave the alarm when the big rock fell and closed the opening. We were very much afraid, but realized that we must dig to find you. It took over a week before we could safely lift the big boulder up, and then we discovered the long tunnel, the underground rooms, the Cave of the Inca Throne."

"You mean you know all about that cave inside the mountain?" Dick cried, in complete surprise.

"Yes, Dick, we know all about it. It contained the Golden Throne of the last Inca. That and many other things which we are only now bringing out, and which will be placed in the

National Museum. The President has decreed that your name must be written on a tablet as the discoverer of the Inca Throne Room."

"But did you know I was alive?"

"We did not know exactly, but we were hopeful," replied the Director, soberly. "When we found the room, and the tunnel, and the pieces of flashlight and your compass, we knew you had reached there safely. You weren't there any more. So you must have gone somewhere. We found where you had hopped along the wall, on one foot, and we reasoned you might be injured. But since you were gone, we knew someone had found you. The entire country has been alerted, the army has been looking for you. We were waiting for the end of the rainy season to organize expeditions into the mountains."

They were flying now over the high, dry barren mountains of the lower cordilleras. An occasional very blue, deep little mountain lake peered up at the passing plane, darkened as the plane's shadow flew over it.

Dick walked down the aisle to where his father and mother were sitting. Government officials, army officers, uniformed men of the different services smiled at him. Dick recognized a Secret Service man from Lima.

"You knew they had found the cave, Dad?" asked Dick, as he reached his father's seat.

"Yes, Dick, we knew."

"But you asked me . . ."

"I am glad you didn't have to tell us, Dick . . . and you won't have to say anything you don't want to. Your word of honor is good enough for me, too, son!"

Father and son looked at each other. Mom, too, was staring at him, tears of pride in her eyes. Then they heard Dr. Ortega's voice.

"Look!" he cried, pointing to the window. "There is Lima. The whole city is waiting for you, Dick!"

"You better get back to your seat now, Dick," said Mr. Collins, "and fasten your seat belt."

Dick met his father's steady gray eyes. He tried to read in them how his father really felt about the whole thing. All he could see was the shine of pride . . . pride and something else Dick couldn't quite make out. Finally he turned, as the plane made a long wide sweep in the clear of the sun-filled sky. The plane was headed down toward Lima!

"Yes, sir!" said Dick, turning.

"And—oh, by the way!" His father's voice stopped Dick as he was about to return to his own seat up front. "I guess Aunt Martha will have that picture for her store window now, eh, Dick?"

Dick looked at his father, and he thought Mr. Collins was keeping back laughter. Dick thought he wanted to shout. He glanced quickly at his mother and saw her eyes full of tears. When he looked back at his father he saw the wrinkles around Mr. Collins' mouth, pushing up his father's cheeks as they always did when his father was really pleased.

"Yes, sir," said Dick again, smiling back at his dad, "I guess she will."

Appendix

THE INCA HIERARCHY AND LAW OF SUCCESSION

QUIPU RECORDS—THE KNOTTED WOOLEN STRINGS USED BY historians to refresh their memory when reciting the history of the past—record twelve Inca Emperors. Inca law was that the first-born male child of the marriage of the Emperor and his sister-wife should succeed to the throne. The first sister-wife was the Coya—the Queen, and Principal Wife. But an emperor could have as many as four "legitimate" wives, mostly his sisters, in case the first wife did not give him a son. Some emperors had as many as fifty wives, but only the "legitimate" ones counted in the law of succession. There are, however, good reasons to believe that very occasionally the nobles and war-lords elected some son other than the legitimate first-born to be Emperor.

If, as later historians think, the average reign of each Inca Emperor was forty years, then the Inca Empire, which ended with the Spanish Conquest of 1530-1534, lasted perhaps 450 years, and was founded about the year 1080—near the time of, the Conquest of England by William the Conqueror (1066).

The known Inca Emperors and their principal claim to fame were as follows:

Manco Ccapac: Founder of the Inca Empire. Ccapac means King, Principal or Sovereign.
Sinchi Rocca: Great leader and colonizer.
Lloque Yupanqui: First of the great military geniuses.
Mayta Ccapac: Brave and brilliant general, fearless and great engineer. Creator of the hanging bridges.
Ccapac Yupanqui: One of the weakest of the emperors.
Inca Rocca: Great soldier, conqueror of many provinces, leader

of great wisdom, engineer, creator of the fabulous aqueducts.

Yahuar Huacca: In great crisis he saved the empire from conquest and destruction at the hands of the warlike Chancas.

Inca Viracocha: Great general and military conqueror who assumed the surname "Viracocha," really the name of the Supreme Deity.

Yupanqui Pachacutec: Last of the really great emperors; like his father, a military man, extended kingdom over far-off lands; some think, too much for his own and his empire's safety.

Tupac Yupanqui: Though not first-born, as prescribed by law, became emperor by election after his heroic conduct and inspiration saved the empire from the fierce Chancas for a second time. Great civil governor as well.

Huayna-Ccapac: Extended kingdom to include present-day Ecuador (kingdom of Quito), saw much civil war and strife and through his decisions laid groundwork for fratricidal wars that opened doors to Spanish Conquistadores.

Huascar (Tupac Cusi Huallpa): Last of legitimate Incas before the Conquest. Killed by his half-brother after betrayal, leaving son who many years later raised flag of rebellion against Spaniards in bloody but fruitless struggle to regain their lost greatness.

Atahualpa: Though not really Inca by right, was favorite of his father, Huayna Ccapac, and had won a bloody victory over his brother when the Spaniards in turn tricked and captured him. His fabulous ransom was supposed to have been worth many, many millions of gold dollars, in an amount really never properly evaluated.

The word *Tupac* means 'brilliant'; and the word *Yupanqui* means 'memorable, to be remembered.' Emperors often took on titles after coronation, dropping the names they had been given at the time of their Festival of Naming, at the age of two.

Glossary

ACCA (ach - ka). A fermented drink made from corn. In ancient times selected women chewed the kernels. The chewed paste was allowed to ferment. Drops from the Inca's drinking cup were considered almost sacred and were bestowed upon favored nobles as special favors. The liquid is white and frothy and looks somewhat like beer suds.

ACACHU (ah - kah - chew). Name of Dick's big Indian guard. It was also the name of a famous general in ancient Inca times.

ADOBE (ah - dough - bay). Mud bricks from which Indian huts were made. Today the most widely used construction material for low cost housing in many Latin American countries. Mud is mixed with straw and allowed to dry in the sun, generally in square "brick" shapes roughly the size of building blocks. Treated with lime and colored wash paints, the houses have a toy village appearance in pastel pinks, green, blue.

ALLIN PUNCHAITA (ah - lean poon - cheye - tah). "May God be With You"; the parting greeting (see JINALLA-TAC CONSUQUI).

ALLIN TUTA (ah - lean toot - ah). "With the going of day"; nightfall; when darkness falls.

APURIMAC (ah - poor - eeh - mack). "Chief of the Speaking Waters," one of the mightiest mountain rivers in the world, flowing somewhat west of Cuzco through frightening precipices in the Andes, eventually joining the Sacred Urubamba River to form the main tributary of the Amazon.

AQUEDUCTS. The Incas were great engineers, and brought mountain streams from thirty and even fifty miles away to irrigate terraced gardens and dry valleys to feed their subjects. Archeologists believe that the reason for the desertion of the "Lost Cities of the Andes" was the failure of the water supply. Some ancient irrigation canals are still in use, and underground aqueducts of marvellous construction are still being uncovered, after five hundred years of being "lost."

ASTO HUARACA (as - toe who - ah - rack - ah). Name of Chief in the Lost City, a direct descendant of the ancient Incas.

ATAHUALPA (ah - tah - who - al - pa). The last Inca ruler. Though not by rights emperor, because he was not the legitimate heir to the throne, he had captured and murdered his half brother, the true ruler, and was in turn captured and put to death by the Spanish conquerors, in spite of the most fantastic ransom ever paid in the history of the world!

AYA (eye - ah). Quechua for "dead"; the dead, the departed, the buried.

AYA CAMAYOC (eye - ah ca - ma - yok). The Guardian of the Dead; head-keeper of the cemetery of the nobles.

AYLLU (eye - you). The tribe or family. The head of the ayllu was head-man, and the family which lived in his ayllu was under his control. Some families were large enough so that the ayllu was an entire village.

BALSA. A tree of tropical America. The extremely light wood is used in the manufacture of life-preservers and rafts. Several balsa tree trunks strapped together form a safe platform for one-room cabins and are used for slow transportation down rivers. In the Inca days, they were used as a means of transporting soldiers in the valleys of both the Apurimac and the Urubamba rivers. The Spanish name for a raft is "balsa." An ordinary man or boy of seventeen can easily lift a whole balsa tree trunk.

BENTLEY, Horacio. The name, although English, is not uncommon, especially on the West Coast of South America. The greatest national hero of Chile is Bernardo O'Higgins, an Irish-born, London-educated lover of liberty who lived and fought for Chile, and Chilean independence. There are many English, Irish and German names in the population of South America.

CATHEDRAL. The main Cathedral in Cuzco is an imposing structure built on the foundations of the great Inca Palace fronting the main or Sacred Square (see *Huacay Pata*). Many of the stones in the walls of the Cathedral were torn from the Inca palace's walls, or from the walls of the great Fortification of Sachsahuaman.

CCORI (core - eeh). Quechua for gold. Actually, the double C means that the pronunciation starts deep in the throat and resembles the harsh German "CH" sound, rasping guttural. There is no exact duplicate of it in the English language, sort of a double H-H, as in HORSE.

CCORI CANCHA (core - eeh can - tcha). House of Gold; hence, the famous and greatest of all Temples of the Sun in Cuzco. Side walls inside the Sun Room, and cornices atop the magnificent Temple, were made of inch-thick solid gold plates. The Image of the Sun was carved on the wall of the room facing the East so that the rising sun could flood the entire Temple.

CHICO (chee - co). Spanish diminutive term meaning small, little, or lad. It is often used in Spain and Latin American countries for "boy" and for calling bell-boys, waiters, etc. As a nickname, it is a term of friendly endearment.

CHONTA (chon - tah). A native hard wood of the Andes. Used for making spears, arrows and daggers, in countries where iron was unknown and hard metals scarce. Sharp daggers of chonta wood are still used for hunting by mountain natives. The color is black, and it can be sharpened to almost razor-like sharpness.

CONCH (konch). Spiral sea shells used as trumpets. Some of them are as much as eighteen inches long and make a deep moaning trumpet sound. Inca troops were called to battle with conches, much as we used the bugle.

CUCUY (coo - coo - eeh). Guinea pig of the Andes. Considered a delicacy in a land where meat was scarce, it is still a widely bred animal which runs around in the native huts almost as tame as cats or dogs. Roast cucuy is a tasty dish much prized by the Indians, especially in the mountains.

CURACA (coo - rack - ah). Chieftain and Head Man of Tribe. Each tribe had its own curaca, some of them claiming noble blood. Some tribes, paying titular allegiance to the Inca Emperor, were in constant state of rebellion. Some curaca daughters married into high Inca nobility, and their offspring attained blood royal status.

CURARAC MIN (coo - rah - rack mean). Quechua meaning "far away," or "a long distance to go." Could be used as verb or adjective.

CUYUCHI (coo - you - chee). Name of the Keeper of the Inca Secrets, son of the Chieftain of the Lost City.

CUZCO (coos - ko). Literally: "The Navel." The Capital City of the great Inca Empire, sacred seat of Inca nobility. Even today mountain natives look upon Cuzco as a sacred town, and for its size, has more churches than any other city in the world. Every Catholic church today is built upon the foundations of the former Inca Temple—the Temple of the Sun, the Moon, The God of Lightning, of Thunder, etc.

FESTIVALS. To relieve the monotony of work, which was compulsory for every man from sixteen to fifty (idleness was not tolerated in the Empire of the Incas) monthly festivals were held at which time there was much dancing and drinking. The greatest of all Festivals was that of the *Intip Raymi* (see below), in the first month of the Peruvian winter, June, starting with the winter solstice, June 22. It was the Harvest Festival. Another very important festival was the *Situa*, the Festival of Purification on September 22, and the *Huarachicu*, the Festival of Puberty when youths were admitted to manhood and service of their King.

GRINGO (grin - go). Spanish-American term for North American; sometimes used as term of contempt, but more often as accepted term as we use "Yankee"; as used in the story, "Gringuito" is term of endearment, meaning "little Yankee."

GUANACO (goo - ah - nack - o). The lowest of the three-type species of Camel of the Andes (the other two being the Llama and the Vicuña). Beast of burden, served also as meat, and the hides for leather, for bed mats, and coverings against the weather over windows and doors.

GUARDIAN OF THE TOMB. In certain sections of the Inca Empire, tombs were dug deep into the ground in conical shape, and enlarged into wide underground round chambers. Here the dead were wrapped in yards and yards of cloth and sat on the ground next to earthenware (and in the case of nobles, gold and silver) dishes, filled with food for the long journey to their ancestors. In some cases, favorite women, servants and attendants were buried alive to serve the departed nobleman.

HAMPI (ham - pea). Quechua for "cure," medicine.

HOSPEDAJE (os - pay - da - hay). Spanish meaning "dwelling," or dwelling accommodations, similar to our signs "Tourists" or "Rooms." An inn.

HOUSE OF VIRGINS. The Temple of the Virgins of the Sun. Girls specially selected in childhood for their beauty or intelligence to become the servants of the High Deity, the Sun. They lived in special temples or houses, were waited on by specially selected maids, and were carefully guarded against the outside public by armed guards. They were known in Quechua by the term of *Acllas* (ak - yass), meaning "white-robed virgins."

HUACAY PATA (who - ah - ca pat - ah). The great or sacred square before the Palace of Viracocha in the center of Cuzco. The square held as many as two hundred thousand people on special occasions, was the scene of the great festivals and triumphant celebrations; and after the Spanish Conquest, it was in this Huacay Pata Square that the Spanish Conquistadores murdered the Indian captives and subsequently killed and beheaded each other in the long struggle for power and gold that followed the end of the Inca regime.

HUARACHICU (who - are - ah - chee - koo). The Festival of Puberty, when the youths of the nobility were taken into the service of their Emperor. It was a festival second only to the great Intip Raymi.

HUAYNA (who - ai - nah). Quechua for "young," "youth"; sometimes taken by the son of a famous man designating "the younger," as Huayna Capac, the Emperor. Huaina also refers to any youth, any young man.

INCA (ink - ah). The name of the tribe that conquered the valley of Cuzco, and in Quechua meaning "lord," "master"; was also the title of the King or Emperor. "The Inca" was the noble head of the country, the Master.

INCA HIGHWAYS. There were four of these magnificently paved highways radiating from Cuzco north, south, east and west. Used mostly as military roads, they were kept spotlessly clean and clear winter and summer by specially trained Road Keepers whose profession was proudly passed on from father to son, from generation to generation.

INTI (in - tea). In Quechua, The Sun, the chief deity of the Incas.

INTI HUATANA (In - tea who - ah - tan - ah). Quechua for "The Needle that Captures the Sun"; that is, the Sundial.

INTI (INTIP) RAYMI (in - tea rye - me). The Great Festival of the Sun. As the greatest festival of Inca days, it is still preserved and re-enacted every year on June 22 by large crews who rehearse for months for the festival. It is a colorful performance given in the great plains outside of the fortress of Sachsahuaman, where Dick's adventure began.

JANALLAC CONSUQUI (hah - na - yak con - sue - key). Farewell greeting, meaning "and He accompany you also," answering the parting greeting of a friend who calls *Allin Punchaita*.

LAPQUEO PARISCA (lap - eh - oh pa - rees - ka). Quechua meaning "big injury," "big illness," or "big hurt."

LEAGUE. A land measure, approximately three U.S. miles.

LLAMA (ya - mah). The most useful animal in the Andes, the Camel of the Andean mountains, source of meat, wool, leather and rugs for the natives, and only beast of burden in the area at the time of the Spanish Conquest. While the llamas are gradually dying out, being killed by trucks and by carelessness, at one time they numbered many millions. The Incas had personal herds of several hundred thousand animals. Llamas stand about 3½ feet at the shoulder, but their long necks make them look like miniature giraffes. They refuse to carry more than fifty pounds on their back and show their resentment of abuse by spitting foul yellow spittle in the face of their tormentor.

MACHU PICCHU (mah - chew pitch - oo). Quechua for "The Male Mountain," or "The Great Mountain," the name of the Lost City of the Andes discovered in 1912 by former Senator Hiram Bingham of Connecticut. The city had been lost more than four hundred years, although persistent rumors spoke of this one and of as many as one hundred other "lost" cities, where perhaps the Incas buried their gold and silver and precious stones which they were able to save from the lust of the Conquistadores.

MINISTER. The name used in Spanish and Spanish American countries for Members of the Cabinet of the President or ruler. Thus, "Minister of Foreign Relations" is known in the United States as the Secretary of State.

MIRAFLORES (me - rah - flow - ress). The name of the beautiful suburb by the sea adjoining Peru's capital city of Lima. Lima, when it was founded in 1535, was called "La Ciudad the los Reyes," The City of the Sovereigns, in honor of Ferdinand and Isabella. It has been incorrectly translated as "The City the Kings." "Los Reyes" in Spanish means the kings, but also, in the case of a King and Queen governing jointly, Their Majesties, or simply The Sovereigns. Miraflores means, literally, "Look at the Flowers."

MISKQUI (miss - key). Quechua for "Little Drop of Honey"; a term of great endearment, and the name of a famous character in the Quechua (Inca) drama "Ollantay," preserved for us through translations into Spanish and English; the drama is still played on occasions, in Quechua in its original form.

MITIMAES (meat - eeh - mah - ees). Quechua for "transfers," people transplanted from one section of the country to another to cultivate the land, or when a conquered tribe was split up so as to minimize its rebellious power and the young men were sent into virtual exile to another part of the empire. Sometimes whole tribes were thus transferred from mountain to sea coast or vice versa.

MOZO (moss - oh). Spanish for "servant," "porter," and sometimes just "man." In some sections to say *"muy mozo"* means a handsome fellow, or a strong chap. In Latin America *"mozo"* generally means a porter, a waiter.

NOBILITY. Inca nobility was jealously protected, and the families of blood royal guarded against any infiltration of non-royal blood. The nobility as a whole were the rulers of the land; they did not work, but were well-fed, clothed and housed at the expense of the state, from the third of all things produced or made that went to the Inca.

PACHACAMAC (pah - tcha - kam - ack). The House of Voices; hence, the Temple of the Oracle, the highest pilgrimage in the empire of the Incas, where the Oracle Room housed the Voice of the Oracle that spoke to the High Priest and counselled the Incas. In part it has been restored by the Peruvian government. It was ruthlessly destroyed by the men of Pizarro when they discovered that the Indian caretakers had spirited the golden statues and the Oracle away, substituting wooden ones which they gleefully turned over to the conquerors. Pizarro ordered the Temple, built mostly of adobe and stone, to be torn down. It stands on a high hill some thirty miles from Lima.

PASHTE (pash - tay). Indian name of both a tree and the fruit of the tree, which resembles a dry sponge, but is filled with little seeds which give off a sort of foam or suds and hence are used as "wash cloths" by Indian natives instead of soap.

PENSION (pen - see - on). Spanish for "boarding house."

PEPE (pay - pay). Spanish equivalent of "Pete," standing for Pedro, or Peter. Usually used as diminutive or term of endearment.

PIQUI CHIQUI (peak - eee cheek - eeh). In the Inca drama, the servant of the King, guardian of the door to the King's chambers. A proud name used by those who served.

PONCHO (pawn - tcho). In Peru and in the Indian highlands, ponchos are made of closely woven wool, and are virtually waterproof. They constitute overcoat, raincoat, and blanket for the natives, who often huddle under them and under big hats during rainstorms to escape the elements.

PRIESTS. In the Inca hierarchy, only the Inca himself was

above the High Priest; and in certain matters of the church, the priests were virtually supreme. They were greatly feared and revered. The High Priest was usually a brother or other blood-relative of the Emperor.

PRINCIPAL WIFE. In Inca nobility, the Inca married his sister, to preserve the purity of the blood; the first born male child was the heir to the throne. But to insure that there would be a noble heir, the Inca could and often did marry three or four "legitimate" (that is, noble-blood wives) usually his sisters. He could have as many as fifty concubines who were his wives in every respect except that their offspring could not inherit the throne. The first sister-wife, especially the one who gave him the first male heir, was the "principal wife," the Coya, or queen.

QUECHUA. The language of the high Andean Indians, still spoken in Bolivia and parts of Peru. There was no written language, and Quechua has been preserved to us as a sound language, written out in our own alphabet. There are therefore many different spellings of the same "sound"; and the correct Quechua word for "word" was "voice"; i.e., sound.

QUE PASA. Spanish for "what's up"; colloquially, "what gives?" Common expression used in all Spanish speaking countries for the equivalent of our "What's the matter?"

QUIPU (key - pooh). Rope or string, usually made of wool, to which were attached a number of knots, representing different events of historical significance. The quipu was the "record" kept for history; it also served as counting machine for the payments of taxes, for census of births and deaths. The color of the strings explained the subjects to which the knots or "numbers" referred.

QUIPU CAMAYOC (key - pooh cam - ah - yok). The Keeper of the Quipu; the Inca historian, census taker, keeper of the records.

RAFTS (see Balsa).

SACHSAHUAMAN (sack - sah - who - ah - man). The greatest fortification of the Inca Empire, one of the monolithic wonders of the world. Granite blocks weighing as much as eighteen tons were pushed and carved into place in a series of three successive walls or stone parapets and the total formed the fortified city that protected Cuzco against all enemies. It is recorded that it never fell to an enemy in battle. The Spanish Conquistadores tried to destroy it and succeeded in tearing down parts of the ramparts, with which they built churches and palaces for themselves in Cuzco, two miles away. But the main walls resisted even the Spanish cannon.

SITUA (see - too - ah). The Festival of Purification. It was the great festival that Dick took part in in the Lost City.

SNAKES. There are many kinds of snakes in Peru which run from those of a few inches long to the giant boas and cobras. Some mountain snakes grow as much as twenty-five feet and there is evidence of whole armies having been killed by these mountain monsters in Inca days. A twenty to twenty-five foot boa constrictor is not an uncommon sight in the forests of South America.

SOROCHE (sore - o - chay). Mountain sickness. Dizziness, nausea, often accompanied by intestinal disorders, fever, and extreme chills.

SUPAY (soup - eye). The Curse, The Evil One, The Devil. Some hold that it meant "the evil eye," but the majority of students of Quechua translate it as The Curse, or The Devil.

TATAI (tah - tie). Quechua for "father," "dad"; in many parts of Latin America the Indians today use "tata" for dad, daddy, or simply "protector." Spanish Americans have adopted the word and use it coloquially for "pa" or "dad."

TOMBS. Of Incas and noblemen have been found in many sections of Peru, some of the finest ones in the dry desert lands where climate has preserved the bodies in almost perfect state of preservation after hundreds of years. Many tombs have been uncovered in recent years and many more are believed to hold Inca secrets of the past in various sections of the land.

TOPU (toe - pooh). Pin in Quechua. Silver and gold topus were used by the women as pins to hold together the folds of their ample blouses; but topu also means "mace" or emblem of power; "pin" in the sense of a small generally round stick or short staff. It was also used as a measure of

land, two or three topus of land being assigned to each
head of a household as his land to grow the crops consumed
by his family. But the land was not his, it belonged to the
state.

URUBAMBA (ooh - rue - bam - ba). The mightiest of all Peruvian rivers, considered by Inca tribes as sacred waters. Also
bears the name of "Vilcañota," from the mountains where
it originates, and from the Sacred Valley of the Vilcañota.

VESTIBULE (of tomb). A sort of bottle-neck entrance atop
the real opening of a tomb or underground chamber. A
special "guardian" was buried in the vestibule to insure the
privacy of the departed one inside the tomb fifteen to eighteen feet below the vestibule.

VICUÑA (vee - coo - nya). The finest of the three "camels of
the Andes"; its soft fleece was used for the weaving of the
Inca's clothes, and for making silk-like tapestries and cloth
for the nobility. Rugs of vicuña are highly prized, and their
exportation today is forbidden, since the once numerous
herds are dying out.

VILCAÑOTA (veal - kah - yno - tah). Literally ("The Knot," a
cluster of granite mountains high in the Peruvian-Bolivian
alti-plano in the perpetually frozen Andes. The river Urubamba begins in the everlasting snows of this great mountain and is fed, as it has been fed for centuries on mountain streams that have never even been explored.

VIRACOCHA (veer - ah - cotch - ah). The Supreme Deity. An
Inca Prince, reasoning that the Sun could not be the All
Powerful God, because the sun was "imprisoned" in the sky,
traveling the same path day after day, established Viracocha
as the Supreme God, but wisely decided to reserve the wor-
ship of this Super God, the Unseen, to the nobility, the
"ones who could understand" an unseen God, a God who
did not reveal Himself to the people. At least one of the
Emperors annexed the title "Viracocha" to himself, a sort
of self-deification.

VISAC (vea - sack). A mountain rodent, a large rat, prized as
game for meat by the natives.

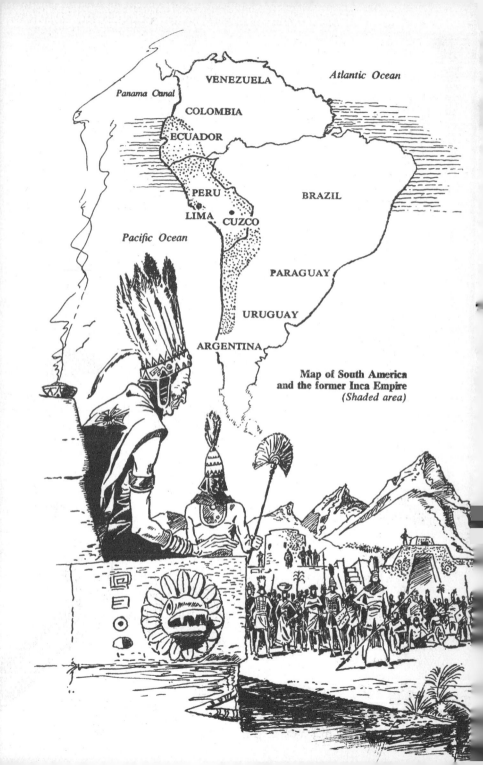

Map of South America
and the former Inca Empire
(Shaded area)